THE SCOT, THE WITCH AND THE WARDROBE

This Large Print Book carries the
Seal of Approval of N.A.V.H.

THE SCOT, THE WITCH
AND THE WARDROBE

ANNETTE BLAIR

THORNDIKE PRESS

An imprint of Thomson Gale, a part of The Thomson Corporation

THOMSON
GALE

Detroit • New York • San Francisco • New Haven, Conn. • Waterville, Maine • London

THOMSON
GALE
™

Copyright © 2006 by Annette Blair.
Magical Series.
Thomson Gale is part of The Thomson Corporation.
Thomson and Star Logo and Thorndike are trademarks and Gale is a registered trademark used herein under license.

Thorndike Press® Large Print Romance.
The text of this Large Print edition is unabridged.
Other aspects of the book may vary from the original edition.
Set in 16 pt. Plantin.

LIBRARY OF CONGRESS CATALOGING-IN-PUBLICATION DATA

Blair, Annette.
    The Scot, the witch, and the wardrobe / by Annette Blair.
        p. cm. — (Thorndike Press large print romance)
        ISBN-13: 978-0-7862-9657-6 (lg. print : alk. paper)
        ISBN-10: 0-7862-9657-7 (lg. print : alk. paper)
        1. Magic — Fiction. 2. Large type books. I. Title.
    PS3602.L333S37 2007
    813'.6—dc22   2007010834

Published in 2007 by arrangement with The Berkley Publishing Group, a member of Penguin Group (USA) Inc.

Printed in the United States of America on permanent paper
10 9 8 7 6 5 4 3 2 1

Dedicated with love and thanks to:

Heather Venneri, for sharing her
wicked wit and Wiccan ways . . . and for
naming Brock.

Jeanine Spikes, with her brainstorming
brilliance and tremendous talent, for
inspiring the vision.

Life is like a carousel, a dizzying affair,
First color and music and nary a care,
Then ponies aplenty and unicorns rare.
Later heights to meet and lows to bear,
Dreams to fulfill with wind in your hair.
Make the journey with joy,
bright and aware.
Reap peace and love if you meet
the dare.
Refuse the risk and end alone in despair.

ONE:
SALEM,
MASSACHUSETTS

The circle of three sat in a sunbeam on a quilt-bright bed beneath the eaves. Victoria Cartwright opened a small silver jewelry casket, removed an ancient brass key, and read its brittle parchment tag for the first time. "Unlock the wardrobe with the magic inside you and meet your destiny."

"Magic?" Melody asked. "Are you coming out of the broom closet, Vic?"

Vickie wrinkled her nose, distracted by the key tingling in her palm. She changed hands. It tingled there, too. She pressed it to her cheek, and the result was the same.

"So open the wardrobe, already," Kira said.

Vickie put the key back in the jewelry casket. "What say I just leave it for the next female Cartwright? My father's probably still alive. He could be screwing up another kid right now."

"But you always wanted to know what was

in the wardrobe," Mel said.

"Sure, I was curious as a kid, but I got over it. I mean, it's been locked all my life, like a big old security . . . wardrobe."

The wide-load construction afterthought jutted from a corner of her attic bedroom, and during one of their imaginary childhood-sleepover scenarios, they had placed inside a mahogany spike-scaled dragon who would come to their aid whenever they called.

"You didn't *know* about Nana's bequest?" Kira asked.

"The key, yes. The destiny, no." Lifting the key by its tag, Vickie rested it on Kira's ankle then Mel's hand, but they looked as if she were being no weirder than usual.

Vickie lay on her side, head in hand, and slid the key through her shawl's fringe. "I never told you because it's nuts. Lili Lockhart, a grandmother on my father's side, a witch by all accounts, left this key to her female descendants a century ago."

"Retro!" Kira said.

"Decidedly, except that it's never worked."

"Bummer. That's like a taunting instead of a haunting."

"No, because only the daughter who inherited Lili's magic can open the wardrobe and complete her spell."

"You mean, you might be a witch, too!" Kira raised her wand like a champagne flute. "To the witchkateers!"

Melody swatted her with a pillow. "Will you pay attention? Complete *what* spell, Vic?"

"Family legend talks about the key spell" — Vickie held up her key — "and a preservation spell on the contents. But the spell that needs to be completed has always been a mystery, which creeps the alakazam out of me."

"Let me reassure you," Kira said, "A spell can let a figurative dragon out of a figurative wardrobe, but *you* get to decide whether to befriend or vanquish the beast."

"That's supposed to reassure me? A drive-by spooking?"

Mel hugged her knees. "Remember how we always wanted to see inside the wardrobe, and your grandmother always said that someday we would?"

"Mel's right, Vic. Nana was psychic. Look at her card-a-day–tarot readings. She was brilliant. She knew you had magic. She knew you'd open the wardrobe."

"This key is not going to work." Vickie closed her fist around it and suddenly found its tingling warmth alluring. "I'm not a witch." She rose with a shiver and turned back to them. "Doesn't the note sound like my destiny's alive or something? Not that I believe any of it, but what if the dragon's not as friendly as we supposed?"

Kira slipped into her flats. "The *dragon* you believe in?"

"It's a metaphorical dragon," Vickie said.

"Right," Mel said, "which is why you waited to open your inheritance until we could be with you."

"I wanted my best friends beside me, so shoot me."

"You wanted backup," Mel said.

Vickie opened her palm to reveal the key. "I wanted to *authenticate* my findings."

Mel grinned. "I know that tone. I interviewed for a cooking show when I couldn't cook, remember?"

"Forget about her," Kira said, "*I'm* into the potential, here. Your dead old granny might have chosen your soul-mate for you more than a century ago. Talk about retro to the max."

"Talk about hocus bogus," Vickie said. "Fair warning; if a hundred-year-old guy steps out'a that wardrobe, I'm history."

Mel looked more closely at the key tag and lifted the corner to peel it open and reveal a second note. "Make the journey with joy. Yours, Lili Lockhart, 1906." Mel's eyes twinkled. "*Maybe* you're supposed to take a trip to the past."

"Thanks," Vickie grumbled, "cause I wasn't freaked enough."

"Mega cool," Kira said.

"Mega flaky," Vickie corrected. "I am so not a witch. My life sucks. If I had magic, I'd fix it, wouldn't I?"

"What are you saying, hon?" Mel touched her arm. "I know you miss Nana, but is anything else wrong?"

"Tell us," Kira said. "We'll help any way we can."

Which is why they'd never know about Nana's medical and funeral bills or her unexpected mortgage. "It's everything and nothing. Of course I miss Nana, but —" Vickie read her friends' looks. "I do *not* need a man. Talk about the dense and the useless. Oh stop grinning. I'm glad you both found soul-mates, but I don't have the stamina to sort through the users, losers, and deserters I tend to attract."

"Every man is not your father, Vic."

"Can't prove that by me."

"Of course, if you used that key," Kira said, "you'd have to take a chance for once."

"I take chances."

"Good, open the wardrobe."

"Yeah," Mel said. "You might find, like

. . . a blueprint of the House of Seven Gables with a treasure-map hidden in the design."

"Covered in tarantulas," Kira added, as she set out yarrow and rosemary, and directed the smoke from her smudge stick to surround them. With a flourish of her wand, she began her chant:

"Protect we three,
From man or dragon,
What will be.
Plus those dear,
Far and near,
Harm it none.
So mote it be."

Kira shrugged. "In case it's a mummy case with Lili's 'preserved' walking dead inside."

"A claustrophobic dragon is starting to sound charming," Vickie said, as she wished for a sword or stake. "How *do* I defend myself against a dragon?"

"A fire extinguisher?" Mel suggested.

"Here goes." Vickie slipped the key in the lock and looked back at them. "When this doesn't work, we go down and play with the baby, right?"

"Right," Mel said, with a maternal grin.

Vickie turned the key and turned away,

dismissing the faint click, but the creaking sound behind her superglued her to the spot . . . until something hit her in the ass.

TWO

Kira raised her wand. "The wardrobe's open!"

"*Your* mama didn't raise no dummies!" Vickie snapped, from behind her. "Something hit me!"

"The wardrobe door," Kira said looking like a happy cat with creamy whiskers. "Hocus bogus, huh?"

Vickie elbowed her. "You can put down your wand now."

Mel aimed the gooseneck lamp at the wardrobe while Vickie approached it. "That's the most beautiful unicorn I've ever seen."

"It's vibrant," Kira said.

"It's gorgeous." *And familiar,* Vickie thought. She touched its gold, spiraled horn, its honeyed mane, and the tiny dragon curled behind its saddle, and she knew this wasn't the first time she had touched it.

"Dragon looks pretty tame. What do you

make of it?" Mel asked, propping the wardrobe door open with a chair.

Vickie fingered the gem-encrusted stars in the unicorn's bridle. "It has to be hand-carved, but I think the rockers were an afterthought. The hole in the center has smooth, metallic markings, see? This unicorn rode a carousel once. Can't you picture it in the bay window of my shop?"

"Way to bring the Immortal Classic some publicity," Mel said. "See, your destiny's a tame old unicorn."

Vickie inhaled deeply. "Do you smell lilies?"

"Cedar," Mel said. "I smell cedar."

Vickie untied the watered silk ribbon around the unicorn's neck to see the giftlike envelope attached.

Kira beamed. "Open it!"

"You must be a hoot on Christmas morning," Vickie told Kira, taking a tarot card from the parchment sheet folded to form an envelope.

"Isn't that from Nana's tarot deck?" Kira asked.

"Lili hand printed Nana's old deck. It's been in the family for years. This is the missing High Priestess card."

"You mean, Nana didn't read with a full deck? Oh, sorry, I didn't mean that to sound like a slam."

"I asked her about reading with an incomplete deck once, and she said I'd get the reading I needed when I needed it. She said all things would come in due course."

"Makes a mystical sort of sense," Mel said. "What does the High Priestess card mean?"

Vickie felt dizzy. "My interpretation would be 'opening to dreams.' "

"Even I'm spooked," Kira said, "after hearing what Nana said, because my instinctive interpretation is to allow your destiny to come to you 'in due course.' "

Vickie shook her head. "Guys, I —"

"Wait!" Kira said. "You opened Lili's wardrobe. You're a witch!"

"I don't believe that, but given the High Priestess card, I have to admit that I've seen this unicorn before. You're gonna think I'm a whack-job, but I dream about it." *On the carousel, where I kiss a man wearing a kilt.* Vickie shivered.

Kira did a wand-wielding happy dance and high-fived her. "Welcome to *my* world. Talk about opening to dreams. Yours are prophetic."

"Wait a minute," Mel said. "I hate to trip your twinkling toes, Kira, but Vic, couldn't you be dreaming about a different unicorn?"

18

Vickie stroked the figure. "How many carousel unicorns with dragons curled around their saddles and lilies around their necks do you think there are with my birth sign, Aquarius, carved above their eyes?"

Kira smirked. "And we have . . . magic!"

"My stars," Vickie said, hands on hips. "You don't seriously believe that?"

"Only one way to find out," Kira said. "Pop quiz."

Mel curled up on Vickie's bed. "If you use me for levitation, don't wake me. The baby kept me up all night."

Vickie grinned, and Kira raised a brow. "This is serious stuff, Miz Vickie!"

"Serious, right, duly noted."

Mel chuckled.

Kira frowned. "When you were six, you wanted to go to the circus, remember? You begged and cried for days, and just when you knew your mother would *never* cave, your father showed up for like the first time in years?"

"Uh, yeah, and they fought like maniacs, about babies of all things. Didn't feel like magic to me."

Kira waited for her to remember *everything*.

"Oh, right," Vickie said. "I almost forgot. Nana came and took me to the circus to get me out of there."

Kira nodded. "Senior year hockey finals. Ron Dumbrowski — accent on the dumb — paid the sign guy to flash 'Victoria Cartwright is a big fat virgin queen,' on the scoreboard before the game?"

"Stop; you're making me hate my life."

"You were so mad, you focused on making the Dumbzer screw up, remember? You *said* you were. So what happened?"

Vickie grinned. "He scored a goal for the wrong team and lost the state title."

"I rest my case."

"Yeah," Mel said, "I'm thinking that a lot of weird and — excuse my honesty — ditzy things have happened around you, Vic. I may have been at boarding school half the time, but even I remember a few zingers."

Vickie folded her arms. "No way."

"Way," Mel said. "Cheerleaders, Thanksgiving football game, tenth grade?"

"Those self-centered snobs said rotten things about you, Mel."

"They did? And you defended me? You're so sweet."

Vickie rolled her eyes. "I didn't *do* anything."

"Right," Mel said, "so we're in the first row, the cheerleaders are in a pyramid in front of us, and you point and say, 'As you sway, fall away,' and they fall!"

"I didn't want them on top of us."

Mel smirked. "How did you know they'd fall?"

"How do you remember what I said?"

"You rhymed and scared the pom-poms out of me."

"Seriously?" Vickie grinned then she sobered. "Hey, they were teetering. Really. I remember being glad the grass was soft, because I knew . . . which doesn't prove a thing."

"It proves wishful magic," Kira said.

"Magic?" Mel asked. "Was that you, then, Kira?"

"Nope. I was a late-blooming witch. Neither did I whisper a rhyme for the breeze to take our exams off the ledge and out the fifth-floor window, because I'd pilfered my mother's romance novel instead of studying the night before."

Mel gave her a thumbs-up, and Vickie chuckled.

"It's true, Vic, and it was all you," Kira insisted. "You're like a loose cannon in the world of witchcraft."

"See," Mel said, getting up, "And I always thought she was a loose cannon in the regular world."

"Thanks, guys. So glad I invited you to

the grand opening."

Kira snuffed the smudge stick. "Vic, you need to make peace with your magic, learn to accept and control it."

Vickie huffed. "Those were flukes, quirks, twists of fate. And did I mention coincidence? *You,* Kira dearest, need to make peace with the fact that I have no magic."

"But you have a unicorn," Mel said. "Get it appraised, find out what you've got." She turned to the sound of the baby crying. "At least for insurance purposes. I gotta go rescue Logan."

Insurance? Great, Vickie thought, another bill she couldn't afford to pay. But if the unicorn had value, it might attract customers, which would help pay Nana's bills.

Vickie followed Kira down the stairs.

"Mel," Vickie said, taking baby Jessica from her. "Where the heck do I get a carousel unicorn appraised?"

Three: Caperglen, Scotland

"Must be Friday, if the hermit MacKenzie's deigned to leave his fancy cave to watch the antiques on the telly." Old Angus slammed his shot glass on the table, startling more than one man into spilling his ale.

"Right, well then," Rory MacKenzie said, letting the door shut behind him, ignoring the inebriated Knight of the Sacred Star . . . the "Star" being the organization, dressed in ceremony, that had helped the locals turn drinking into "lodge business" more than a century before.

"Turn on the telly, will you, Liam?" Rory asked.

"Give it up, damn your eyes!" Angus shouted. "Drummond's unicorn sits at the bottom of the sea. It might be your family's curse, but it's our families who suffer." Another shot of single malt Scotch whisky silenced the superstitious duffer.

The MacKenzie curse, Rory thought.

He'd cut his teeth on talk of that. Uncanny how his "mad" age-old search to end it had been shot through with vigor-reincarnated of late. He scratched his tatty beard and claimed his favorite bar stool. "You're in rare form tonight, Angus. Took to the bottle a wee bit early today?"

Angus refilled his shot glass. "Damned hermit. You're as mad as old Drummond," he muttered.

"Ach, go vent your spleen in the loch, and sober up, you old blatherskite," Rory growled. "I'm here to watch the telly, not listen to your twaddle."

In the days before the curse, according to local history as told by Angus and his ilk, visitors from all over the world swarmed to Caperglen to ride Drummond MacKenzie's Immortal Classic Carousel. Because of it, the village thrived . . . until Drummond broke his engagement to rumored-witch Lili Lockhart.

After Lili fled to America, Drummond destroyed the carousel — and village prosperity — by breaking up the set of zodiac figures and sending the Aquarius unicorn to Lili. The villagers said Drummond had been bewitched, and *they* suffered his curse.

Whether fact or fiction, the unicorn, Caperglen's prosperity, and Drummond's happiness, never resurfaced. The Immortal Classic became a broken whirligig in a pavilion on the family property. And the MacKenzies became pariahs, from that day to this.

Rory's grandfather, another in a long line of carousel artisans, had, in fact, carved a unicorn from Drummond's original plan and repaired the carousel, but he failed to resurrect it. According to legend, only Drummond's unicorn could bring the Immortal Classic and the village of Caperglen, back to life.

Rory dreamed of reversing the curse. Talk about mad. Lately, he'd been dreaming about the carousel, itself — music merry, lights bright — turning beneath a pale blue sky, and himself kissing a woman beside it.

Aye, sure, and he might have time for a woman, if he ever found the unicorn.

Maybe his dreams were responsible for his new zeal, or his zeal was responsible for the dreams.

"Mad and cursed," Angus mumbled.

"Seems so," Rory said. "But it's a matter of public record that the ship carrying the unicorn docked safely in Salem Harbor the year Drummond sent it. I found the ship's records on the Internet."

Angus stilled, shot glass half way to his lips.

Like clockwork, Liam set a bowl of tattie drootle before Rory.

By his fourth ale, Rory was paying more attention to a bit of a dispute over a golf game than to the antiques.

"Rory!" Liam shouted. "Look, a unicorn!"

The lodge went silent, and Rory about choked on his potato soup, because he saw someone who looked amazingly like his dream woman, there on the antiques show, bold as brass, laying claim to a carousel unicorn with the sign of Aquarius carved on its forelock.

"That *our* unicorn?" Angus asked, shocked sober.

Her name was Victoria Cartwright. Her unicorn belonged to her ancestor who brought it from the old country more than a century before — all the proof Rory's mates needed for a lynching. His own thoughts darkened as he became one with their dissonant ire, and while no proof could be found, and no sense made of their garbled shouts, the general consensus fit his mood. "She stole our unicorn!" "Off with her head!"

"Wheesht!" Rory snapped to silence them.

The woman invited viewers to "come and

"see" her unicorn at her vintage dress and curio shop, The Immortal Classic, on Pickering Wharf in Salem, Massachusetts.

"Why don't she just take out an ad," Liam said.

Rory raised a quieting hand. "Her shop is named for the carousel, did you hear?"

"Odd that you call your shop the Immortal Classic," the carousel expert said, "since the workmanship on this figure indicates it could have been carved by the Scot whose Immortal Classic Zodiac Carousel won him world recognition at the 1867 World's Fair in Paris."

In counterpoint to the woman's pleasure, Rory's heart firmed to tempered steel. Did curses get passed, like blue eyes and mahogany hair, from generation to generation? If so, he'd fight Victoria Cartwright for Caperglen's treasure with a claymore honed by decades of village bitterness.

"Did you know?" the appraiser asked, "that your shop was named after a famous carousel?"

"No," she said. "No, I'd never heard of it. I made the name up, I thought, in reference to the kind of classic clothing that never goes out of style."

"But you come from Salem, right? Land of witchcraft? That's enough to raise the hair on my arms," the art dealer said. "I wonder if fate, or magic, gave you the words?"

"Coincidence," Victoria Cartwright said with conviction. "Good advertising. So, the Scot who built the Immortal Classic Carousel was my unicorn's carver, then? How weird is that?"

"Drummond *might* have carved it," the man said, "except that his figures were last seen on his carousel around 1880, I believe, and no collector since has come across one. It's generally believed that they were destroyed by fire, as so many carousel figures were over the years."

The reverent appraiser touched the unicorn's glass marble eyes, its fine carved-and-painted tartan saddle blanket, the sign of Aquarius below its forelock, every feature that proved it Drummond's. "It almost has to be a Drummond," he said, echoing Rory's thoughts.

"Why?" Victoria asked.

Rory picked up his tankard. Too much knowledge and he wouldn't have time to claim it before dealers and collectors started circling.

"Until later in the nineteenth century, astrological magic was linked to the occult," the appraiser explained. "Because of that, I only know of the one carousel artisan who took a chance with astrological signs mid-century. But, as I said, nothing of Drummond's has ever come up for auction. Anywhere."

The carousel aficionado tilted his head toward the unicorn. "Nevertheless, this looks like the real thing. Without knowing whether it's a Drummond or not, because of it's age, its condition and patina, its rare astrological reference, and because the semiprecious stones set into its bridle are real, I'd put a price of one hundred and fifty, to two hundred thousand dollars on it. If we can prove it's a Drummond, we can safely double that. At auction, the sky's the limit."

"I'd never sell," the woman said. "It's a family heirloom."

Rory groaned. On that they agreed, except that it was *his* family heirloom. Her adamance was a classic case of good news/bad news. Reclaiming the unicorn might prove as great a challenge as finding it, he thought, but with her determination, she might just keep it long enough for him to get to America. The hermit in him cringed at the thought.

"With more research," the appraiser said, "your unicorn could prove to be a national treasure. Congratulations."

Liam turned off the telly.

"That's our unicorn," Angus said, without question, his gaze expectant, like every other gaze turned Rory's way.

This was as close as any MacKenzie had got to respect in more than a century, and by God, Rory wasn't going to let Caperglen or the MacKenzie name down again. He tossed back the dregs of his ale and slammed his tankard on the sleek mahogany bar. "I'll go fetch it, shall I?"

A resounding cheer followed him out the door, warming him as he walked the length of Caper Burn toward MacKenzie Manor.

If Drummond Rory MacKenzie had carved Victoria Cartwright's unicorn, a hidden compartment sat beneath its saddle. *Ach,* and if he found the compartment, that unicorn was *his* national treasure, not Victoria Cartwright's.

FOUR

"Thanks for doing this, Mel," Vickie said, holding the ladder while Mel went up to retrieve the shop's Halloween decorations from the dormer attic above it. "I'm not good on ladders."

"This one is a bit rickety," Mel said. "You should think about replacing it. Where did you say the box is?"

"I don't know. Nana used to go up."

"I found — oh, here they are. All set." Mel came down with her arms barely meeting around a box so big it doubled Vickie's guilt over Nana's treks up there.

"Good thing it's not heavy." Mel set the box on the table. "And I found this between the floorboards. Looks like the envelope we found on the unicorn, doesn't it?"

"My stars," Vickie said, "you'd think Nana would have noticed it at some point over the years."

"Well, it was smack in the center of a

sunbeam, and the mouse nibbles look fresh, so maybe it wasn't sticking out before. You think Lili put it there for you to find?"

"That's a disconcerting thought."

"You didn't find the unicorn and the High Priestess disconcerting."

"Geez, get with the program. I'm still having nightmares."

Mel smiled. "Maybe this'll help you finish Lili's spell?"

Vickie groaned. "Who needs enemies with friends like you?"

"Oh, stop complaining and open it."

"Where have I heard that before?" Vickie brought the envelope to the window. "It's another tarot card, the Hermit. See? Lili's telling me to go it alone."

"Talk about skimming the surface," Mel said. "I read a lot about the High Priestess after you found it, and it can refer to looking beyond the obvious. Plus I saw that the Hermit reinforces the High Priestess."

"As the High Priestess reinforces the Hermit," Vickie said. "I go it alone."

"Damn," Mel said. "No wait, the Hermit card could mean quieting and opening to what could be."

"Like?"

"I don't know," Mel said. "Hermits?"

Vickie laughed. "What did you do, memorize what you read?"

"You got a problem with that? Somebody needs to pull you out of that rut you're stuck in."

"Okay, I get it. The Hermit can also mean accepting wise counsel. *Wise.*" Vickie smoothed the card and tried not to grin. "So, who can we get to counsel me?"

"Me, damn it."

"That's what I thought. Okay, I'm braced, oh wise one."

"I think the cards together mean *not* going it alone," Mel said. "Think of them as an invitation back to the world of relationships."

Vickie grinned. "Okay. I'll replace Brock."

"The butterfly vibrator Kira gave you? You named it? No, wait, you wore it out?" Melody hooted. "Though, Logan does like it when I bring out our vibrating rabbit."

"What did you say?"

"You know? Rabbit for two?"

Vickie put her hands over her ears. "TMI, TMI. Get it out of my head!"

Melody smiled. "You killed two 'Brocks,' and you're freaked by —"

"Don't say it! I have to look Logan in the eye the next time I see him."

Mel chuckled. "I should give you back to your customers."

33

"You should give me amnesia."

"You need a man."

"I need a lobotomy."

"Okay, I'm out'a here."

"No, wait," Vickie said. "I'm sorry. It's just — I know Logan. I don't wanna think about his, you know . . . 'Brock' . . . in action."

"In a way," Melody said, "I understand."

"Stay until the next trolley. The tour-guides are talking-up the unicorn, so I get an hourly rush. Too much to handle alone."

"I wish I could help like the old days," Mel said.

"Thanks, but, you saw my sign, I'm looking for a part-timer. You're busy with your job and family, you lucky thing."

"I told you I'd fix you up with —"

"I do *not* want to go on a blind date with Logan's cousin's brother-in-law's next door neighbor. If I wanted a knight on a white charger, I'd find my own."

"Fine," Mel said. "But if you *did* want one, what would you be looking for?"

Vickie dusted the unicorn's Plexiglas case and considered the qualities she'd like in her dream man. "The knight I want will speak to my heart. He'll be gentle and kind and we'll be of one mind. He'll like to cook while I read a book. He'll love my hair and pull out my chair. He'll kiss to please and weaken my knees." Vickie lowered her voice. "He'll worship my bod while I adore his rod." She grinned. "That should do it."

Mel fanned herself. "I'll say." She quirked a brow. "You do know that you wished in rhyme?"

"A whim."

"A spell."

"Please, you sound like Kira."

"She might be right. You're a natural."

"No, I'm a lost cause. Ooh, and so is that hunk outside. Yum." Vickie stepped closer to the window to get a better look at the shag-maned stranger across the street. "A sexy lost cause. No way could we turn him into a knight."

"Who?" Mel said.

Vickie pointed with her chin. "Tall guy, face carved in stone, ancient leather jacket, tight jeans, firm butt. Does he look familiar to you?"

"No," Mel said, shaking her head, "But between his build, his wild beard, and that chip on his shoulder, he looks like he should be carrying a club. Wow, he's really checking you out, Vic."

"Yep," Vickie said. "It's the Neanderthals who do."

■ ■ ■ ■

Rory MacKenzie stood on the far side of the world in a bustling city of witches and vampires and magic-to-go, across from Victoria Cartwright's Immortal Classic Vintage Dress and Curio Shop.

Through its window, he saw a vision — a sorceress disguised as a dream — beside the glass-encased evidence of his family disgrace, or so he hoped.

As if she sensed his interest, the woman from the *Roadshow* met his assessing gaze with one of her own through a diamond-paned bay window on the porch level of a fussy wooden Victorian painted the color of fresh heather, with ripe eggplant and clotted cream for trim.

She disappeared too soon, but a minute later, she emerged from the house to lean on the pumpkin-lined railing of the wraparound porch. Like a brazen selkie maid, she took no note of the harbor breeze scrambling her long honey hair, plastering kiss curls to her brow and molding her vintage seafoam gown and lavender shawl to her full, lush figure. Her heels were high, her shoes purple, her gaze direct.

Rory raised his chin and matched her look

as he crossed the street. If this was Lili Lockhart's descendent, he tasted a bit of old Drummond's weakness, savored the sweet of it on his tongue, and stepped up his pace seeking more . . . until he remembered its cost.

Sobered, he stopped at the base of the porch steps atop which the siren stood. "Miss Cartwright," he said with a nod, prepared for any jiggery-pokery she might toss his way.

She stiffened at his words, hesitated, flipped the end of her shawl over a shoulder and held a hand against her heart. *To calm its beat, or protect herself? From him?*

"Victoria," she corrected, soft and skittish as a selkie maid.

At the sound of her siren's voice, Rory's mouth went dry, his mind went blank, and the silence stretched. He fingered his beard, the fullness of it hiding emotions he'd rather keep to himself.

He cleared his throat. "Victoria . . ." The silence stretched too long. "You looked better-fed on the antiques show," he said in a rush.

Victoria stilled, firmed her spine, and turned away.

"Rory MacKenzie," he said climbing the steps to keep up with her retreating form.

"Hermit by nature."

Victoria stumbled on the stoop, caught herself, and scowled back at him.

He shrugged. "Rusty manners, I guess you could say."

"No kidding." She entered her shop and let the door shut him out.

Rory faced a sign taped to the glass. ROOM FOR RENT and BOOKKEEPER/ HANDYMAN WANTED. APPLY WITHIN.

Despite the frightening sense of destiny riding him, Rory went in after her with anticipation. Not only the prospect of Drummond's unicorn to claim, but gob-smacked by the fetching, hot-tempered gatekeeper standing square between him and success.

Except for the Halloween decorations and a strong scent of cinnamon, her shop could be a sunny-day attic with its trunks of clothes, shoes, and shelves of colored glass through which daylight cast rainbows on button art, butterflies, and butter churns.

Stars, he saw, in wind chimes, astrological charts, and such, with mirrors lined like plates in a cupboard on a shelf, too high to reflect anything but the shadows and each other. *Smoke and mirrors,* he thought. *Illusion.*

The selkie had enough customers to keep

a proprietor busy, though perhaps not quite prosperous.

Like a hedgehog in a thorny thicket, Rory braved his way through a timeworn maze of clothes racks and memorabilia as he headed for the unicorn, or its temporary owner, whichever he reached first.

When he emerged on the other side, he found Victoria snapping a picture of a brunette he thought he should know. Victoria raised her head from her camera and eyed him up and down . . . as if he stood in a case with a price tag on his privates!

"So, how *was* he?" the brunette asked nodding Rory's way, as if for a score on his shagging skills.

"The opposite of a knight," Victoria said. "It starts with an 'A' and has a 'hole' in it."

Rory flinched when the shot hit home.

"Bummer," the brunette said. "What happened?"

"Red-beard said I was fat."

"Who, the Neanderthal?"

"I did not!" Rory snapped, afraid he might have done. "Besides, I'm partial to a woman with meat on her bones. Who's a Neanderthal?"

His response raised Victoria's ire. She skewered him with a look that placed him on a level somewhat lower than the belly of a serpent, making him feel less welcome than the Monster of Loch Ness come to call.

"My beard is as mahogany as the hair on my head, not red, and I meant to say that you're thinner than I expected," Rory said.

"Thinner, but not thin." Victoria raised her chin. "You seem to have examined my figure at length."

"Aye, you could say that." Rory baited her by boldly doing so again, at his leisure, a payback for her own brazen perusal.

"Stop it," the bonnie selkie snapped.

"Some things canna be helped, nor would we want them to be." Rory tried for a grin as rusty as his manners, and thought he might have pulled a grimace instead. He'd have to find a mirror in which to practice to be sure he could smile. At any rate, he failed to charm her. "It's what's under the bonnet that counts, ye ken? Not the body work."

"I'm not a car," Victoria snapped. "What do you want?"

Rory frowned — an expression he'd long-since perfected. "Do you treat all your patrons so rudely?"

Victoria noticed that several of them awaited her answer. "My customers are never rude, unlike you," she said loud enough for them to hear, side with her, and reproach him in disapproving silence, which they did brilliantly.

"I came to see the unicorn," he said, giving up on charm as he placed his satchel on the wide-planked floor.

The brunette stepped between them like a mediator. "Hi. I'm Melody Seabright, a friend of Vickie's."

"Ach, and you're the Kitchen Witch," Rory said.

"I know!" Melody Seabright's smile reached her eyes.

"Aye, and now I know why you looked familiar. An American telly star first day in the States! I heard such things could happen. How do you do, Miss Seabright?"

"I'm fine, thank you, and, please, call me Melody."

"I'm Rory MacKenzie. Rory. From Scotland. I liked the program where the bees took over your kitchen." He turned to the frowning unicorn-thief, her eyes as wide and lucent as the priceless ocher marbles Drummond had used on his carousel figures. "Weren't you on that show as well, Victoria, at the end?"

He'd caught her off guard, scared her witless, or softened her sharp edge. Hard to tell which.

"Did I look well-enough fed that time?"

she snapped with an edge that could cut glass.

"You looked . . . like a dream." Rory chose the redeeming truth to get to the unicorn, not because he wanted to see Victoria Cartwright smile, which was just as well, because she didn't.

The Kitchen Witch star looked from one of them to the other and indicated the street outside the window. "When we saw you out there, you seemed like a rhyme — Victoria's wishing rhyme — come true."

Victoria tried to object but Melody shook her head. "Humor me," she said, "both of you. Rory, are you married?"

"Ach, no."

"No surprise there," Victoria said with intended insult.

"Is that a requirement to entering your establishment?"

Melody chuckled. "Hardly. Are you by any chance a knight at one of your country's famed Scots' lodges?"

"Aye, sure," he said, hoping his beard hid his confusion. "I'm a Knight of the Sacred Star down at the lodge where I like to go and watch the telly."

"Close enough," Melody said, "even without a white charger."

"Oh, but I have a white charger. I have

several. I carve carousel chargers for a living, you see, so the unicorn caught my eye." The truth, as far as it went.

"Victoria," Rory said with a bow. "My wooden charger is at your disposal."

Judging by her gasp, not only had his cheeky pun failed to charm her, he had annoyed her the more.

"Thank you," she snapped, "but wooden chargers are way more trouble than they're worth."

FIVE

"Never decide until you've tried one," Rory said. "Some wooden chargers are specimens of piercing beauty and should be taken for at least one good . . . gallop . . . before a decision is made."

Melody choked on a laugh. "I'd love to hear more, but I was on my way out."

"Don't leave now," Victoria said, unable to hide her alarm.

The Kitchen Witch embraced her friend and headed for the door. "Mr. MacKenzie?" she asked, stopping to look back. "Do you like to cook?"

"Aye," he said, "and I've a rare talent for it, though I'm not as fine a chef as you. Planning to boil some haggis, are you?"

"Boil his charger while you're at it," Victoria quipped not quite beneath her breath, "and put it out of business."

"We'll exchange recipes," The Kitchen Witch told him. "Nice meeting you." She turned to Victoria. "Read the card in your pocket again, and be careful what you rhyme." She gave Victoria a wink and a thumbs-up. "Congratulations on maybe getting it right."

"I don't want to get it right," Victoria called after her. "I don't have time to get it right!"

"You're afraid to!" Melody waved over her shoulder. "Try something new for a change."

Victoria stepped her friend's way almost in a panic, moving aside enough for Rory to get his first look at the unicorn.

To his dismay, the saddle blanket was not painted the MacKenzie tartan. He'd hoped the lodge telly distorted colors, but stripes of aqua crossed by teal were not navy and emerald. It wasn't even an *old* version of the his family tartan. He'd try to find it on the Net or e-mail a picture to Liam and see what he could find out, though the paint might not be original. The tartan could have been painted over.

It could still be Drummond's unicorn. But how to search for a hidden compartment when the unicorn was locked up?

"What do you think?" Victoria asked returning.

"It's brilliant," Rory said, as enthralled by

the coveted carousel figure as by the sparring enchantress who claimed it. "It's totally un-got-at."

Victoria's ire dissipated, in view of his enthusiasm, he supposed. "Beautiful and pristine," she said. "Yes. I'm head-over-heels in love with him."

Her gaze and features were so transformed by her adoration of the unicorn that Rory could barely look away. "You think it's a him? Why?"

Victoria raised her chin. "He's handsome and he's got a fine . . . horn."

The air between them crackled as their gazes locked, her cheeks a merry pink, his turtleneck shrinking neck-tight.

"Aye, but horns are like wooden chargers," Rory said, invited by her cheek to give as good as he got. "They canna be judged until put to the test."

Victoria raised her chin, her cat's eyes as piercing as the ceremonial dagger he wore with his dress kilt.

Rory could almost feel the prick of their blade points. "How many men do you know wear lilies 'round their necks?" he asked.

Stumped for less than half a beat, Victoria rallied. "The wreath is a tribute . . . placed there by his lady fair," Victoria said, "for . . . deeds of great valor."

"Ach, and you win, though I'd question *what* deeds, his horn being so fine and all. Did you notice that his eyes match yours? As gold as the sun over the loch before it says goodnight."

Victoria shook her head. "They're a darker gold than that, I think."

"Then you've seen the sun set over Scotland?"

"I . . . no, not actually. But I can rightly claim the unicorn's sign. I'm an Aquarius as well."

"Aye, and that would make you a free spirit, as opposed to the pragmatic likes of me."

"The lack-mannered likes of you."

Rory tilted his head, conceding her point. He'd not apologize again.

As Victoria slipped a wrist-bound key into the case lock, her wall phone rang.

Rory fisted his hands to keep from showing his frustration. He feigned patience as he waited, and heard enough to know that she was turning down an offer for the unicorn with practiced ease. If he wasn't careful, she'd sell it out from under him. *Ach,* and how to keep that from happening?

Victoria looked uncomfortable talking on the phone while a customer waited to ask a question, which brought her help wanted sign to mind. She'd never find a better handyman, plus he kept his own books on the computer.

He needed to rent a room as well, because claiming the unicorn might prove a wee bit more time-consuming than he hoped. He'd best stay near, and on Victoria Cartwright's good side, providing she had one.

After the phone-call, she served her customer and asked if another needed help before she returned. "Still admiring my unicorn, I see."

"He's a rare beauty," Rory said, caught again by the dreamlike quality of Victoria's own beauty, though her suspicious look brought him back to his purpose. "That canna be the first offer you've had," he said.

Victoria inserted her key into the case lock. "No, and they're becoming more generous. You never told me your zodiac sign," she said releasing the lock.

"Dabble in astrology, do you?"

"No more than in the books and charts that come and go. But the unicorn carries my sign, so —"

Rory lost track of their conversation as he took his place before the masterpiece that might be capable of restoring his village and family name to dignity. He nodded his thanks and tried to remember her question.

"Ach, my sign. It's Taurus."

Victoria gave him a look of smug satisfaction. "The sign of the bull — determined, stubborn, obstinate."

"And sensual," Rory added. "We're all of us Taureans sensual. Did you spray the scent of lilies in here, Victoria? Chemicals won't be good for the original paint. Neither will the sun, so you might want to move the unicorn from the window."

His hostess caught her breath, as if struck, but not by the bite of his reprimand, he'd wager. No 'twas something that made her look at him in a more enlightened manner.

She watched him stroke the dragon saddle cantle and the painted tartan saddle blanket as he made a covert search for a latch to a hidden compartment. "It's the Taurean's sensual nature that makes a lass forget the gruff," he said to distract her from his probing hands.

"Forget?" said she. "I think not. Not this lass, but the Taurean's song might help. Do you sing?"

"I don't know," Rory said. "I never had cause. Would you forgive me my rusty manners, if I tried?"

"Your lack-wit manners, you mean. Not in this lifetime, not for a song, though you could dance for your forgiveness."

Rory looked about to see how much of a fool he'd make of himself, if he did. "Your shop's gone empty."

"For now," she said.

"Ach, I see. Well then, are Taureans as known for their dance as for their song?"

"I have no idea. I was simply trying to make you pay the price of your insult."

"I cut my teeth on restitution," he said. "I know how to pay. What dance would you have me do?"

"The chicken dance," she said, eyes merry, a true shock to his senses.

Rory scowled, refusing to be charmed. "Never heard of it."

Victoria shut the case, near catching his fingers, and locked up the unicorn. "The chicken dance is a hoot," she said. "Too bad."

What would it take to remain on her good side, in her company, in her employ, perhaps even in her home? "Do you live here in this house?"

"It's been in my family forever. Why?"

"I like it," he said. "And you have a room for rent?"

"Not to someone who's insulted me."

But Rory had seen her flash of interest. "Restitution it is then," he said, "but perhaps, we could amuse each other?"

"I doubt it."

Trust did not come easy to this one, Rory thought. "I'll match you my version of your chicken dance for your version of my highland fling. You show me yours, and I'll show you mine."

"In your dreams, MacKenzie."

He skewered her with his gaze. "Aye, and you've got that right, darlin'."

SIX

Victoria's shock made Rory wonder if she somehow, on some obscure level, understood his reference to dreams.

Her astonished gaze met and mated with his, and Rory knew the cool silk of her lips against his. He knew the serenity and sensuality of holding her in his arms, and he ached to become reacquainted with every lush inch of her full and delectable mouth.

Reacquainted?

Aye, and he was mad after all. The likelihood made him surly, which wouldn't help his cause, but bloody hell, surly was the skin in which he breathed best. "What?" he asked, at her look of wonder, after too long a time to be comfortable, and with no further patience for civility.

Nevertheless, Victoria smiled. "You noticed the scent of lilies surrounding the unicorn."

"Well you shouldn't have sprayed in there,

if you didn't want —"

"That's the point."

"What point?" Rory snapped. "I find —" Well, he couldn't say he found it odd the way she'd stepped from his dreams now could he? "I find your . . . need for a wooden charger of much more significance than my keen sense of smell. I wish you'd stay on topic, Victoria. Your confusion is making me dizzy."

How daft had he sounded? It wasn't the dream reference she found significant, but his bloody sense of smell. Wonderful.

Victoria bit her lip, but a misplaced giggle emerged to further stun his dyspeptic system. No one giggled in the face of his gruff.

"No one smells the lilies in there, but us," she said.

Had Lili Lockhart left her mystical calling card? "How can no one else smell so strong a scent?"

"I know."

Lilies, of all things, binding their senses. "Is that your Salem trolley I hear?" Rory asked, to turn the subject and make a grasp at sanity.

"Saved by the bell," Victoria said as if she'd sidestepped a pitfall. She shivered and rubbed her arms beneath her shawl.

Rory removed his tatty leather jacket and placed it over her shoulders, and with a surprised nod of thanks, she clutched it against her, and turned to welcome her customers as if they were old friends. So different from the welcome she had *not* given him, though to be fair, he had given the impression he thought her plump. 'Twas a wonder he hadn't choked, with both feet in his mouth like that.

From the locust swarm of customers emerged a two-foot lad with baggy coveralls who climbed into a doll cradle that rolled him gently to the floor as its rockers snapped.

Rory picked him up, despite his wail of mortal-wound proportions, which stopped the second the lad found a thatch of mahogany beard to denude.

"Ouch, blast it!" Rory said, and the lad giggled.

Victoria and a stranger ran over.

"Is he all right?" Victoria asked.

"I am not paying for that cradle," the woman said. "In fact, I should sue for my son's injuries."

"You've no cause," Rory said. "The boy was surprised is all. I saw it happen. He rolled; he didn't fall. It's a toy an inch off the floor. Victoria, take a date-stamped picture of the giggling lad, here, and the cradle, as is, to capture the facts."

Victoria went for her camera, and took several, while the boy plucked Rory's beard, hair by painful hair, giggling more at every wince.

"It's just that a mother worries."

"Right," Rory said. "So, let's be certain. Go with Victoria and strip the lad to his nappy to be sure there are no hidden bruises. Victoria, more pictures," Rory said as they disappeared into another room.

Ten minutes later, the lad wanted back in Rory's arms.

"He's bonnie, clever, too," Rory said to sweeten his mum as he picked him up.

The woman gave a flirty smile. "No wonder my boy's so taken with you." She kissed her boy, pressing close. "You should bottle that brogue," she said. "I'd buy the lot."

Rory handed the lad over. Blast, but he wished his bloody brogue worked half as well on Victoria.

By the time the lad and his mum left, she and Victoria were friends, though Victoria regarded *him* differently. "Thank you," she said. "I have a sign asking people to keep their children in tow, but it doesn't always work."

Rory picked up the cradle and examined

its rockers. He'd flaunt his skills with an eye toward landing her handyman job, searching for a key to the unicorn case, and repairing the damage he'd done with his well-fed remark. "I'll fix this," he said.

"You're kidding? Why?"

"It's made of wood. I told you; I carve carousel horses . . . out of wood."

"No, I mean, why would you take the time to fix it? You don't know me."

Ach, but he'd like to. Rory finger-combed his beard. "I . . . saw the accident coming, and should have stopped it. I feel responsible. I'm a top woodworker in Caperglen."

Victoria shook her head. "I mean, don't you have anything better to do today? Someplace else to go?"

"No, I came to see the unicorn, as I said, and frankly, Victoria, I hoped for a more thorough perusal. I might be able to help you identify the carver."

With half a dozen customers waiting for her attention, Victoria looked from him to them and back. "Okay, great, fine. You can examine the unicorn after we close. Fix the damned cradle. Fix anything you want back there. You might even dig up my fix-it list." She waved him toward the room where she'd taken the lad and his mum.

It was a cluttered backroom/storeroom/

workroom/office, where linseed oil, wood glue, and a computer keyboard shared a dangerous communal intimacy. Overall, it looked like the eye of a brazen selkie storm, which made him hope that a spare key to the unicorn case lay buried somewhere in the debris.

While clearing a work surface, Rory found Victoria's fix-it list, dated two years before. He also found a stack of invoices, a large stack. Among them, an overdue hospital bill with a staggering bottom line, and a mighty bill for a wake and funeral. She'd lost a loved one, had Victoria, and not four months before, around the time he started dreaming about kissing her by the carousel, oddly enough.

He was sorry for her loss, sorry her bills remained unpaid. The room for rent signified her money problems, but she hadn't let a unicorn sale settle them. Too bad her stubbornness worked against him. Her bills were an excellent motive to sell, but even they'd failed to sway her.

Contrary, defiant, unconventional, Victoria wore a dress years out of date — to promote her dress shop, he supposed — but she wore it with style and aplomb, as if she were setting a new style rather than wearing the old. A madcap combination of savvy, independent, and clueless, she seemed to be a twenty-first century woman who thrived amid the trappings of the century before. She also thrived around people, unlike him.

In happy solitude, Rory repaired the cradle, a tired set of folding library shelves, a fine corner curio, and a Windsor chair, and lost track of time.

At the sound of a crash, he ran and pushed his way through a crowd to find Victoria in their center, teetering at the top of an ancient wooden stepladder. "Are you daft?" he snapped, holding her by her waist. "You're going to break your bloody fine neck up there."

White-knuckling the edge of a wobbly bracket bookshelf, Victoria Cartwright all-out grinned. "You think my neck is fine?"

SEVEN

Rory looked back at the customers surrounding Victoria, their arms out as if they
might catch her, though not a one stood
close enough. "How did this happen?" he
asked.

"I dropped the picture I was trying to
hang with my shoe."

"With your shoe?"

"A spiked heel makes a great hammer."

"Of course. But why didn't you call me?"

"Are you kidding? It's taking you all
afternoon to fix a toy cradle."

Rory scratched his nose. "I see. Tell me
exactly how this happened?"

"When I tried to catch the picture, the
ladder tipped and caught my skirt, front and
back. I can hardly move. Damned drapes
got in my way, which they do every day, but
I can't take them down. Nana loved them
this way."

Like a thunderclap, the rod snapped and

fell from the window, drapes and all, taking out a revolving bookrack of shoes and a blue-spatter watering can of marbles, hundreds of colorful glass aggies spreading across the floor like ants at a picnic.

One customer righted the rack and another the watering can. The rest collected shoes or chased marbles.

Rory shook his head. "Tearing the drapes down wasn't the answer, lass."

"My hands didn't move. Did you see my hands move? I didn't. I wouldn't. Nana loved those drapes." Victoria's eyes filled.

"Ach, lass, don't."

"I'm caught," she said, her sudden frailty unnerving.

"I thought I heard you rhyme," he said, looking for her inner spitfire. "Are you *sure* that wasn't one of your powerful wishes Melody talked about?"

"Are you *sure* somebody didn't pee in your gene pool? Sounds like you're straining your brain."

A customer chuckled as he went out the door and Rory felt a rare tug on his lazy mouth that might have been a smile looking to take root on foreign soil. "You rhymed strain with brain. Should I fear for my brilliance?"

"Too late for that. Just get me down before

the little gray matter you do possess atrophies."

Rory chuckled deep in his throat. "Your blethering shivers my vitals, hellcat."

The shelf bracket let go under the strength of her grip, and the shelf hit Rory in the head.

"Bollocks!" He winced as the shout increased his pain, and climbed up to steady her, because her hand-hold had disappeared.

When the stars stopped dancing before his eyes, Rory found that Victoria's waist beneath her shawl fit the span of his hands, a fine waist, not skinny, nor plump, but perfect, soft and strokable.

A rose glow washed up her neck and brightened her cheeks as she searched his poor head for the spot where the shelf cracked it.

"Aye," he said, squeezing her with more than a wee dram of mischief. "My brain's sprained after all, but not so much that I don't know who to blame."

She ran gentle fingers through his hair, which made him itch to return the favor, until she found the painful knot. He held his wince, because he liked her hands on him more than he disliked the pain.

"That's some goose egg, MacKenzie." She

warmed the bruise with the heat from her hand, and he could swear it was healing. He moved his thumbs upward from her waist until they grazed the low rise of her breasts.

Victoria's entire body quivered. "My skirt," she whispered, and cleared her throat. "It's stuck, remember?"

"Right. Where?" Rory asked, unwilling to release her.

"In the ladder."

"I repeat, 'Where?'"

"Oh. Second rung down, front right, and third rung, maybe, back left. I can't look back to check."

Rory frowned. "I'd like to see how you rhymed that trick."

Victoria narrowed her eyes. "Not to get *your* churlish attention, I assure you."

"That's me in my place."

"See that you stay there. Now, do you have enough brain power to get me out? If I move either way, I'll rip my mother's dress."

Rory climbed farther up, till his chest spooned her bottom, an entirely unnecessary, but wholly satisfying, exercise that woke another of his lazy parts.

He had become immune to the opposite sex, as he became immersed in his search for the unicorn, but Victoria had changed that in his dreams, the way she was changing it now, in fact.

Rory looked about, half afraid this was another dream. "Your shop seems to have emptied."

"For another few minutes, until the next trolley. It stops out front." She bent her legs so she could see where the ladder pinched her skirt. "I love this dress," she said, her breath in his ear sending shock waves to all his right and ready places. "Please try not to tear it."

Rory tried to come up with a solution, but something else came up instead. He saw that her lips were close enough to kiss. How would she react if he did? The tickle of her breath on his lips enticed him.

Hers parted on a sigh.

A rush of lust caught Rory unaware and made him dizzy, or was that the concussion? "Right," he said. "Though you've warned me about using my brain, I think I need to close the ladder a wee bit for its teeth to release your skirt."

"Oh."

"I'll get down, shall I, and close it a bit? Your skirt should come free in both places when I do. I'll hold you to keep you from falling."

"Oh."

"Have you swallowed your vocabulary,

Victoria?"

"No."

Rory climbed down. Perhaps her one-word answers meant that she was as affected by their proximity as he was.

To shut the ladder bearing her weight required a firm hand on her firm backside, and a deal of strength, which hurt his poor head, both of which Rory managed, one infinitely more pleasurable than the other.

When her skirt fell free, his strength gave out, and the ladder snapped open, knocking Victoria into his ready arms.

Her grin shot straight through him, softening something inside, as if she were peeling away a layer of defense, a leather layer, but Rory was too captivated to care.

A throat cleared behind them and Rory turned in surprise, Victoria in his arms.

"Logan!" Victoria said, and Rory wondered if this was her boyfriend, or worse, her husband. Why hadn't he considered the possibility?

"Rory," Victoria said. "This is Logan Kilgarven, Melody's husband. Logan, this is Rory MacKenzie, fresh from Scotland, to see my unicorn. He's working as my handyman this afternoon."

"Looks like a dandy handyman," Kilgarven said.

"He rhymed," Rory said to Victoria, setting her down. "Am I in for another bruising?"

"You might be," Kilgarven said. "Fresh from Scotland, eh? Been to the States much?"

"Never, though carousels all over your country sport my carved and restored figures. Why?"

"Your brogue sounds fake to me, and your speech patterns belie your roots."

Rory stroked his beard. "I talk to customers in all parts of the world by phone everyday, ye ken, so I canna be rollin me r's and droppin me g's at every turn and be understood." Rory extended his hand. "Rory MacKenzie from Caperglen, Scotland, at your service."

Kilgarven shook his hand with a nod, though Rory had hoped for the smile the man held firmly in check.

They stepped aside as a new batch of customers came in.

"I enjoy your wife's show," Rory said.

"So do I," Kilgarven said. "As I enjoyed yours just now."

Melody's husband was none too pleased about finding Victoria in his arms.

"He was rescuing me," Victoria said, rescuing him back, and Rory appreciated the attempt, though when she went to help a customer, he felt abandoned.

"Your knight on a white charger. I know," Kilgarven said following Victoria. "Mel told me." He ran a hand through his hair. "She thinks you should keep him."

"What?" Victoria and Rory said, a bit loud for a public forum.

"I'm just the screening committee," Kilgarven said. "Don't shoot the screening committee. If I approve him, I'm supposed to suggest that he rent your room."

"That's absurd," Victoria protested, shepherding them away from the customers and toward the porch.

"That's Mel," Kilgarven said. "I just thought you deserved fair warning. Kira's been consulted, by the way, and she agrees."

Victoria grinned, about knocking Rory on his figurative arse once more. "Serious stuff," she said.

"Dangerous stuff," Kilgarven countered. "I think it's hormones, in Mel's case at any rate. Kira's just being Kira. Nevertheless, MacKenzie, let's go for a walk so I can do my screening best, give my wife a full report, and go cut a deal for my next documentary. Vickie, be a doll, will you, and give Mel a call, so she doesn't wear a path in the new carpet?"

"Fine, I'll tell her you're harassing my knight, as ordered."

"Now wait a twaddlin' minute," Rory said. "You may have wished for a knight on a white charger, Victoria, but you honestly don't think I'm him?"

"No. Melody thinks you're him. I'm back to thinking you're a lack-wit shoddy-mannered Scot with more beard than brains."

EIGHT

Before she called Mel, Vickie waited on customers, finished cleaning the mess the drapes made, and peeked out, often, to watch the stiff-spined filmmaker and the long-haired hermit facing off on her porch.

A Scot hermit, heaven help her. *Open to dreams,* she thought, rubbing her arms as she looked out at the Scot and wondered if he owned a kilt.

She pictured him wearing one. Oh yeah; that could work. Her rampaging hormones sure thought so. Rory the hunk, naked beneath his kilt. Naughty girl. If she kept it up, she'd kill another Brock.

Scratch that, she'd rather kill the Scot. With lust? Get serious. Besides, Logan might kill him before she got her shot.

Logan talked while Rory leaned against the porch rail finger-combing his beard.

When faced with an uncomfortable situation, Rory probably combed his beard the

68

way Logan ran his hands through his hair. There was a lot of both going on right now. Damn, but she wished she could hear them.

After her last customer, Vickie turned the shop sign to closed, and left the door ajar as she dusted nearby stock, but Logan and Rory spoke too low, the rats.

Eventually, Logan relaxed, and leaned against the rail as well, his hands in his pockets, both men open, if not quite friendly. Rory had somehow earned Logan's approval.

Vickie didn't know if she wanted to rent Rory a room. He'd alluded to it, but that didn't mean he wanted it.

She speed-dialed Mel on her cell phone. "What do you think you're doing, you matchmaking twit? You want a strange Scot sleeping in a bed in my house?"

"Sure," Mel said, "but I was thinking he'd be more comfortable in your bed. You could send Brock to a rest home."

"Are you out of your mind? Rory's a stranger. He could be an axe murderer."

"Rory, huh? That slips off your tongue rather easily. Don't worry, I'll buy you some axe-murderer spray as a bed-warming gift."

"While you're at it, get some of that fruity massage oil to match the way you think."

"Vic, if he has an axe, he uses it on wood.

He's a world-class carver. Logan looked him up on the Net. He has references. He's a well-respected businessman. More important, he's a hunk who weakened your knees before you knew his name. Never mind that he shows up after you cast a spell for a knight on a white charger."

"I did no such —"

"Consider the possibilities," Mel said. "That's all I'm saying. I'll bet he'd ace worshipping your bod while you adore his —"

"Melody Seabright Kilgarven!" But Vickie's knees, among other parts, tingled at the thought. She remembered when Rory stood close behind her on the ladder, his body cupping hers, and her tingles tripled. She shivered. "What makes you think he needs a room?"

"His travel bag with the airport tag was a tip-off."

"I didn't see a bag."

"You were looking at his bod."

"They could use your imagination in Hollywood, Seabright." But sure enough, Vickie found a well-used leather satchel on the floor about three feet from the unicorn. She moved the Boston Airport tag to read his ID. "Rory MacKenzie, One Caper Burn Lane, Caperglen, Scotland."

"I told you."

"Smartass," Vickie said. "Wipe that smile off your face."

"What makes you think I'm smiling."

"The twenty-five years of friendship you're risking with your drive-by matchmaking. So he's traveling. So what? I'm not renting him a room."

"I dare you," Mel said. "No, I double-triple dare you. Take a freaking chance for once in your celibate life."

"Ouch! And I take chances all the time."

"Not. The wardrobe would still be locked if not for us."

"Yeah, yeah, yeah. So maybe I don't like change."

"No kidding, Rapunzel. Cut your hair and blow that tower. Step into a world that's a little bit scary and a lot exciting. There's a Scot hunk with a hard bod and orgasmic promise waiting for you to grab yourself a handful."

"Of what? Never mind," Vickie said. "He's a *stranger!*"

"You're advertising a room near Halloween in Salem. You thought maybe you'd know the vampire who moved in?"

Vickie sighed. "Can Jess or her D.A. call in a favor and get a background check on him?"

"You suspicious thing," Mel said on a laugh, because she knew she was winning, damn it.

"I'm cautious," Vickie corrected turning at the sound of the door. "And smart."

"And you need to get laid."

"That's a negative. Gotta go." Vickie lost her breath at the blue-eyed Scot coming her way. Scowl and all, he carried his own sizzle.

He wiped his brow with the back of an artist's hand. "I got out with my skin, but 'twas a near thing. Volatile, these American suit-types."

"What? A big Scot like you afraid of a —"

"Shark. The man's a shark."

"I was gonna say pussycat. You should see him when he's with Mel and his children. I swear, you can hear him purr."

"Well it was awkward as arse out there and I only heard him growl. Maybe he's a shark with his own kind, because at home, he canna —"

"You are such a . . . man." Oh yeah, she thought. One, who used his muscles often. Hell, his muscles had muscles.

"Men have their uses."

"Like exercising their wooden chargers, you mean?" Vickie ignored the picture her mind conjured, otherwise, she'd jump the hunky son of a Scot.

72

"I was going to say we can fix broken antiques, but I like your take better. Come." He led her, speechless, to her backroom, as if he owned it.

"All of them?" she said shocked by clear surfaces and stacked papers. "You fixed every broken piece back here?"

"I found your list."

"You found my Achilles' heel," she said, admiring the workmanship on the curio.

"The frame on this picture you dropped needs a clamp and a bit of wood glue," he said. "Easy to fix, and the painting is fine in every way. I feel as if I should know the artist, but I canna find a signature, unless its that wee design in the corner."

Vickie liked the way his brogue got thicker when they were alone, as if he let his guard down. "That's Salem's Paxton Wharf in the eighteen-hundreds," she said, "painted by my many-greats grandmother. The Paxtons built the ships in the scene. The castle in the background is still there, rotting on a small island offshore."

"Your many-greats granny was talented."

"Yes, but there's a sadness to the scene that sucks me in, so it's not my favorite example of her work. They say she spent a great deal of her life on the wharf waiting for her lover to come for her." Vickie disliked

73

the story. It felt almost like . . . a memory.

"And did he?"

Mesmerized by the intensity in the Scot's look, she missed the question. "What?"

"Did he come for her?"

"No, she married a local and lived miserably ever after." Vickie turned from the story and the rugged, intense Scot, who seemed to embrace it. "Let me pay you for your time."

"Not necessary, but join me for dinner?"

"No, but you can join me. It's the least I can do. I have a standing order for pizza every Friday night. It should be here any minute."

"I'd be delighted."

Vickie offered him the painting. "Would you accept this in appreciation, since you won't allow me to pay you?"

"Are you a mind reader, too, Victoria, as well as a rhyming wisher?" He accepted the piece of her family artwork with a great deal more pleasure than he accepted the prospect of pizza, Vickie thought, though in no way, at any point, had he smiled. "Thank you," he said. "It . . . speaks to me."

"Nana used to feel the same way. If she heard you echo her sentiment, she'd say it was destined to be yours."

"I don't believe in destiny," the Scot said.

"Neither do I." Vickie closed her shawl against a chill.

NINE

Rory helped her set Nana's old Formica table in the shop's backroom with paper plates and such.

"It's a wee bit knackie, your kitchen set," he said, running his hand over a chair back.

Upholstered in red and gray plastic, each back was centered by a raised red rose set in a recessed gray square, the rose and square both outlined in brass upholstery tacks.

"Gaudy, you mean," Vickie said, "but ultra-modern when Nana was a bride." With a wave of grief, Vickie looked down and opened a bottle of cola.

"I'm . . . sorry for your loss," Rory said. "I can see that you miss her."

"I do. Thank you, but how did you know?"

He indicated the stack he'd made of her papers. "The funeral bill, then you got misty-eyed when you talked about her. You must get lonely now that you're alone in this big old house."

"What makes you think I live alone?"

"I asked Logan. I was afraid you might be — I mean . . . well, I asked, and I have a proposition that might solve our problems."

Vickie straightened. "What problems?"

Rory came as close to an eye-twinkle as Vickie had seen. "Give me the handyman job in exchange for the room."

She spilled plastic utensils all over the table. "Are you out of your mind? Besides, I need somebody who can keep books."

"That's me. Do we have a deal?"

"Of course not."

"But your friends —"

"Are certifiable. They are." She ran in the house to answer the kitchen door, and get the pizza. "I only want a part-timer," she said coming back, "and a month's rent is way more than the job is worth in a month. Plus I planned to rent the room for more than a few days." She opened the box.

"I'm not here on a flying visit. How long a lease do you require?"

She plopped a piece of pizza on his plate, sauce splattering his turtleneck, though he pretended not to notice. "I'll work at no charge, if that'll help. I'd rather not face the bloody paperwork of a work visa, at any rate. That way you'd have rent *and* a handyman/bookkeeper. It's a win/win situation?"

"It's a too-good-to-be-true situation." Who worked for nothing these days? She'd like to keep him around just to find out what he really wanted. "How many carousel carvers do you think will show, now that I took Drummond on the *Roadshow*?"

Rory juggled his pizza, and lost the fight. "Drummond?" he asked pulling a foot-long cheese string from his lap.

Vickie tried not to laugh. "I named the unicorn after the possible carver."

He took a napkin and wiped his lap.

"Wait," Vickie said going around to his side of the table. "Wow. Face down. Cool. Let me get it."

The way his head popped up, Vickie figured he expected her to swipe at his package the way he'd been doing.

"Have at it," he said with a cocky head-tilt.

Vickie grabbed a bottle of stain remover off the shelf behind him, and sprayed his crotch.

"Bollocks!" Rory shouted as he jumped from his chair.

Vickie sprayed the back of his neck just for fun, and he ran from the reeking mist.

"Are you daft?" he asked from halfway

78

across the room.

She showed him the bottle. "Stain remover, see? Throw your jeans in a washer and they'll be good as new."

Rory wiped the back of his neck with a napkin. "Did I have sauce there, too?"

Vickie bit her lip on a giggle. "I was toying with you. How many carousel carvers do you think will come to look at my unicorn?"

Her surly Scot scratched his beard, as opposed to smoothing it, cautious maybe, as opposed to frustrated or thoughtful. He shrugged. "One, possibly two."

"That was my guess, too. Will you excuse me for a sec? I need to make a call." Vickie went out to the porch and closed her hand around the cell phone in her pocket.

Despite her attraction to the shag-maned Scot with his wide shoulders and a brogue that could charm the moon from the sky, he worried her. She'd be nuts to rent to him. But how to resist the income with a mountain of debt?

Sure Rory had saved her skin with the little boy, having her take pictures, in case of a lawsuit, and charming the g-string off the kid's mother. But he'd had *her* purring, too. Since when could a man charm her with snark and get away with it?

Vickie took out her phone and hit speed dial.

"Hey," Mel said, when she answered. "Did you jump his bones yet?"

"Twice. Once on Nana's ugly old table, and once on the unicorn case. We got a standing ovation from the tourists in the trolley."

"So what's your problem?"

Vickie sighed. "I think he's trying to charm me out of my unicorn."

"Do tell."

"That wasn't a euphemism."

"Well he wasn't using any charm on you when I was there. Growls, yes. Charm, not so much. Has he changed personality?"

"No and no."

"But you're charmed anyway? Interesting."

Vickie rolled her eyes. "Mel, stop gloating and listen. He wants to rent the room."

"And you want to rent it. So what's the problem?"

"I can't decide if his offer of a gallop on his wooden charger works for, or against, him. Then there's the matter of a background check. Get this. He's willing to be my *free* handyman/bookkeeper. Any chance the judge knows anything yet?"

"Just got off the phone with her. Rory

MacKenzie lives on One Caper Burn Lane, Caperglen, Scotland, like his MacKenzie forebears for centuries. He's a successful carousel carver, has never dealt in antiques, has no arrests, not even for jaywalking. In short, he has nothing to hide. So, what are you gonna do?"

Damn it. Mel was right. Whoever took the room would be a stranger. And something in Rory MacKenzie spoke to her on a gut level, something basic and familiar and . . . vital.

His discomfort around people and his terminal crankiness amused her. She liked his determination and work ethic, his athletic body and dark Scot's features, even his mahogany, not-red, hair. She liked *him,* damn it. "I should be committed for considering this."

"Yes!" Mel shouted.

Vickie hung up. She found the Scot on his back on the floor beside the unicorn case, trying to examine the unicorn's underbelly.

"See anything I should know about?"

Rory jumped and smacked his head on a bookshelf. "Bollocks!"

"Wow, two concussions in one day." Vickie's chuckle escaped as she bent to help him up, though he was so big, she felt foolish and — oxymoronically — petite in the attempt.

"What can I do to talk you into renting me that room?" he asked. "I have a headache, and I'd like to lie down."

"Here's the deal. I was going to ask for a three-month trial period of any applicant."

"Fine," Rory agreed. "That's fair. I'll rent the room for three months." He reached for his back pocket. "How much per month?" he asked. "I'll pay in advance."

Vickie's heart raced. Three months in advance would put a temporary stopper in every compounding debt. "A thousand a month," she said, "plus a month's rent as a damage deposit, which I'll return when you go."

"For *one* room? Do you have Scot's blood in you, lass?"

"I'm renting more than a room. You'll have the run of the house."

"Which I presume does not mean that I get to come and go on all fours through a hole in the scullery door?"

She huffed. "It means you get free use of the living room, the remote, the library and kitchen, the computer —"

"How about three square meals a day?"

"That's right, you cook. So yes, great idea. I'd love it. Thanks."

Vickie stopped baiting him when he

started peeling hundred dollar bills from a wad that any red-blooded American would bank, and fast. "Cash? What are you doing with all that money on you?"

"I hate debt," he said.

"You'll get robbed!"

He opened her palm, placed the cash inside, and closed her fingers over it. "Victoria, darlin', I just was."

TEN

Victoria's sudden color matched a shade not unlike the pearlescent coral Rory often painted his carousel mermaids. "You are not being robbed!"

Like a caged tigress, she paced, regal and fit to kill, skewering him with her hungry cat's eyes. "I checked the Net for the going rate. For sharing a house this size, in this city, at this time of year, I could have asked for fifteen hundred a month." She threw the cash at his head. "Check into a hotel for two hundred a night. Your stash'll be gone in three weeks." She turned, arms crossed, to stare out the window. "Feel free to leave anytime."

He supposed she was right about the cost of local rentals. "Did you advertise the rental, Victoria?"

Still showing him her back, she nodded.

"You advertised it but it's still available?" he asked.

"I put the sign out this morning. The ad will be in tomorrow's paper for the first time. I'll have a renter by noon."

That was it then. He had no choice, but he'd have to tread warily. She suspected his motives, and damned if he wasn't charmed by her perception, her temper, the lush curves that fit his palms so well. Carving figures was his business, and Victoria Cartwright's had been sculpted by a master.

Crivvens, she might have bewitched him already.

He'd come for the unicorn, bloody hell, and he refused to fall for the stunner. He'd not repeat old Drummond's mistakes nor let the Caperglen citizens accuse another MacKenzie of falling under a witch's spell. True, the more real time he spent with Victoria, the less magical she seemed. Then again, she came to him in dreams with all-seeing eyes, hair of spun gold, and seductive sea-selkie kisses.

But would a witch jam herself into a ladder? Perhaps not, but she might try to scramble his brains a time or three.

She'd caught him on his back beneath the unicorn and questioned his interest, which meant time was short, so he needed to stay, whatever the cost.

"I apologize for the insult, Victoria." He

picked up the cash she'd thrown. "I'd consider the rent well-spent for a good shower."

She turned. "All it would take is a shower?"

"I boarded a train at dawn, yesterday, and flew all night. I've been varnished, dusted, sauced, cheesed, in more ways than one, and chemically sprayed. I'm knackered and I smell like a ferret's armpit. I need a wash and a soft bed, lass, if you're of a mind to forgive me."

"Consider yourself . . . on probation."

Rory went for his satchel. He'd find the compartment at first chance, top Victoria's high offer, return the unicorn to Caperglen, and the MacKenzies to respectability.

If lady luck, or lady stubborn spitfire, smiled on him, he might enjoy a wee bit of harmless pleasure as well. He hadn't forgotten the sizzle on that ladder. No, nor her shivering wide-eyed interest either. "That's it then." He cleared his throat. "I'm your handyman and you're my landlady."

"Heaven help us."

She led him from the backroom into a raw-beamed blue and yellow kitchen that smelled of pumpkin pie. Her cabinets had no doors. They were sitting on the floor leaning against every surface. Her table, chairs, and curio cabinet were oak, classic and beautifully aged.

Rory put down his satchel, lifted a cabinet door, took a hinge-pin from a clutterbox on her counter, and pushed it into place, then he grabbed another.

"Maybe I was smart to rent to you," Victoria said, sitting at her round claw-foot table.

Rory peeked at her beneath the cabinet door. "You doubted it?"

"Am I sane?"

"I'm thinking that the verdict is still out on that."

"Good. I pride myself on keeping people guessing." Victoria nodded toward the cabinets. "I took the doors off to paint them before Nana passed, because she insisted, and, well, thanks. I tried to put them back myself, but I broke the heel on my favorite spikes."

"Rubbish. Not you? How did you get the pins *out*?"

"Nana did it. She was a lot handier than I am."

Rory chuckled inwardly, and attached another door. With the third, he knocked something from the woodwork to the floor, and a cat pounced on it from nowhere, like a . . . catapult.

"Who's the gymnast in zebra stripes?"

"Tigerstar. She has A.D.H.D."

"What?"

"She's hyper. Keeps bringing home notes from the teacher."

"Ach, and no wonder. She looks like a tiger, but she's dressed like a zebra, and she's too small to be either. Anybody would have issues. At any rate, she's having a tinker with something I just sent flying. You might want to fight her for it to see what it is." But it hit his shoe, and Rory got to it first.

Victoria came for it. "What is it?"

"Just an old envelope."

Her hands shook for some reason Rory couldn't imagine as she unfolded the thing and took something from inside.

"Jings," he said, looking over her shoulder. "It's an old joker."

Victoria sat at her round table looking quite pensive.

"What's wrong?" Rory asked raising the last cupboard door, her cat trying to climb his leg.

"It's the missing Fool from my grand-mother's tarot deck."

"Tarot? Oh, fortune telling cards." But Rory didn't like the sudden gravity in her expression. "You're thinking you were a fool to rent to me, then?"

"Do *you* normally take crazy chances?" she asked.

"Ach, no, I don't even leave my cupboard doors off their hinges."

"Well I hate change."

"But you're a free spirit; you said so yourself."

"At my choosing, not someone else's."

"Aye, I ken." Rory shook his head. "But this new living arrangement," he said, unwisely digging himself into an eviction, "is a mighty big change, though I've been told that change can be good."

"So Melody and Kira tell me." Victoria placed the card on the table. "The Fool, as pertains to our situation means a new phase, heading into the foolish unknown, toward risk and adventure. I wonder if Nana knew it was there?"

"Maybe that's why she wanted you to paint the cupboards."

Victoria frowned. "Nah. This is from . . . Nah. Maybe if I did a spread and I got say, the Two of Swords, which would be an opposing card —"

"You're killing me here," Rory said. "Do I stay or do I go?"

"Oh sorry. Bottom line? No matter how foolish my impulse to keep . . . to rent to you may seem at the moment, the Fool allows for embracing folly so . . . you stay. I've found several of these lately, all different."

Rory slipped the last hinge pin in place and wiped his brow with the back of a hand. "Hard work," he said, but 'twas her decision he'd been sweating. "So how many more cards do you need to find?"

Victoria shrugged. "However many it takes, I suppose."

"To do what?"

"Who knows?" Victoria rose and fluffed her hair, a whiff of lavender assaulting Rory's senses.

"What?" she asked watching him.

He pointed to the old black iron skillet of mounded pumpkins on her table to distract her. "Creative use of a skillet."

Victoria tilted her head. "I thought it worked. I'll show you the living room."

Painted ivy trailed along the arch of the door through which he followed her.

Her white-walled parlor, furnished and trimmed in shades of green, was striking, despite its sofa-clutter, bric-a-brac, and naked windows that needed a wash. The room's claim to beauty shone in its Victorian wedding-cake trim staircase, also in shades of green, from mint to sage.

"Too bad your granny was a junk collector." Rory touched one of the antique carousel music boxes lining the pale green mantel, and elicited a tinny tune. "You haven't the heart to clear her mess, I take it?"

"Excuse me, but those music boxes have been in my family for generations. They're my heritage, thank you very much, and they're priceless."

"Glass cases would protect them."

"Every glass case that comes my way goes into the shop to display my stock."

Rory cranked another and sneezed. "Ach, and they could stand a dusting."

"Feel free." With a flip of her wayward curls, Victoria turned to lead him up the stairs, throwing the end of her shawl over her shoulder to slap him in the face. When she did the same with the other end, he knew she'd intended to smack him. Twice.

"Thank you," Rory said. "I needed that."

"The library," she said leading him in, "is my favorite room in the house."

Rory stopped inside the door. With its beams and Mission furniture, the entry seemed breathtakingly reminiscent of the library in his ancestral home, right down to the scents of cloves and rare Scotch whisky.

The built-in desk, where important keys might hide, cut into a set of bookshelves in a window corner. Framed zodiac drawings, and rough draft carousel-figure designs in Drummond's style topped several bookcases, and made Rory think he'd come to the right place.

An old yellow folding ruler, opened to form a star, hung on a wall between bookcases. Starfish filled shadow-boxes. Star molds formed a wall arrangement in tin, copper, and brass.

Around a bookcase corner, cozy in their secluded setting, he found three caramel leather sofas, centered by a star rug that matched the sofa quilt. The sofas squared off to face the focal point of the room, a fireplace with a straight-cut Mission-style backdrop and mantel. Rory lost his breath at the symbol of the Sacred Star Lodge on the wall above.

Below that, two shelves held a series of woodcut blocks. He picked one up, because it looked familiar. The workmanship and artistic style reminded him of the Fool card they'd just found, but it also reminded him of something else. Something he couldn't wrap his mind around at the moment.

"That's the Two of Cups," Victoria said.

"What does this one mean?"

"In this case, it suggests a . . . truce."

"Does it now? Are we fighting?"

"Not at the moment."

"Close enough then." He held up the block. "Where did these come from?"

"One of my ancestors carved them. She printed the tarot deck with them. The Fool we found belongs to the original set."

"These are carved from basswood, which is what I use to carve carousel figures. Basswood is from the linden tree, a native to Southern Scotland."

"That's an odd coincidence," Victoria said.

"A lot of people carve carousel figures from basswood. I like your fireplace." Rory put the woodcut down, pleased by every coincidence, like the opening in her fireplace, a perfect brick circle, rare, and identical to his own.

As if Victoria sensed his pleasure, though not his shock, she gave a hint of the smile that already threatened to enslave him.

All of it was a surprise yes, but a welcome as well, as was the Gaelic message in her mantel-front, carved but not worded like his own.

Drummond had commissioned *his* library mantel carving, which said, "Make the journey with joy." On Victoria's, Rory knew that one word meant "home," and another, he believed, meant Rory — Drummond's middle name, which his family and friends had called him.

Victoria's ancestor *must* have been Lili Lockhart, the witch who frequented his family home before Drummond broke their engagement. The pentagrams at each end of her mantel message were unique, however, to this library.

Rory recognized the pentagram from the one in Drummond's old room — his room now — a memento of Lili, a magic symbol that generations of MacKenzie women had wanted, but feared, to discard over the years.

Rory ran his hand over the words, trying to come to terms with the implication in the room's design.

"It's Gaelic," Victoria said.

"I ken, but what does it mean?"

"Drat, I was hoping you could tell me. We've never known."

"I'll e-mail an acquaintance, and ask him to get it translated. I wish I could send it to one of the village elders, but the old codgers don't care to use a computer."

"Don't you have any friends you could e-mail?"

"Do you not ken the meaning of the word *hermit,* Victoria?"

ELEVEN

"I thought you were kidding," Victoria said, mocking him. "Who's a hermit these days?"

Rory finger-combed his beard. "We don't all live on top of each other, ye ken, and some of us have good reason." She would never understand what it meant to live like a pariah in one's own village, the shame of being born into a family of the exiled and disrespected.

"Skeletons in the family closet?" she asked at his silence.

"Aye," he said, surprised at her perception. "In a big way."

Victoria rubbed her arms. "Me, too."

His head went up. Was her skeleton a sorceress who'd bewitched a man into sending her the source of Caperglen's prosperity? "We have something in common, after all," Rory said.

Victoria brightened, as did the room, and he became hers to command. *Ach,* and she must be Lili's kin after all, because here was him, bewitched, first day in the States. "This room alone is worth the price of rent," he said. "I apologize for my rude assessment of your rental fee."

"Apology accepted." Victoria let her shawl fall open, and Rory admired what he could see of her well-camouflaged curves.

She had a lush old-fashioned hourglass figure, did Victoria. Generous breasts, and hips a man could sink into with pleasure. 'Twas the kind of figure he most liked wrapped around him in sleep, but especially in lust.

Ach, but he'd best turn his thoughts to safe ground. "This is quite the room," he said, "designed after a different century than the rest of the house."

Rory sat at the opposite end of the same sofa as Victoria, his bruised body appreciating its butter-soft cushions.

"The house was designed by my old granny," Victoria said. "The woman who painted Paxton Wharf and carved the woodcut blocks. But in her will, she asked that this room be left as is. Would you care for a drink, by the way?"

"Ach, and I'm not company. You don't need to serve me."

Her hyperactive cat came from nowhere

and landed hard in his lap. Nut-cracking hard.

"Bollocks! You broke 'em," he said, scooping the beastie off his damaged goods when her claws started to come out.

Victoria claimed her cat with a laugh.

Rory crossed one leg over the other wishing Victoria would soothe his aching parts, but that kind of wish had already got him spot-cleaned.

She petted the purring black-and-white striped cat. "Sorry," she said. "Tigerstar is nature's most savage predator."

"Perfect name, considering the stars dancing before my eyes, not to mention the ones that fill your house and shop."

Victoria's smile hit and quivered in the center of his chest like an arrow in a bull's-eye. "You noticed!" she said cuddling the beast. "Tiger has the same birthday as Nana, don't you, puss? She was more Nana's than mine at the end. So devoted."

She'd damned near castrated him, Rory thought, but she was devoted.

"She was the runt in a litter of blacks," Victoria said, smoothing the cat's silky fur to show him a jagged black star on her left hind leg. "Melody's son Shane found this on her coat and knew she was meant to be mine." She purred, the cat not Victoria, though Rory had hopes in that quarter as well.

Victoria's smile went soft. "Tiger is a tabby with questionable ancestry, but the best way to describe her is 'blotched,' because her stripes are erratic. The star formed where the stripes met and crossed, though 'botched' might be a more accurate description. Look at her eyes."

Rory raised the cat for a face-to-face and scratched her behind both ears. "One blue eye and one green," He said. "You canna decide what you are, can you, little Star?"

The cat meowed and licked his nose, and a chuckle rose in him before he could stop it. "Doesn't matter. You're my kind of people, er, cat, raggle-taggle and take-me-as-I-am."

Victoria's expression could only be termed besotted.

This must be one spoiled cat. "You don't need to explain the predator part," he said. "I've had an example."

Victoria's eyes twinkled. "You never know when she's going to pounce, or where she's going to land."

"Wonderful."

Victoria tried to hide her amusement by petting the cat dangerously circling his lap.

He liked having Victoria so close, but Tigerstar nudged his hand with her head, so Victoria took hers away, and let him have a go.

Rory got the cat purring, and Victoria chattering — about her library, her house, and her family, though she never mentioned her artistic old granny by name.

His dream woman seemed as dangerous and seductive as her possible forebear. She wore her dresses long, loose, and flowing, so long, he'd not glimpsed so much as an ankle during the entire ladder episode.

So, why was *he* besotted?

She dressed from another century, a voluptuous handful of scatty woman, who bore a knack for wreaking havoc, as displayed in her shop this very day. But she was sweet, funny, and enticing. He admired the way she'd treated every new customer as a friend, worlds better than she'd treated him at first sight. Perhaps she hadn't found him anywhere near as extraordinary as he found her.

He questioned her now in such a way as to keep her talking, to absorb her energy and admire her without revealing his attraction, or his interest in her past and her unicorn.

They chatted deep into the night, a strangely satisfying exercise, though Rory learned nothing to aid his research.

When her Gothic-arched long-case clock struck two in the morning, Victoria jumped from the sofa. "My stars, look at the time. I talked half the night."

"Yes, you did, but I listened and asked for more, did I not?"

That rattled her. "We have to go to bed," she said.

Rory experienced a disconcerting urge to smile, but resistance came easy, because he didn't know how. "If you'll show me to my room," he said, ignoring her double meaning. "We have work to do tomorrow."

"Oh dear, where to put you?"

"Victoria, you placed an advert for a room you hadn't prepared?"

"No. Yes. Well, I thought I'd rent to a woman, so I do have a room with fresh sheets and no dust, but the less frilly rooms are full of broken overstock."

"Frills it is, then."

His bedroom reminded Rory of a museum.

"This was Nana's room," Victoria said with a hitch in her voice. "She collected antique wall mirrors."

No joke. Good grief, 'twas a disconcerting array, twenty or more on every wall, hung and on shelves — ovals, squares, triangles, hearts, moons, stars — each and every one revealing his shock, though none revealing Victoria.

Some, he'd swear, were fairy-painted by the same hand that decorated the rounding boards, shields, and mirrored panels on the Immortal Classic Carousel. The same hand that had painted Paxton Wharf at the turn of the century?

That's why the painting spoke to him. He might be familiar with the artist's work. But if Lili had painted the trim on the Immortal Classic, Rory hadn't been aware of it until this moment.

The rest of the room was just as amazing. The art deco bedroom set was carved with tulips. A heavy ruby-cut-to-clear vase topped a lace dresser runner and held a "bouquet" of antique hand mirrors. The high backed deco bed wore lavender satin ruffles and cream lace.

"Victoria?" Rory looked for her reflection. How had she found a spot that didn't reflect her times sixty? "Come in," he said, entertained at finding her outside the door. "I want to see you in the mirrors."

She waved so he saw her hand. "You can unpack while I take my turn in the bathroom," she said, "then I'll show you where to find towels and such, and you can have your turn, in peace and privacy, after I go up to bed."

A clear message if ever he'd heard one.

In the end, Victoria didn't take as long for her nightly ablutions as Rory expected. He stood watching her climb the stairs to her attic bedroom alone, without him, foolish notion, and damned if he didn't have to plant his feet and fist his hands, so as not to follow or reach for her.

It didn't bode well for him or his goal that he'd never been more drawn to a woman.

Rory mocked himself for his premature infatuation, and refused to believe that his heart had been touched by anything more than an odd dream in which a blonde of Victoria Cartwright's approximate size, features, and figure had starred.

He shook off his lethargy, went into the bathroom, and came face to face with a medicine-chest mirror that looked as if someone had hit it square in the center with a . . . spiked heel? From there, the crack had spider-webbed.

With his reflection fractured, his thoughts became as scattered and intriguing as his landlady.

But when he examined his surroundings, speculation fled in the face of the huge state-of-the-art bathroom — spa tub and all

— that he'd paid to share with a sexy, if untidy, free spirit, who might, or might not, be a witch.

Then Rory's heart skipped, for there beside a wicker clothesbasket, a pair of pink-as-cotton-candy knickers graced the bathroom floor.

TWELVE

Maybe Rory MacKenzie could do without people, Vickie thought as she dressed for bed, but animals seemed to love him. Tigerstar had followed him to his room as if he had catnip on his heels. She'd even curled up on his bed.

Vickie knew exactly how her cat felt. Given half a chance, she'd follow Rory and do the same. How frightening was that, hours after meeting him?

She wished Nana was here to talk to.

She remembered their last conversation so well. "Pay attention to the star," Nana had said, telling her to have faith in the future.

But Vickie had taken her literally, because Nana was dying and nothing was simple. "The tarot Star," Vickie had said. "It's missing," and Nana had squeezed her hand, so Vickie repeated her lessons. "Have faith in the future. Open my heart —"

"And your home," Nana had said.

Vickie had nodded and continued, "Enjoy harmony —"

"And destiny," Nana whispered, which wasn't part of the lesson, but her grip had eased, because she'd traveled to a plane without pain.

Even now, the October wind seemed to whisper "destiny," in a repetitive chant, as it rattled the windows.

Of all the woodcuts Rory could have chosen, he'd picked the Two of Cups, which also meant "connection and attraction." But simply telling him about "truce" had seemed more prudent, under the circumstances.

The funny thing was, the Hermit opposed the Two of Cups, so either Rory was about to make some changes, or they were in for a rocky cohabitation.

Getting beneath the covers, Vickie thought again about the dream she started having as a child in this room, a dream that flowered to scintillating life after she'd moved in with Nana a year ago.

Of course she would think of that now, but her Scot boarder didn't wear a kilt. If he did, she wouldn't have been able to resist his soft bedroom eyes as she'd turned to come upstairs.

Her dreams had once been as innocent as

she was, but they'd matured with her. In the last year, the dream had turned into a kiss, the kind that usually led to more, but never did.

When she found the unicorn, Vickie began to react physically to her kilted Scot's kiss. And after that she'd come to dread the dream, because she woke feeling lonely, and needy for a man, for fulfillment as a woman. But tonight for some reason, she wanted the dream.

Vickie walked toward the carousel in a breeze at dusk during that magic time of evening when the sky brightens and the universe reveals its majesty, before the stars come out to play.

So familiar was she with the scene, she no longer questioned the carousel's presence in a wildflower glade, devoid of people and landmarks. She didn't care that the amazing carousel figures ran with the clock, rather than counter to it. She simply rejoiced at the sight of it, like a puff-ribboned gift wrapped in a rainbow.

The lilies swaying in the breeze teased her senses, the scent stronger as she took to circling the carousel's kaleidoscopic whirl. Its magical figures came to life with their star-studded bridles, flowers, flags, and fringes, each zodiac figure flying in tune to the steam organ's spirited beat.

As usual, hers was a circling search she would repeat several expectant times before she found herself wrapped in her kilted lover's arms, never sure how she got there, but greedy for his remembered kiss nonetheless.

The longer she circled, the more she ached for his lips, for the way they made her feel. Lips that seemed starved for hers, sensual, practiced, a promise without words, implied but never fulfilled.

If she could find the unicorn, she would find "him," but they were both illusive, the Aquarius figure and the brawny Scot in his tartan kilt and black pirate shirt, never present on the first, or the tenth, go-round. Vickie sometimes felt as if she circled for hours before she found them, but she never gave up, not until dawn lit the sky and the search was taken from her.

Yes, some nights she circled for naught, and perhaps tonight was one of them, but not if she could help it. Like the wind, Vickie picked up her pace, believing more than ever that she would find him, that hurrying would make it so.

Threatened by a cloud of regret, she finally came upon them at last: the kilted man and the horned beast, side by side, and waiting . . . for her.

The carousel no longer seemed to turn, though the music accelerated to an effervescent beat. Then the wind set up a clamor and whipped up the Scot's kilt, and Vickie got herself a fine flash of mighty glory. Her heart sped at the sight, and her woman's body awakened in a new and exciting way.

The sky turned a brighter blue, the man and beast as bright as if the sun shone upon them.

Vickie stopped before her knight, and neither he nor his horned white charger vanished, as sometimes happened. Yet rather than finding herself snatched into his embrace and lost in her lover's kiss, the Scot stood his ground, paid her no mind, and gave his attention to the unicorn.

Vickie tried not to pout or tug on his sporran.

She had rarely seen his face, and didn't remember it, but tonight she recognized his profile, stone-chiseled and aristocratic, surly and stubborn.

She knew the feel of his powerful build against hers, the warmth of his breath along her neck, the silk of his shag-maned hair beneath her stroking fingers.

He gave his studied attention to the unicorn, his long, tapered fingers catching her fancy. He touched the figure's gold-spiraled horn, its blonde mane, its gem encrusted bridle. And then he took to fondling the lilies around its neck, and Vickie lost her breath.

With a finger, he stroked the inner cavity of a lily, as if its petals were made of silk, or a woman's intimate flesh, his finger dipping deep into its center and sliding out again, each stroke slow and mesmerizing at first, then deeper and faster, until Vickie felt as if he stroked her at her center, and she moaned.

Shocked by her reaction, she stepped back, and for the first time ever, her would-be lover turned to regard her, his morning-glory eyes knowing, lust-hazed, and as familiar as his mahogany beard and chiseled features.

The face of a dragon set free.

He didn't smile, but she didn't expect him to.

He did, however, examine her, in bold and brazen detail, his gaze stroking its way up and down her body, resting in all the right places, leaving hot prickles in its wake.

When Vickie thought she might catch fire, he stepped her way and raised his hand to stroke the hair from her cheek and place it behind her ear, his gaze, like his touch, as light as air, more moving than any kiss, more physically exhilarating.

He pulled her hard against him, his caress playing low on her spine, his body no longer a chimera but solid in all the right places. And he opened his mouth over hers in a kiss so sensual, licks of fire shot to her pulsing womb, bringing her to flower, branding her as his.

He grasped her around her waist, his thumbs teasing beneath her breasts, a new and amazing sensation, and her nipples peaked in need.

Vickie gave herself over to his kiss, to rising pleasure, their bodies so close that her center met his, curve for curve, like pieces of a perfect puzzle, the melding of their various and sundry parts both alarming and enticing.

She wanted him closer still.

As the sun rose, the glen, the carousel, and her dragon Scot faded and disappeared, and panic filled her.

"Rory!"

The sound of his name of her lips woke Vickie with a start. She sat up in bed, pulsing with a need to bring him inside her. Him. Rory.

Why him, of all people? Why had she dreamed about a kilted Scot before the cranky Scot came to her door?

Vickie threw off her covers, and went to the window, the sky the dusky blue of her dream, dawn on the rise.

Why Rory?

She'd dated on and off, met attractive men. Less surly men. Outgoing nonhermit types. Men who smiled but didn't make her heart race, didn't make her yearn, didn't become her lover in dreams, or otherwise.

Why had finding the unicorn escalated her awareness in the dream? Why had tonight's dream increased in sensuality? How could the man who crossed an ocean to see her unicorn be the man who beguiled her in sleep? "It's not freaking possible."

Vickie watched the horizon, refusing to contemplate her wayward mind in sleep. A bright apricot dawn rose over Salem Harbor, and she turned to beginning her day.

She had given her phantom lover Rory's face. She'd placed him by the carousel because he slept downstairs.

Dawn. A new beginning. A man in her life. "A boarder. Nothing more."

A bold woman might climb in his bed, tell him about the dream in which he starred, and beg him to give her release.

Vickie chuckled. "As if I would. Bold is one thing, Cartwright, enticing entirely another. The first you might fake, the second you'll never pull off."

She'd stay away from his room. He could make his own bed. The mirrors gave her the creeps anyway. Fat, multiplied by fifty-three. Barf.

She felt pretty when he called her Victoria,

not Vickie, in his knee-weakening brogue. Nobody used her full name. It had always been a word on her birth certificate, as if it belonged to someone else. But the way it rolled off Rory's tongue, as if it had three r's in it, sounded beautiful.

She got a kick out of Rory's rusty-fusty Scot manners, now that she knew he wasn't rude on purpose. A hermit, he said, and damned if she wasn't starting to believe him. She'd like to see a smile, see his face beneath the beard, but she certainly wasn't ready to jump his bones.

Well, she was . . . but she wasn't.

As if he'd let her. Vickie imagined his face if she tried, and she laughed. "Well, you can't hide up here all day. You have a shop to run." And she needed some quiet time after her dream, and before she faced her boarder again.

Between the time difference and jet lag, he'd sleep for a while yet. Nevertheless, though her mother's old nightgown was thirty years old and ruffled from neck to toes, she found the robe Mel had given her the Christmas before, still in its box, and put it on before she went to the kitchen.

She scooped Chai tea mix, heavy on the caffeine, into hot water, stirred, squirted a mountain of whipped cream on top, and grabbed a box of chocolate-frosted breakfast tarts. Then she opened her research book about vintage women's underwear, and started reading.

"Crivvens, do you call that breakfast?"

Vickie shrieked and knocked over her mug. "Damn it! Look what you made me do!"

Rory searched her kitchen drawers, and found a dish towel to mop up the froth. "Pour yourself another," he said throwing the towel in the sink. "Is this what you're drinking?" he asked, picking up the canister of Chai and reading the directions. "I'll make you another," he said. "You've obviously not had enough caffeine to make you civil."

"So speaks Sir Freaking Galahad."

Rory placed her mug before her then he took the towel from the sink, wrung it out, and hung it on the stove handle. His mocking bark must be a laugh, because he slapped the counter. "Bitch, bitch, bitch," he read, indicating the towel.

"Victoria? Did someone have this made especially for you?"

THIRTEEN

Vickie curled her eager middle finger prudently around her warm mug, concentrated on her research book, and tucked her bare feet beneath her chair.

"You should be wearing slippers," Rory said, catching her move. "It's October. The floor is cold."

Vickie shivered. "I'm not cold."

"Right." He ran upstairs.

He was big, huge, bigger than her kitchen, shot through with testosterone, and so adorably sleep-mussed, she'd nearly lost her breath at first sight. Must be the aftereffect of her dream creeping back into her system, because he'd already pissed her off, and she was still hot for him.

Okay so it wasn't the dream. She'd been attracted from the first. Damned Two of Cups.

Even without a kilt — well, especially without a kilt — but she meant wearing other than a kilt, the beard-scratching Scot looked yummers, despite the bitch comment, even in torn sweats, big stockinged feet, and pillow-spiked mahogany hair.

He came back down the stairs carrying a pair of his socks and stooped down beside her. "Give me your feet."

"I beg your pardon."

He grabbed one, and she nearly kicked him in the chest with the other while trying to fight his hold.

"Daft woman doesn't have the sense to keep her feet warm." He caged one troublesome foot between his thighs while he shoved a sock on the other.

Vickie pretended she was trying to get free while she worked her toes into stroking distance of his package.

"No, you don't," he said, grabbing her thwarted foot and stuffing it into a sock. "I'm not getting kicked in the bollocks by a tiger first thing in the morning."

"Speaking of tigers," Vickie said, spying the striped stalker. "You should know that —" Too late. Tigerstar landed on his shoulders.

Rory yelped, shot to his feet, and turned in circles, but Tigerstar clung.

"Victoria!" Rory called, each syllable well enunciated.

"If you stop moving, she won't have to use her claws."

Rory stopped, and Tigerstar relaxed, stretched out, and became his furry neck muffler, her tail undulating in his face.

Rory shoved a quick thumb toward his right shoulder.

Vickie nodded. "I noticed."

He opened his mouth to speak . . . and spit out a tail.

Her amusement didn't earn her any points with her boarder. "Oh bring her over here. I guess the show's over."

Rory stooped again, this time with his back to her.

Vickie tried to pull Tigerstar off while testing Rory's shoulder muscles. "She must like you. She wants to stay."

"I can tell; she's broken the skin in at least three places." Finally free, Rory stood, and rubbed the back of his neck.

Vickie's giggle stopped him. "I'll be prepared next time," he said.

"I doubt it."

He ignored her, opened the fridge, and scratched his chest.

"Hey, you're a multitasker," Vickie said baiting him, a perversely satisfying pastime. "Can you eat a banana while swinging from a tree?"

"No, but I'm fair certain I could paddle your backside and pull up a rusty laugh."

Vickie felt a jolt. Indignation and longing in one beat. She realized what a leap in familiarity they'd taken in twenty-four hours.

He stood there with the fridge door open, like they did this every day.

Rory. In her dreams. In her kitchen. Slipping her bare foot between his thighs. His hands on her bare feet, putting his socks on her. This was taking the notion of "opening to dreams" a bit far, she thought.

"Jings, there's a god-awful smell in here?" He snapped the cover down on a container. "Making your own blue cheese, are you?"

"Wha'd'ya know," Vickie said. "I thought the fridge was empty."

"Other than your six cans of squirt whip cream, you mean? Aye, it's empty. Is there nothing to cook for breakfast?"

"Cook? There's the problem. I don't."

"Aye, I ken." He opened the cold cuts drawer. "Jings, you have two eggs, half a tomato, half a pepper, and two slices of —" He sniffed it. "Fresh ham and a nice aged cheddar."

"Oh yeah, I took care of Melody's kids yesterday, and she insists I feed them the food she brings."

"Smart woman. May I have what's left?"

"And you think *I* eat a weird breakfast."

"Spices?" he asked.

"No thanks," she said. "I like my tarts *au natural.*"

"That's how I like mine, too," he said, his brow quirked in a suggestive manner.

"Dream on, laddie."

"Darlin', I don't have a choice."

Vickie looked down at her book. What had he meant by that?

The flat of Rory's hand covered both pages. She looked up to see what he was doing.

"Rewind," he said. "Do you have any herbs or spices that I can use on the breakfast I plan to prepare?"

"Herbs, yeah, kitchen garden out back. Nana planted . . . something."

"Glory be; the selkie has a kailyard." Her tenant went out the side door and left her to wonder why every time she mentioned dreams, he gave her an answer that made her shiver. "What the hell's a kailyard?" she yelled.

Five minutes later, like a bad penny, he was back. She knew this because he dropped grass on the page she was reading as he shoved a bush up her nose.

"Smell this. Isn't it grand? That's fresh

rosemary. And this . . ." Rory switched greens.

Vickie turned and sneezed. "A bug flew up my nose!"

"Poor bug. Did it die?"

"I don't know, but you might."

"I'm all atwitter," he said.

She grabbed a tissue.

"This is basil and this is sage. You have an herb garden. Oh, and you have a medieval garden as well. Both your Virgin's Bower and Dragonhead are in flower, but the Virgin's Bower is running amuck and climbing all over the Dragonhead."

"The hussy!"

Rory scratched his nose, which she was beginning to take as a sign of amusement. "You also have a vegetable garden," he said. "But you're letting your tomatoes go to seed, Victoria."

"Yeah, well, there's never anybody around to pick my tomatoes when I need them."

Rory stared down her robe, directly at her breasts, and seemed to lose his ability to speak.

She pulled the ruffles together at her neck. "Pervert."

He gave her an eye-twinkle, nearly, but not quite a smile. "I like your tomatoes," he said. "I'd be happy to . . . pluck them any time you ask."

She almost wished he was flirting, but he was only doing what any testosterone factory would; he was hitting on the nearest female with a pulse. "What's a kailyard?"

"A kitchen garden." He went back to preparing his breakfast. "I'll buy groceries for myself later," he said, "if you don't mind sharing the storage space you don't use."

"No, yes, great, good idea. Care to buy double and I'll pay for half? Might be nice to have something different to eat once in a while."

"I don't even want to think about what you normally eat. Never mind. I wore an example last night."

"What? You don't like pizza? How foreign of you."

"I don't mind it once in a while, but a standing order?"

"I am *not* going on a diet!"

"I didn't say that you sh —"

"I won't. It's not healthy!"

"*Eat* healthy, then. Eat what you want, all you want, but eat a vegetable once in a while is all I'm saying."

"Oh."

He opened and shut several cupboard doors. "Where's your coffeepot?"

"I don't have one. Care for a caffeine

alternative?" She raised her "Witches Brew" mug. "Pumpkin pie Chai."

"A cup of normal coffee," he said, walking toward the window, sounding rather sad. "Is that too much to ask?" He was talking to himself.

Amused again, Vickie bit her lip. "You might want to scout out the nearest coffee shop. Soon."

Her hunky Scot proceeded to rattle the rafters with banging pans as he pulled Nana's old cutting board from the back of a cupboard. From another, he extracted a Swedish Modern jadeite mixing bowl in mint condition.

"Hey, don't use that. I gotta sell it in my shop."

"Is that what you've been doing with your kitchenware?"

"Some, but jadeite's hot. And that style is blazing."

"How much do you want for it?"

"Five hundred bucks," she said without cracking a smile, but he damned near did. She'd have to try harder. "I was only half kidding."

He shook his head and found a frying pan as well, but when he noticed she was watching, he raised a brow, so she turned back to her book. "Gastronomic geek," she said beneath her breath.

She went to get another scoop of Chai, and he slapped the counter.

She jumped three feet. "What the hell?"

"The back of your robe," he said.

"Whatever it says, Mel meant it in fun."

"Your Melody is rising in my estimation. It says, 'I don't need your attitude. I've got plenty of my own.' "

"She's taken."

"Who Melody? I'm not talking about taking her? I said —"

"Yeah, yeah, yeah."

"A wee bit argie-bargie this morning, are we? Bad dreams?"

Vickie looked up so fast, her neck cracked. "Ouch, damn it."

"Ouch is right. I heard that." Rory led her to her chair. "You must've slept wrong."

"I'll say."

"Want me to massage it?"

Oh yeah. Give it to me, baby! "If you want."

She'd gone to heaven. His hands on her neck felt almost as good as . . . "That's enough. Thanks. Feels better. What you're cooking smells . . . done." She'd almost said "delicious," but she wouldn't give him the satisfaction.

A minute later, he sat across from her, an omelet overflowing his dinner plate. "Want half?" he offered. "It's huge."

I'll bet it is, and yes please. Upstairs, my bed, right now. "No thanks." Vickie sipped her Chai so he wouldn't see her drool — for more than his omelet.

He pulled her book out from under her nose, examined the pictures, and whistled. "You wear this stuff?"

"Please," she said.

"Okay, *please* wear this stuff."

She took her book back. "I need to value the vintage underwear I acquired, so I can offer it to collectors, but I'm not sure what to charge."

"Should be easy for you. Quadruple the going rate."

"Thanks, grumpus." She took another breakfast tart. "Seriously," she said. "Did you find it difficult to sleep? Was the bed uncomfortable?"

"I did dream . . . about a carousel," he said. "You were there, by the way."

Vickie aspirated dry pastry crumbs and coughed like an aging smoker. Air. She needed air.

Rory pulled her from her chair.

She saw stars, while he grasped her around the middle and broke her in half. A piece of tart flew across the kitchen, and cleared her windpipe. Her throat was raw, but she didn't care.

Rory forced her to sip her Chai, then he downed the rest as if it were whisky.

"Thanks," she wheezed, trying to rise.

"Sit," he ordered, a hand on her shoulder. "You're white as a sheet."

"I think I need to lie down."

"Good idea." Rory lifted her and carried her up to his bed.

"How brazen of you," she rasped, grateful for his mattress at her back and the pillow that already smelled of his old-fashioned spice cologne, the same scent her grandfather had used.

"You needed a lie-down. I didn't dare try and carry you up another flight."

"Thanks, Rhett, but enough with the well-fed digs. 'I don't give a damn,' is good enough for me."

Rory sat beside her. "Victoria. I wanted to get you into bed fast."

"That's better," she said.

"You have the most beautiful figure I've seen in an age. Hell, in my dream last night, I examined it at length . . . though you were dressed of course."

Warning! Warning! That had happened in *her* dream. Vickie's limbs prickled and she shivered.

Rory tucked the covers to her chin and

covered her brow with his palm.

Vickie tried not to sigh at his touch while thoughts of meeting her destiny, opening to dreams, and an over-the-top attraction scared the bejeebers out of her. She rose leaning on her elbows. "You have to go back to Scotland."

With his hands on her shoulders, he eased her back down. "Because I dreamed about you? That's one shoddy reason. I have no designs on your virtue, Victoria."

"There you go," Vickie said, her throat feeling better. "That makes two shoddy reasons."

"Excuse me, but do you *want* me to have designs on you?"

"No! Absolutely not. It's an ego thing. Being desired makes a girl feel secure is all."

They'd had similar dreams, she thought, a mighty good reason why he should go, but she wanted him to stay, to see where her dreams would lead. Hers might have nothing to do with his. She might have been gutting a fish in his dream . . . on a carousel?

"Who gets the shower first?" he asked. "Or maybe you're so weak you need my help taking your shower?"

"Is that you having no designs on my virtue?"

"No, that's me testing boundaries and

house rules."

"Test this: I dreamed about you last night, and I examined you as well."

When the unflappable Scot stood, fast, Vickie figured he understood her reaction to his announcement. "Quite the startling revelation, eh? If you'd been eating dry pastry, you'd be in this bed."

"Wait," he said, "I'll go get some."

FOURTEEN

Victoria snuggled deeper into his bed while Rory wanted nothing more than to climb in with her.

"Why do Scottish carousels run clockwise?" she asked.

Rory changed focus in half a beat, because he found the possible source of her knowledge troubling. "How do you know they do?" He sat again.

She sighed and closed her eyes. "The same way I know the color of a Scottish sunset, I suppose." She looked right at him. "Television?"

"Ah," he said, but needles pricked him beneath his skin.

He soothed her throat by knuckling her neck. "Feeling better?"

She looked at him with surprise, and he reclaimed his hand. "Our carousels turn clockwise because the originals were fashioned in medieval times to teach young boys to mount their steeds from the correct side and to keep their seats at increased speeds."

"Oh, that makes sense, so they must all have been horses back then."

"Aye, and crude beasts they were."

"No unicorns with lilies round their necks?" she asked.

Rory remembered dipping his finger into the center of a lily last night in his dream as he imagined he was stroking Victoria. And, crivvens, hadn't she looked then as if she might feel that stroke, much as she looked right now?

"I gotta go shower." She shoved him out of her way so fast, he landed on his arse. She stepped over him, and kept going, without an "oops" or an "excuse me."

At the door, she looked back. "House rule number one: I *always* get the shower first. And boundaries will be decided by me as we go."

An hour later, Rory stood in the shower, his emotions in turmoil. Relief . . . he'd found the unicorn. Guilt . . . claiming it would negate Victoria's claim. Panic . . . they'd dreamed about each other. Lust . . . a sweet unprecedented lust, ever since he met her. Hell, since before he met her.

Rory looked down at himself, rock hard for a woman he hardly knew.

"Insane." He scrubbed his chest. "Impossible." He scrubbed elsewhere and imagined stroking Victoria the way he'd stroked the lily.

"Bollocks." He should take the next plane back to Scotland — but if he arrived without the unicorn, he'd be stoned at the gate.

Already doomed, he may as well ride out the tempest named Victoria, though he'd like to ride *her* instead. Lust. Nothing but. A day in her presence and hard as a pikestaff. And no wonder, he'd been half in lust with her before he arrived.

She made him want to run as much as she made him want to stay. "Right," he said, turning off the shower. So he might as well stay and get to work.

His fate rested in Victoria's hands. Aye, and what a thought, for if he must suffer for his cause, he knew exactly what he'd like to place in her hands as he did.

Getting to work in the backroom later, Rory looked for a key to the unicorn case. He sorted bills, correspondence, and receipts. He boxed wood glue, varnish, stain, and linseed oil, but he found no keys.

He trisected the room. Workshop, here, under the fluorescents. Office, there, where no light could dim the computer screen. The knackie table in the window corner.

He went to ask Victoria to explain her bookkeeping system, and found a witch in blue, hands on hips, frowning at a shelf of vases by his knee. "See that fan vase, the ugly gray? Throw it away."

"I'll put it behind the rest," Rory said, but when he picked it up, it slipped through his fingers. "I swear I had a grip on it."

Victoria brought the dustbin. "Did you want me?"

"Aye, stop rhyming and dreaming; you're making me twitch."

The selkie with long royal blue sleeve points, grinned. "You're as guilty of dreaming as I am. As for the other, start worrying when I figure out how to rhyme 'shrink' with 'charger.' "

"Bollocks!"

"You're right; I could shrink them, too."

"Ach, you already are."

"Nothing but fear. Buck up, you twitchy Scot."

"You wouldn't," he said. "You couldn't."

"Now you've got it. I won't, because I can't. My rhyming talent is a figment of Mel's overactive imagination."

"Selkie promise?"

"Sure, whatever the heck that is." Victoria swept up the shards. "No biggie."

"Aye, and that's not what I want a lass

saying about my charger, ye ken?"

She grinned. "Is it a biggie?"

Rory returned to the backroom, so as not to give away the answer. He'd rather have her make the discovery first-hand. "I'm ready to learn your bookkeeping system," he called.

"Coward," she accused as she joined him.

"If you're so brave, ask and you shall see how very big my charger can be."

"A rhyme I'll keep in mind."

"Bookkeeping system?"

"Don't you ever smile?" She opened an old oak filing cabinet, retrieved a large brown paper sack and placed it in his hand. "There you go."

Rory looked inside. "This would make an accountant weep." He sifted through bills, paid and unpaid; envelopes, open and sealed; receipts, dunning letters, and cancelled checks. "Tell me this is not the sum total of your record keeping."

"Every slip is from January first of this year." Pride, not distress, colored her tone. "I keep my records up to date."

"What records?" Rory shouted.

"I have all the important papers."

"You do know how to use a computer?"

"Sure, but Nana always kept her . . . hmm. Guess Kira and Mel are right. I don't like change."

"You rented me a room."

"Ah, but I fought a good fight against it."

"Did you now?" Rory fingered his beard, and examined her at his leisure. Yesterday, a sea-mist selkie maid with a row of aqua beads hanging from her ears. Today, a royal witch with a gown and cape hiding her figure. Rory wanted to comb his fingers through her wild honey hair.

Her scatty whatever-will-be style enchanted the hell out of him in some ways, though it annoyed the hell out of him in others. Her, he wanted to take to bed, but the odds of getting her there, for more than recuperative purposes, were less than naught.

"Rory?"

"I apologize for my impatience," he said, placing her records by the computer table. "Do you have a ledger book or a computer program into which I can enter this info?"

"I have an accountant."

Rory shook his head. "The man must be a saint."

"She is, and she doesn't shout, either."

"I'd wager her rates are astronomical."

"No charge, just a standing order for all the clothes she wants at half price."

"She must be one of your best customers."

Victoria noticed the clean room and looked at him as if he were a specimen under glass. "Are you always this strong-minded and obsessively neat, because I think you have issues."

A rusty laugh escaped him, his first in ages. "I have a keen appreciation for order and discipline, yes, which I assure you is quite normal in a Scot. While you, on the other hand, swan through life with nary a care in the world."

"I don't know how to swan, thank you very much. And I have as many cares as anyone. I'm simply not as much of a tight-ass."

Rory quit the room, crossed the shop, and went out the door.

"Hey, you came looking for me," Victoria said following him to the porch.

"Aye, I sure did." He crossed the street.

"Running away from home?" she called. "Too spooked to stay?"

He turned her way, surprised and touched that she would refer to her home as his.

"What?" she said. "Did you forget your blankie?"

He shook his head. Little use in responding to her taunts, though, truth to tell, he found her highly amusing. "I'm going to purchase bookkeeping and website software."

"Really? Where?"

"Be so kind as to stop mocking me, if you will, and point me in the proper direction. This is for your own good, ye ken?"

"If I had a nickel for every time somebody told me *that!*" She pointed. "A couple miles in that direction."

"Bollocks! Do you have a bicycle?"

"In the garage. It's open. The chain might be loose."

"Like the bookkeeping," Rory muttered.

"Hey, MacKenzie," she called. "Do you want money?"

"No, I want bloody brains for agreeing to this arrangement." But he was so charmed, he turned for another look, and the royal witch blew him a kiss.

Rory turned away. Crivvens, he was in so much trouble, he should dive into Salem Harbor and swim home.

If Lili didn't get him from the grave, because he'd come for her unicorn, Victoria would surely get him with a high-voltage testosterone surge.

FIFTEEN

She'd thrown him an air kiss and damned if his jaw wasn't trying to crack, literally, into a smile, until he saw the inside of her garage.

A needle of a bicycle was hiding in this haystack of broken furniture.

Climbing around, Rory found a box of junk, rifled through looking for keys, and found a painting that shifted his heart into overdrive. He examined the familiar scene, a carousel in a glade of wild lilies against a pale blue sky, two lovers kissing in the foreground. His dream.

But who painted it? He took it to the window to find a signature, but there was none. "Bollocks!"

Had Lily orchestrated his dream a hundred years ago? Or was Victoria the witch who'd ensorcelled him in dreams and lured him here?

Question on question. The more he learned the more he needed to know. The longer he stayed, the less he wanted to go. "Listen to me. I'm bloody rhyming."

Rory tucked the painting into the box, put it where he could find it later when he could wrap his mind around its implications, and continued looking for Victoria's bicycle.

By the time she joined him, his hormones had got quite well under control, thank you very much, and Victoria had slipped from enchantress to the foundress of his black mood, a deal more comfortable to manage than dotty adoration.

"Back already?" she asked, as if she couldn't see him on his knees, black with grease and dirt.

"Are you daft?" he snapped. "I haven't bloody left yet. After I extricated this rattletrap from the furniture graveyard you keep here, I found this moth-eaten hand pump to fill tires that are like to split halfway down the street. Now I need to thread this wanking chain on these bloody gears." His voice had risen with every word. "Any more questions?"

Victoria backed up a step. "So, no groceries?"

His fury must be evident, because she raised her hands, as if he might shoot. "Okay, I'll order out. How about a Mexicali pizzarito? Do you like jalapeños?"

With a power surge born of fury, Rory locked the chain in place and rose, prepared for battle.

"I can't believe you fixed that chain," she said. "I hope it doesn't fall off again. Oops!"

Rory growled. Victoria ran.

Ten minutes later, he was still cursing when a lorry from Mike's Bikes pulled into the drive.

Rory wiped his hands on a rag. "Did she send you to fix the bike?" he asked the driver.

The man shook his head. "She sent me to bring you this and take that one away." He pulled a bike in reasonably new and well-fitted condition from the back of his van. "Said you needed as many saddle bags as we could fit." The bounder grinned. "For groceries and software?"

When Rory noticed her peeking out the shop window, Victoria jumped aside and dropped the curtain.

As the driver put her junker in his van, Rory got directions, then he rode around to the front of the Immortal Classic, where Victoria magically, and repentantly, appeared.

Rory blew her an air kiss before he pedaled away.

Several hours later, he foraged in her

garden for basil, oregano, tomatoes, zucchini, and peppers. As his spicy ground beef simmered, he finished chopping tomatoes for her ancient food processor, and Victoria came into the kitchen.

"Smells yummers in here." She leaned over the frying pan, spooning a taste. "Oh my stars," she said, with the kind of ecstatic expression he'd like to see in other circumstances. "What is this?"

Rory wiped the erotic fantasy from his mind as he covered the processor. "It's going into a stuffed zucchini casserole."

"Oh, don't ruin all this good meat with yucky vegetable stuff."

Rory ignored her, hit the button on the processor, and everything in a ten foot range got tomato-sprayed.

Victoria yelled for him to "shut it off," and the louder she did, the harder it was to find the switch.

She braved the shower and turned it off.

Blessed silence.

Rory wiped his face.

Victoria licked her lips. "Needs salt."

Rory felt his cheeks warm. "I'm an excellent cook."

"Sure you are. You just don't know how to use an *American* food processor?"

"It's broken. The cover, I assure you, is on

as tight as it can go."

"Right, but the spray came from beneath the cup thingy that's supposed to catch the mushy stuff. Looks like it should fit tighter . . . here." Victoria settled the receptacle in place with a snap. "Try it now."

"It's your kitchen," Rory said, expecting a deluge, but the bloody thing worked.

"I'll shower while you finish," Victoria said.

"Ach, and who's going to clean this mess?"

"I'd say whoever made it cleans it."

"Then whoever made the mess will be the only one eating dinner."

"Zucchini? Yeah, right," Victoria said as she left. "Woe is me."

Rory admired her sassy mouth and kept thinking of ways to put it to better use.

He put dinner in the oven, and by the time he cleaned the kitchen, and himself, his zucchini casserole, garlic bread, and roasted red peppers were ready. Now, he thought, oven mitts on hips, how to get the selkie sorceress down the stairs?

A fan placed behind the food helped send the scent wafting up the stairs while Rory set the table.

Not five minutes later, Victoria stood in the kitchen, shiny clean and free of makeup, in baggy sweats and fuzzy pink bunny slippers, upon which Tigerstar had pounced, clung, and now rode . . . standing, with her front paws around Victoria's leg.

"Is she a magic cat?" he asked.

"Nope. Just psycho."

Rory watched Victoria try not to eye the steaming casserole in the center of her table, but she did get close enough for a premeditated sniff. "That looks and smells incredible," she said.

"Aye, and it is."

She straightened a napkin. "You set two places."

Rory uncovered the casserole. "I thought you might be hungry?"

"I am, sort of."

"Would you like some of my yucky vegetable stuff?"

Unabashed, and sensually sweet, Victoria smiled. "Yes, please."

"Then by all means, be my guest."

"You're a doll."

She took one bite and made that face he knew from his dreams, as if she'd come to life in his arms — hell, as if she'd *come* in his arms — and Rory became as hard again as when he woke, as in the shower, as when he had her in his bed.

Crivvens, a sex maniac after one day.

If he wasn't careful, she could have "Rory MacKenzie's Downfall" engraved on her mantel. He'd lived a celibate life for years, and here he sat with a stranger rushing his blood south. A stranger who might have painted his dream. Between her comments of this morning and the painting, he was beginning to wonder how closely her dream resembled his. How daft was that? Doolally is what.

He caught her orgasmic response to a taste of his dinner, and shifted in his seat. "Like it?" he asked.

"It's incredible. Wonderful. You're a master." Victoria's grin shot straight to his sex.

Rory sighed. "Victoria, if we're going to live together, I think we should set down a few rules."

She raised her head, her look wary. "We also need rules not to kill each other by," she said. "And by that I mean, rules to keep you from killing me."

He eyed her. "I was thinking the same thing. To begin with, if we share dinner, we share cleanup."

"Deal. And if I piss you off, you back off. Sound safe?"

"And sensible, like putting my privates in a witness protection program."

He saw her grin when she looked back

down at her food.

They discussed carousel figure carving through dinner, and Rory said goodnight after they cleaned up, because Victoria was hell on his libido.

Settled into his comfortable, if a bit too fussy bed, he opened her book of vintage ladies underwear — more fool him — and began to peruse it with interest.

Rory waited for Victoria with the sky paling blue, the moon coming full, the stars waiting to shine, and the fairy crickets song to lead her.

Because the unicorn, with its matchmaking magic, had brought her in the first place, Rory stroked its gold-swirled horn as he waited for her.

When Victoria finally rounded the carousel, their gazes met and held, their hearts and minds like one, and Rory remembered the taste of her, the feel of her along his length . . . though he couldn't remember why he remembered.

His blood coursing through his veins, he knew the seductive sensuality of holding her in his arms, and he ached to explore every curve and dip of her lush and enticing figure.

He read a corresponding excitement in her expression, and hoped she yearned for him in the same intense and astonishing manner in which he yearned for her.

The breeze toyed with her wayward curls, and plastered her tartan-draped pale blue frock against the round lush figure he planned to explore in every way. Then he realized that the tartan she wore tonight was his.

She came toward him, and he waited to scoop her into his arms for a kiss, an embrace, anything . . . everything she was willing to give.

Victoria's eyes were bright with excitement, and memory, as if meeting like this had happened time out of mind and yet . . .

Soon, she would be close enough to touch, but suddenly he needed to know why he had this absurd rush of longing for a stranger.

Her eyes . . . they spoke to his hollow heart, of shared dreams, lifetime regrets, and unfulfilled destinies.

They made him remember broken hearts and a last-call boat whistle that sounded like a death knell, the two of them stopping, and running into each other's arms for one last bittersweet kiss.

Ach, but where would he find so clear an image? And why did it hurt so bloody damned much?

When Victoria stopped short of throwing herself into his arms, because for a minute

Rory feared, and prayed, she would, he denied a strong need to crush her in his embrace . . . and a stronger need to turn and run.

The pull, the excitement and fear warring inside him, were that strong, but Rory stood his ground, and reached without hesitation.

Their hands touched as if for the first time, less of a welcome, more of a caress, holding, holding, then slipping away. Memory stirred again. A picture in his mind — him kissing her fingers, her kissing his — and she laughed, making him think of songbirds on a spring day, them making love in a rowboat on Caper Burn.

Ach, and another memory so clear, he could feel himself harden as if he slipped inside her in truth, there in the bottom of the boat.

Rory knew this woman — he knew her to his artistic soul, and he wanted her with a need as old as time, a century of need. He lifted her and placed her on the carousel, the now-turning whirligig snatching her away from him.

Panic rushed him, though it should not, because by its very nature, the carousel would bring her back.

When he could no longer bear the wait, Rory jumped on and went after her, bracing himself from pole to pole, moving as fast as the music, his heart skipping with the beat when he saw her.

He took her hand and led her to the rocking chariot, a dragon brought to dark and vigorous life with a gloss of pearlescent mahogany over muted scarlet.

Rather than allow him to set her inside, she indicated that he should precede her, and so he sat waiting, wondering.

She climbed in and stood before him with a gleam of wicked intent, and then she straddled him. That she anticipated his deepest desire, stunned Rory out of mind. But shock turned to appreciation, which turned to pleasure, then lust, then the heady mandate for fulfillment.

As the dragon rocked, Rory's ready sex met Victoria at her arching, undulating center, her movements sensual and seductive as bloody hell, as if she worked to bring him inside herself, despite the clothing between them.

With Victoria's wide-eyed nod of approval, Rory slipped the first of her bone buttons from their silk loops, then another and so on, until he exposed her shift and corset to his hungry gaze. He tested the weight of her breasts in his hands through each titillating layer, the sensitivity of her nipples to his stroking thumbs, and in so doing, he tested them both for endurance.

Victoria closed her eyes, raised her chin,

and her head fell back, her hair tickling his hands, as he cupped her bottom and nuzzled her budding nipples through her shift.

Her keening cry and obvious release at so simple a touch, drove him wild.

He released her lush breasts into his hands. With the dragon chariot rocking, the carousel and its music speeding along on its endless journey, and the scent of lilies filling the air, Rory fed off Victoria's breasts as they rode toward a realm where dragons ruled the skies and pleasure came in starbursts.

"Victoria!"

Sixteen

Rory woke calling Victoria's name, his sweat-slick body hot, tangled in blankets, in a strange bed, stranger surroundings, every bloody mirror reflecting his sexual frustration.

Whatever insanity dogged him, Victoria Cartwright had filled his erotic dreams for the two nights he'd spent beneath her roof. Torture, pure and simple, to endure her tantalizing presence by day, when he could touch her only by night.

Had Victoria created the dream painting he found in the garage? Did her dreams match his?

Rory tossed aside his blankets. Did she lie in her bed, right now, slick from a near mating so real, a bead sat at the tip of his cock? He took himself in hand, and imagined her finishing what they'd started.

Would she lie on her back, raise her knees, or spread them in sexual abandon? He watched her in his mind's eye, until he replaced her hand with his own, found her perfect center, dipped deep into the warm wet silk of her, opened his mouth over hers, and she cried her release against his lips.

Rory swore and covered his brow with the back of a hand. And he'd thought he'd gone comfortably celibate.

Four months since the dream began. Four months since Victoria found the unicorn.

Two nights beneath her roof. Two nights of sexually heightened dreams.

An eerie coincidence or a fated connection?

One connection: the unicorn.

Was the figure a catalyst? Was it Drummond's? Should he leave it behind and return to Caperglen with his sanity, and perhaps his man parts intact. The unicorn could well be Lili's revenge on Drummond for breaking their engagement.

A hundred years' worth of revenge?

Rory got up to pace.

When he'd seen Victoria on Melody's show and thought she looked familiar, he'd called himself daft.

When he saw her later on the antiques show with the unicorn, he lost that argument. He *wasn't* daft.

His first day in the States, his heart beating double-time, he saw his dream woman in the flesh, standing on the porch. No wonder she'd come to life in every dream since.

Fact or fancy?

He'd think he subconsciously placed Victoria in his dreams, if he had met her *before* the dreams started.

Rory made a rude self-deprecating sound and turned his efforts to showering and preparing a breakfast whose scents would draw Victoria, one she could neither resist nor mock.

After putting his creation in the oven, he heard what sounded like a tumble down the stairs. He ran and found her sitting at the bottom.

"I'm fine," she said, getting up and walking sedately into the kitchen.

"Did you hurt yourself?" he asked.

"Nah, I landed on my padded end."

"Fine padding. Want me to rub it for you? Apply some salve?"

Victoria laid her crossed arms on the table, placed her wet head on the pillow they formed, and closed her eyes.

Rory felt another surge of desire, another smile forming deep down. He poured her a mug of her pumpkin-scented caffeine and brought her head up by gently tugging on the neck of her robe. He danced the mug before her eyes. "Did you shower with your eyes closed?"

"I can do that," she said, eyes closed. But she sniffed, and they opened. "Bless you." She cupped her mug, sipped her brew, and sighed. "The nectar of the goddess."

"Perhaps you should keep a mug by the bed to get you safely down the stairs of a morning. The canister says it's good cold."

Victoria fluffed her damp hair, forcing the burnished mass into a titillating tangle, took another sensual sip, and cracked her first morning smile. "What *is* that divine aroma?"

"Homemade cinnamon rolls." He took them from the oven, and brought the cake tin over to tantalize her. "Plain or frosted?"

She gave her hair a two-handed fluff, her breasts coming to a standing pout, which was so bloody distracting, he nearly dropped the cake tin, rolls and all. "I like them slathered in frosting," she said.

Just ask, darlin', and I'll slather them until you come. "Aye, sure, anytime."

"What?" she said.

"I'll slather you — your . . . roll, your cinnamon roll, with frosting. As you say."

Victoria cocked her head, as if he were daft, and surely he was. He slathered and got hard, and placed her breakfast before her. When she didn't look away, he licked the frosting from his fingers the way he'd like to lick it from hers.

"Are you for real?" she asked stopping him.

"Huh?"

She held up the roll.

"Oh, because I like to bake?"

"And cook, and dig food from the dirt."

"It's called gardening. It's a hobby, like cooking and baking."

"You really are a hermit, aren't you?"

"Aye, people I can do without. My land's acres from my nearest neighbor and that's how I like it."

She halved the bun, slathered the center with butter, closed it, and licked her fingers in orgasmic ecstasy.

The look on her face when she took her first bite upped his testosterone level to volcanic proportions. "So, how did I get so lucky as to get you in my kitchen?" she asked.

Ach, but he wished she was asking about getting him in her bed. "You found the unicorn and took it on the *Roadshow*."

"So watching the *Roadshow* is another hobby."

"Aye, you could say that."

"And the unicorn is important enough for

you to have traveled half way around the world?"

Oh, he'd got himself into that one, hadn't he? Damned testosterone. "It's a rare figure, I think. And yes, I still want that thorough look. But finding you, and this place, was serendipity. More than I ever expected."

"Thank you." She swung her hair from side to side and gave it a full ten-fingered fluff. "Mel is one smart cookie for thinking of the *Roadshow*."

"Your friend has some good ideas."

"Hey, don't think she cornered the market. When she became the Kitchen Witch, she couldn't toast bread without a fire extinguisher. I made the sample hashed squash she ruined on her first show."

"Are you jealous of Melody, then?"

"Don't be dense. She's one of my best friends, but her first hashed squash was mine. Ask her. She'll tell you."

"Fair enough," Rory said, setting another slathered roll before her. "How do you make hashed squash?"

Vickie huffed. "I don't remember, but only because it was Nana's recipe and she showed me what —"

"Right. If you could cook, you wouldn't eat so much pizza."

"I like pizza. I don't *choose* to cook. It's

not that I can't. On the rare occasions I do, I have both successes and failures, like everyone else."

"Aha!"

"What?" Victoria asked. "You don't trash the occasional hash?"

"Never."

She looked beyond him, her merriment giving her away. "Where's there's smoke . . ."

Rory turned as his smoking omelet burst into flames.

"Bollocks!" He grabbed the skillet, swore, grabbed a potholder, and ran the inferno out the side door.

As he stared at it, wondering what to do, Victoria cracked the door open, her arm coming out waving the skillet lid.

Rory took it with silent ingratitude and smothered the fire. After freezing his bollocks off for a stubborn minute, he left the charred pan on the stoop, and returned to the kitchen.

"That's what you get for being so cocky!" Victoria said sipping her Chai with a sexy smirk.

"Aye, cocky," he said, tugging at his earlobe, "I am that."

Victoria looked as if she caught his double meaning.

Rory raised a brow. "You rhymed, and I

burned my first meal."

"I did not rhyme."

"You rhymed hash with trash and there went my breakfast up in flames. Are you sure that wasn't one of your wishes, like your knight, and that falling curtain, and . . . are you a witch, Victoria?"

She fluffed again, her hair becoming a seductive silk swirl of scrambled waves. He'd never seen a witch who looked so innocent. Ach, and what did he know? He'd never seen a witch.

"I don't rhyme on purpose," she said, "and damn it, I keep telling everybody. No! I am absolutely and categorically not a witch."

"Everybody?"

"Never mind. If I were a witch I'd fix the money pit I've dug myself into. I'm so not a witch that with Mel wearing my clothes on her show, and advertising my shop in her credits, I'm not making enough money to live on."

Rory sat across from her, took a roll, and placed it on her plate. "Have another. I see your point, but considering the state of your books, I'm not surprised."

"Can we change the subject? Money talk is depressing."

He grabbed a roll for himself. "What

uplifting subject would you prefer?"

She quirked a brow. "Have you ever seen the Chariot Card from a tarot deck?"

Rory stilled. "Canna say as I have."

"It symbolizes the bringing together of conflicting forces with strong willpowers, sometimes male and female, to work together toward a common goal."

"And your point is?"

She shrugged. "Guess I have chariots on the brain this morning."

And if that wasn't disturbing enough, she bit into another buttery, cinnamon roll, and this time *he* had the near-orgasmic reaction. She opened her eyes. "Have you ever carved a dragon chariot?"

Rory fumbled his roll and frosted his palm.

"Have you?" she repeated.

He stood to get a kitchen towel. "Never," he said, looking her straight in the eye.

"Okay," she said. "Did you ever get laid in a dragon chariot?"

SEVENTEEN

Rory's gaze turned icy hot. Vickie shivered. No man had ever given her a sweet physical stroke at her core with a look. "I repeat," she said. "Ever get *laid* in a dragon chariot?"

He raised his chin, his bright blue eyes narrow. "I've . . . *dallied* in one."

Aha, and so have I. The sexual awareness between them hummed and thrummed like Brock on high.

Rory's erection became evident, and he saw that she saw, but he stood his ground.

Vickie could barely turn her gaze from the sight. Did he have a sexual interest in her?

Yeah, right.

"And you, Victoria?" he asked. "Have you ever dallied in a dragon chariot?"

Vickie carefully considered her answer. "Not in broad daylight."

"At night, then," he asked, serious, alert and assessing.

She shrugged, trying not to give anything away.

"And with whom did you dally?" he asked.

"Damn it, MacKenzie. The dragon in question is breathing fire, yet you keep throwing it back at me."

"If I carried a sword, that would be called a parry."

"Oh, you carry a sword all right. It's long, thick, and poised for action."

Rory's lips might not have curved but his eyes held a smile that hit her like an arrow to the heart.

"My charger thanks you, Victoria. Does this mean you're up for an attack?"

Vickie didn't know what she wanted more, to kiss him, jump his bones, or drag him up the stairs — except that they were strangers, said an unwanted spark of sanity. Horny strangers . . . who'd been jumping each other's bones in dreams?

"Did you dally in that chariot awake or asleep?" she asked, trying to get the dream out there, without being the dumbass to suggest they might be having the same one.

"I think you know the answer," Rory said.

"Damn it," Vickie snapped. "Will you just say it?"

"I canna."

Vickie released a breath. "Listen, *my* ride

in the chariot freaked me out. But it wasn't real."

Rory stilled, gave a half nod, placed a chair beside hers, and sat.

She turned to face him.

"So I didn't have my mouth on your breasts last night?" he asked, raising the voltage between them to the power of heat lightening.

Victoria shook her head, because her tongue was stuck to the roof of her mouth.

Rory chuckled deep in his throat. Having control over Victoria's mute button made him feel powerful. "You've lost your tongue again, lass, because it *didn't* happen?"

Aware that his desire was greater than his caution, Rory undid the sash on Victoria's robe. "Don't be afraid," he said.

"I'm not," she whispered.

"I shouldn't be doing this," he added, unbuttoning her virgin white nightgown of ruffles and lace while she watched.

"Why are you?" she asked, a token protest at best.

"I need to confirm something."

"You could ask."

"You could stop me."

"I'm thinking about it."

"Don't worry, I'm not trying to get you naked."

"My luck."

With a double take, Rory saw Victoria's gaze fixed on his busy hands, very near her breasts, which he took as a sign to continue. "I want to see if the fiery burst of stars I saw tattooed on your left breast in my dream is — Good God, it is real!"

He caught the rapid pace of her heart beneath the fist he should remove from her person, though she neither closed her gown nor pushed him away. He didn't bare her nipples because her blue and yellow star spray decorated the low inner curve of her left breast at her cleavage. He had no reason to bare them, save one, to put his mouth where his mind was.

"I've always believed that dreams don't come true," she said looking up at him, "but if you saw my tattoo in your dream, you must truly be hung like a bull."

"You saw no such thing!"

"Huge," she said. "Mighty huge." She spread her hands so far apart, he nearly choked. "This long," she said.

"That's a daft guess . . . based on . . . a minute ago when you ate me up with your look so I had no choice but to grow while you watched."

"Not a guess. You wear a kilt in my dream, MacKenzie, and the wind picked up as I

159

rounded the carousel one night, and you came into plain and extraordinary view."

"Aye, chilly man parts are part and parcel of the ancient Scottish tradition, but I didn't know you'd caught a wee peek."

"There was nothing tiny about it." Victoria placed the flat of her hands high against his thighs, her breath sliding warm up his neck, her fingers squeezing a bit, and the closer her lips got to his, the more Rory felt like that bull. Heavy-hung and ready for stud.

"I got me a fine flash of glory that night, MacKenzie, and I don't need to lower your zipper to prove it."

"Ach, but I wish you would."

Rory grew while her heartbeat quickened, and he opened his palm against that beat, and what lay full between, and she didn't douse his lights.

"In the chariot, what made you act so bold as to —"

"Straddle you?" She slid her hands closer to the center of his need. "I felt secure being in control of a potentially hazardous situation," she said.

"You rode a dragon to avoid its flame? Brave brat."

Victoria stilled. "I hadn't thought of it quite that way."

"Aye, take it from the dragon. You might have got singed."

"I've wanted to move beyond the kiss for months in the dream, but I didn't know how far beyond, and I didn't know how to get there."

"Months?" Rory repeated, her hands sliding nearer, his rod getting harder. "How long have you been having these dreams?"

"Since the first time I slept in Nana's attic. I was a child and dreamed of meeting a kilted boy. Later, a chaste kiss, and so on. Over the years, a man sparked a woman's desire. But we never went beyond the kiss . . . until you got here." She touched her brow. "No wonder you looked familiar. How long have you been having the dream?"

"About four months."

"You started dreaming around the time I found the unicorn? Then you came to see the unicorn, and we started taking the kiss further? How weird is that?"

"Last night," Rory said, to steer her away from the unicorn, "did we go all the way in your dream?"

"No," she sighed, "but I'm hoping that when I wake up tomorrow, I'll be less . . . frustrated." A crimson wash rose up her neck.

"Let me explain my feelings this way," he

said, "though I shouldn't put them out there at all. I've been dreaming day and night about taking our kiss to the next level, ever since I got here. Last night was extraordinary."

"Oh."

"Right," Rory said. "But don't worry. You're safe while I'm awake. I would never —"

"Because I'm too well-fed."

"Victoria . . . you have a body I adore, and my proof-positive arousal aside, are you saying you want to take the dream to its natural conclusion?"

"Well, duh. Did I look like I wasn't having fun?"

"So I could carry you up the stairs right now and —"

Victoria pulled away so fast, a sea wave might have crashed over him, the chill was that brisk.

"Back up, buster. Do you think I keep a carousel upstairs? A dragon chariot? I want the works *in the dream.* We don't even know each other in real life."

Rory leaned back in his chair. "Right. Except for stars on breasts, flashes of mighty glory, and a pulsating mandate to meld our bodies like none *I've* known."

"Right," Victoria said. "Except for that."

"So, I take it your answer to my offer is 'no'?"

"Yes. No. It's a no. A definite no, in real life."

Rory rose, seeing Victoria's nightgown open, her star-kissed breast mocking him. "I need a shower," he said, hands in pockets.

Victoria eyed the evidence of his acute discomfort with what could only be called self-satisfaction. "Better make it a cold one." And the saucy minx winked.

As Vickie slipped her seventies high-waisted aqua eyelet dress with angel sleeves over her head, she thought she and Rory should probably now add some rules to keep from climbing into each other's beds, especially since he gave every indication of finding her attractive.

Go figure.

Poor bull-hung laddie hadn't slept any better than her the past couple of nights. She'd blush every time she looked at him now.

Before she opened the shop, she drove to Cups, her friend Wisteria's tea and tarot shop.

The town's premier matchmaker — Salem-witch style — Wisteria matched couples whether they wanted her to or not.

And though Vickie was bursting with news of shared erotic dreams, she kept them to herself.

She bought a pound of "wicked" coffee, a spare coffee maker, and Wisteria sold her some oat cakes and shortbread, which she said "her Scot" would like, then she stopped Vickie as she was going out the door. "Make your dreams come true, pet. That's all I've got to say." She squeezed Vickie's shoulder and shut her out, the shop bell tinkling something magical.

Make your dreams come true . . . a simple sentence, a loaded suggestion, under the stimulating dream-filled circumstances. "Well, damn."

At the Immortal Classic, Vickie placed the coffee maker, fixings, and treats beside Rory's desk.

"Coffee!" he said looking up from the computer. "Ach, and biscuits from home. I could kiss your —"

"My what?" she asked.

"Sorry; I remembered what I kissed in my — our dream, and forgot what I was going to say."

"You could kiss my feet."

Rory looked down. "Even your toes are sexy," he said. "I like a girl with aqua polish on her toes." He looked regretful. "But any kiss is bound to lead to trouble. Do you want trouble? Because my wooden charger is up for it."

"Wooden chargers, swords, rods, they're all as dangerous as hell," Vickie said, without saying "no," to keep her options open, and she strutted into her shop with a swing in her step and a grin on her face. Sexy toes, eh?

Her ability to turn-on the gorgeous long-haired Scot jazzed her with an energy that felt mystical, as if she could rhyme for anything she wanted.

Hell, maybe she could rhyme her sex life into order. She'd start with Rory flat on his back, charger at the ready.

But it was time to open the shop, so Vickie turned to the task of making a living, and managed to keep from flirting with Rory for the better part of the morning.

At eleven she screeched in sheer frustration, and Rory came running.

"What's wrong?" he asked.

Vickie fisted her hands. "I've been robbed!"

EIGHTEEN

"How much did they get?"

"A snow globe."

"Is that all?"

"It's a St. Louis World's Fair snow globe, a valuable collectible."

"Do you know who took it?"

"Yes," Vickie said, pointing toward the middle-aged fashion plate at the trolley stop. "Her."

"Did you say anything?"

"Uh, yeah. I said, 'I'd prefer that you purchased the two-hundred dollar snow globe in your three thousand dollar purse.' "

"You did not."

"I did, but she ignored me and left."

"I find that hard to believe."

"Are you mocking me?"

"Crivvens no, I'm speaking from experience. I canna ignore you in my sleep."

That made Vickie smile, but a glance from her shoplifter ruined her fun. "Look at her, all diamonds and innocence. I wish the globe would burst and take a leak in her trendy purse."

While passengers got off the trolley, a child costumed for Salem's Haunted Happenings accidentally caught the shoplifter's purse-handle on his plastic sword, dipped it, and the globe hit the sidewalk, splashing water and glitter on the shoplifter's pink suede glam shoes. When the sword broke, her purse hit the ground as well, and belched a wide assortment of trinkets.

The shoplifter threatened the boy's mother but Vickie went to the porch. "Do you need help?" she called. "It wasn't the boy's fault. I saw everything." The shoplifter backed off, picked up her debris, and walked sedately down the street leaving wet shoe-prints behind.

In the shop, Vickie found Rory scowling. "That's another of your rhyming wishes come true," he said. "I wouldn't believe it, if I didn't keep seeing it."

"I don't remember rhyming. And what's so bad about a shoplifter getting what she deserves?"

Rory raised a hand. "Just don't be making *any* wishes around me."

"Worried about your mighty fine package, are you?"

He crossed her lips with a finger. "Do not toy with my package."

"I've been thinking that might be fun."

Rory raised his chin and tugged on the nonexistent cuffs of his navy turtleneck. "I refuse to rise to your bait. I'm going into the house to do my laundry."

"Got room for a little extra in your batch?"

"How much extra?"

"Everything in the hamper?"

The tight lines around Rory's eyes relaxed as he scratched his nose. "I'll bet there've been times you waited so long to do your laundry that you had to raid the racks in here to get dressed."

"I've never run out of clothes in my life. Go iron a sock, you neat-freak."

"Iron your own socks!" he said on his way out.

Vickie phoned Kira.

"Is the Scot yummy?" Kira asked in lieu of a hello.

"He's cranky if you want the unvarnished truth, not that he would stand for anything unvarnished, because it wouldn't be obsessively perfect."

Kira hooted. "You're attracted to him."

"Define attracted."

Kira made a tsking sound. "You're avoiding the question."

"No. I'm avoiding the answer, but I will tell you that I enjoy baiting him until he gets annoyed and uppity, which is cute. How weird is that?"

"Has he made a pass at you?"

Not unless she counted their dreams and his morning breast search. "He cooked me dinner last night and breakfast this morning."

"Usually that's a good sign, but you're an exception in every way."

"Gee thanks."

"Hey, I was hoping you wanted advice about catching him in your feminine snare."

"No, but I was hoping you could recommend a spell a nonwitch could work to warm and sweeten a prickly Scot?"

"Who's the nonwitch?"

"Funny. Now give me a spell."

Kira chuckled. "Let me think. Oh, I know. You'll need a jar of honey."

"Got it."

"But you'll have to try and take a picture of him."

"Got it."

"Already? I'm so proud. What was he wearing, or what wasn't he wearing?"

"Long story. Later. What else?"

"Jeez, you're no fun. Take his photo, put it in the jar of honey, and put them in the microwave for a few minutes so the honey warms and sweetens his personality. Turn on the microwave, and say, 'Sweet as me, you will be. Harm it none. So mote it be.' "

Vickie leaned against the counter. "I hate spell-speak."

"You're in deep denial, witchy-poo. Spell-speak trips off your tongue whenever your emotions get the best of you."

"They do not! Oh, all right. I'll do it, but only because I'm desperate. Gotta go. Thanks."

Rory came back to the shop later that afternoon. "Your laundry is done," he said.

"I didn't think you were gonna do it. What changed your mind?"

"If you must know, it was the thought of getting into your knickers. I'm thinking of building a shrine to that cherry one-piece."

"It's called a teddy," she said, turned on, despite herself, by the thought of his hands on her underwear. She got the feeling he knew he got to her, because he raised a sexy brow, stroked one of her earlobes, and as she shivered, he slipped his hands into his pockets and whistled his way back to the house.

The rest of the afternoon flew by. After she closed, she followed a roar of machinery, and a string of Scottish curses. Rory stood in the living room trying to clear his face of soot while an ancient vacuum hose spewed dust like a frenzied snake. The only part of Rory's face not black was his wild eyes.

"Pull the plug," she shouted, surprising him, and he stepped back, and tripped, ass over head, knees-up over a bullet vacuum.

"Catch it," he shouted.

"Pull the plug." She made a pulling motion.

Rory rose to his knees, pulled on the offending hose, and snapped it off. The connector directed a stream of dust straight at him.

No longer in range, Vickie ran over and pulled the plug, while Rory coughed up a lung.

She urged him to the sofa and got him a glass of water.

"Thank you," he said, putting the glass on the coffee table and eyeing the dead monster. "What kind of vacuums do you people use?" His words conveyed so much dignity, he might have been wearing Armani, yet he looked like a chimney sweep who'd lost a fight with a rabid squirrel.

She sat beside him. "Since my parents got that vacuum as newlyweds, I think it's a wonder the motor has any whirr left. You plugged the hose into the wrong end. See, two connectors? One sucks, the other blows."

Rory's chin came up. "I beg your pardon."

"Loaded statement, eh? But I kid you not, it's definitely broken, because it's *not* supposed to blow the dirt from the bag back out again. That end is for air to blow the dust away."

"Perhaps the bag was too full."

"Now that I think about it. I'll bet it doesn't have a bag, which would explain why the interior was filled with dirt rather than air. "They must have stopped manufacturing bags for this model about twenty years ago."

"Guess your mother cleans as often as you do."

"She'd clean more, if she wasn't dead."

"Ach, and I'm an oaf. I didn't know you'd lost your mum, too." He pulled her close, getting her dirtier, but she didn't care.

"She died when I was in college."

"I'm sorry. Was she ill?"

"No. Yes, but we didn't realize it. She dieted until her heart gave out. She'd look in the mirror ten times a day and shake her head. I'd stand beside her and tell her she was beautiful, but she didn't see me."

"Perhaps you need to forgive her?"

Vickie shrugged. "I'm madder at my

father. He gave her pet names like Cookie Cheeks, Hot Cross Buns, McNugget, anything edible. He'd laugh and she'd wince. After he left us for a toothpick, my mother went on a diet to die for."

"Which makes my remark on meeting you unforgivable, and yet, you just called someone a toothpick."

"But I didn't mean . . . If I were skinny, I'd . . . Maybe I should stop calling Mel and Kira stick people?"

Rory toyed with a lock of her hair. "If I called you Cupcake," he said, "it'd be because I wanted to lick all the frosting off you so I could go looking for your creamy center from the inside out."

Vickie put some space between them. "No way!"

Rory warmed her with his look. "I'm just saying that perception is everything."

"You mean that she might have had an eating disorder without my father's help?"

"More than likely; they both had issues, and you got caught in the middle."

"I never told an outsider this crap before, and, you know, you've given me something to think about."

"Good. How do I become an insider?"

"Don't bother. Insiders are a real disappointment. Stay out. It'll be better for both of us."

"Okay . . . but forgive me for my well-fed remark?"

"Are *you* cleaning this mess?"

Rory raised his right hand. "Oath of a neat-freak."

"Then I might forgive you."

"I await your verdict with baited breath," he said with one of his charming scowls. "Do you have a vacuum from this century?"

Vickie got her vacuum and set it down in front of him. "I changed the bag last week."

"I stand before you a repentant man."

"You stand before me a filthy man."

"Are there other ancient appliances around here that can get me into trouble?"

"Yep." Vickie smiled at the possibilities. "Nana was a real packrat."

"Wonderful."

"Supper's on me tonight. By the time you're finished cleaning this, you can have your turn in the shower."

After she was clean again, Vickie threw on a witchy low-cut black caftan, heard the water from Rory's shower as she passed, and found the living room clean.

In the kitchen, she cut the two-year-old cradle-breaker from the picture and put Rory's half in her giant economy size jar of honey. "This should make you plenty sweet, brogue boy." Just to be sure, she put it on high for ten minutes, recited Kira's chant, and went for Chinese takeout.

When she got back, Rory sat at her kitchen table, and raised his coffee cup in a salute. "Jings," he said eyeing the bag of food. "I was afraid *that* was supper." He nodded toward the sugary gold slime oozing from the sides and bottom of her microwave door.

"Yikes," she said.

"I'm telling you, your appliances are out to get me. Whatever's in there blew up and sent me running for cover."

"That's not the effect I was going for."

"Effect? I thought it was dessert, and so did Tigerstar by the way. She thought it was a giant lolly."

"Oh, I hope she's not sick later."

"Warning well taken. She'll not be sleeping in my bed tonight."

Damn Kira for having her say "sweet as me," in a spell. How stupid was that? She was as cranky as the Scot. She should have said, "sweet as Mel." Vickie sighed. "I'll clean it up later."

"It'll be hard as rock candy by then. Those stalagmites and stalactites will require power tools."

Vickie crossed her arms. "So why didn't

you clean it while it was soft?"

"Because things happen around here that spook the briefs off me and I didn't want to upset the balance of your madcap universe."

"At least my life's not dull as a hermit. Let's eat."

"The longer you wait, the harder it's going to get," he said.

"Promises, promises."

"I keep my promises, Victoria. Don't tease a sleeping dragon if you don't want to catch fire."

NINETEEN

She might like to get singed, Vickie thought, but catching fire, not so much, and she didn't know how to say so without giving away her attraction.

"I'll clean the microwave," Rory said, "as long as you can promise that whatever effect you were going for didn't have anything to do with my important parts. I'm partial to my package, ye ken?"

"So am I," Vickie said. "Where would my dreams be without it?"

"True," Rory said, rolling up his sleeves.

It took all his considerable strength to yank the microwave door open, and when he finally did, the glass cracked.

Vickie wished she had her camera to capture the look on his face. "I told you I'd do it later," she said.

He shook his head as if to clear it. "What is it with me and your appliances?"

"I don't know. You got some bad karma to

work off?"

"Define bad karma."

"I'll take that as a yes. But hey, you didn't break your coffeemaker."

"Because it's mine, I'll bet. Ach, ouch. There's glass in here."

"Did you cut yourself?"

"Aye, a scratch, but you might have warned me." He looked more closely at the inside. "And what's this?" He took a steak knife from a kitchen drawer, sawed along the microwave ceiling, and pulled out the honey-slick picture of himself stuck to the knife blade. "Victoria," he said. "Do you have anything you want to tell me?"

Vickie considered an escape route. "You won't like it."

"Understatement," he said. "I hate every possible explanation."

"I asked Kira for a spell to sweeten you."

"Tart, am I?"

"As a pickled egg with lemons on top — and cranky, crotchety, crabby —"

"Surly and cantankerous," he added. "Always have been. You think a spell is like to change me? You are a witch, then?"

"No, Kira's a witch. I just thought —"

"I am who I am, Victoria. Take me or leave me."

"I hear you, Rory. That's all I ever wanted

from a man, for him to take me as I am." She took out two forks.

Rory set down the knife and opened the two containers of Chinese food. "I'm not fond of your rhyming wishes."

"Well that's not taking me as I am, is it?" She ate lo mein from the box. "I agree, though. The rhymes drive me crazy, but I'm beginning to worry that my 'wishes come true,' like our dreams, are caused by the magic I don't want to believe I have."

"Rhyme a wish to send your magic away then." Rory stabbed a boneless spare rib from his box.

"You want me to be a witch to stop me from being a witch?"

"Aye, I ken the irony. So you can't do it then?"

"I'm fresh out of powdered toadstool."

"You don't know how happy that makes me."

"Switch containers," Vickie said. "I might be a loose cannon witch, but if I am, you've been caught in the crossfire."

"Bloody lucky me."

Vickie didn't think Rory was ready to hear that opening the wardrobe meant she supposedly inherited old Lili's powers. She'd probably let enough skeletons out of the family wardrobe for one day.

Maybe Kira was right. Maybe she did need to accept her power — if she had any — and make peace with it. Then she could at least harness whatever it was, if only to tuck it away.

"My knack for wishing seemed worse after I found the unicorn," she admitted. "Then worse still when you arrived."

He moved his chair closer as they ate from both containers. "Don't go blaming me for your magic," he said.

She waved away his comment with the last sparerib. "My dreams might be construed as a prime example of my magic, but what about your dreams? Do you have a knack for magic?"

"Not possible."

"That's what I say. Magic; I'd like to bury it in the backyard and forget it exists, except for the dreams. Those I want to keep . . . and improve on."

"Aye," Rory said, setting down his fork. "So do I. Come along, I'll remove the petrified honey with a hammer and chisel tomorrow, and replace the microwave as well."

She threw away the take-out boxes and he left the forks in the sink. "You're a bad influence on me, Cartwright."

"Are you kidding? I sorted my socks this morning!"

He pulled her against him, his arm around her, and walked her up the stairs. "Now that we've eaten like cave dwellers, let's go warm up by the fire."

"That sounds promising." Maybe the honey had worked.

"I don't fancy going to sleep this early anyway," he said. "Our parallel dreams are beginning to worry me."

"I hear you."

She opened the humidor to release the tobacco scents of cloves and whisky, then she chose the corner of a sofa near the hearth while Rory set logs on the fire and got a blaze going.

"I recognize the scent of your tobacco," he said, standing. "It's an old family favorite."

"Nobody smokes it. Nana replaced it every once in a while to keep the scent. What can I say? I'll probably do the same."

Rory sat at the opposite end of the sofa, a disappointment, until he placed a pillow on his lap and crooked a finger. "Lay your head here, darlin'. We've had a long day."

Vickie couldn't think of another place she'd rather be, so she lay on the sofa and put her head in her Scot's lap.

Tigerstar pounced on Rory's shoulder, and he chuckled, stroked her, and handed her over.

"You're getting used to her," Vickie said.

"More or less. Scared the bejesus out of me the other night when she landed on my chest while I was sleeping," he said. "She shows no mercy with her claws, not even on a naked chest." Rory had to rest his arm across Vickie's breasts to pet her cat. Good cat, she thought.

Vickie sighed so Rory would know she was there. "What did you do?"

"Knee-jerk reaction," he said. "What do you do when a bug lands on you? I shoved her off."

"Oh, oh."

"Right. So after I got her out of the dust-bin, calmed her down, and apologized, we came to an understanding, didn't we, Star?"

"You could have put her in the hall before you went to bed."

"If I'd known she was sleeping in the bowl of the overhead light, I might have."

"Oh yeah. That's why Nana had the switch disconnected."

Rory shook his head and toyed with the lace on her dress beneath her breasts.

She never knew a man whose silence could bring contentment. Though she had only known Rory for a short time, he made her feel oddly complete. His presence in her life felt right. *He* felt right in her home.

Vickie got sleepy, but she loved Rory's attention, and tried not to close her eyes.

When she opened them, dawn filtered through the stained glass windows on either side of the fireplace, and she found herself on the sofa in Rory's arms, her head tucked into the hollow of his neck, his hand cupping a breast, his erection nuzzling her in just the right place.

Feeling wicked, she pressed against him.

Rory groaned and surged in return.

No dreams of kisses or breast-nuzzles had disturbed her sleep. No memory left her wanting. She had the real thing, a man next to her, solid and strong-armed, pulling her into him. Two people who fit each other as if God had carved them from the same lump of clay, broke them apart, and made them flesh.

"I didn't dream last night," she said.

"Ach no, but I feel as if I'm dreaming now." His words fanned warmth against her neck.

She tilted her head. "Why do you think we didn't dream?"

"Because we were already holding the one we seek in sleep? No need to search?"

Vickie shivered. "There's something frightening about our dreams, isn't there?"

"And exhilarating," he said.

Her Gothic floor clock chimed seven, and Vickie tried to pull from Rory's arms, but he held her in place. "Bide a while. I like holding you all warm and sleep mussed."

"Work," she said. "I have to open the shop."

"It's Sunday, sunshine. You open the shop at noon. I dusted your sign."

Vickie sighed, snuggled close, listened to Rory's heart, his even breathing, then his soft snores and she drifted as well.

"Mom! I found Vickie! She's sleeping with a man!"

TWENTY

The scent of lavender lingered but Rory felt a disturbing chill as he sought Victoria's sleep-warm body. He opened his eyes and came face to face with a wee lad, his elbows on the sofa, his hands cupping his chin.

Victoria stood with a babe on her shoulder, Melody Seabright beside her.

"Ach, and who's this braw laddie?" Rory asked, ruffling the boy's hair as he sat up.

"I'm Shane. Did you hear, Mom? I'm a braw laddie." He turned back to Rory. "Aunt Vickie said you act like a cranky caveman, but she promised you wouldn't bite."

"Did she now?" Rory eyed Victoria. "Then I'm thinking she doesn't know me as well as she ought."

"This is entirely too juicy for a mom on the run, with a six year old in tow." Melody gave Victoria a look. "We'll discuss it later." She checked her watch. "Meanwhile, I'm supposed to shoot a clambake in Maine in an hour, but the universe is against me. Logan is stuck at the Chicago airport. My mature sitters are on a cruise, and though my timing sucks, can you watch the kids until this afternoon, Vic?"

"Mom, you said 'sucks.' "

"Hush, sweetheart."

"I'm *not* a mature sitter?" Victoria asked.

Shane laughed. "Mom means old like the Grands."

"Don't let the Grands hear you call them that. I gotta run." Melody kissed Victoria's cheek. "Do you mind?"

"Of course not. Wait, I'll walk you down." Victoria placed the babe, no bigger than a button, in Rory's arms, slipped into her shoes, and left.

"Well, mighty me." Rory looked at Shane. "Who have we here?"

"My sister, Jessica. We call her Jess, jor stinky-pants. She got named for the judge that matchmaked Mom and Dad. She gives cemetery tours. She was our neighbor but she got married and we bought her house."

Rory's facial muscles twitched. "I assume the judge is Jess, not stinky-pants, and I'll bet you'd be a bundle of answers, if I asked the right questions."

Shane nodded. "Ask me about Auntie

Vickie. She used to babysit me when I was a kid."

Victoria came in and took the baby. "You two can grill and spill later. Rory, after you shower and dress, you can make us a nice Sunday breakfast."

"Lucky me." He stood, ran a finger up Victoria's neck, and tapped her nose.

Shane followed him into the bathroom. "Why don't cats have lips?"

Rory looked down. "Don't they?"

"If they do, they're sucked right into their mouths."

"No kidding. Go find Tigerstar so you can show me."

"In a minute," Shane said, so Rory ended up brushing his teeth to the lad's detailed instructions. Victoria came in, a baby in one arm, a stack of clothes in the other, his black briefs bearing a happy-face sticky-note.

Rory put them on a shelf in the closet. "They're wearing a smile because?"

"They're my second favorite."

"And your first favorite?"

"A kilt in the wind." She took Shane's hand. "Mr. MacKenzie might need some privacy, sport."

"What's a kilt in the wind?" the lad asked as they left.

When Rory stepped from the bathroom,

Shane was sitting on the stairs to Victoria's room waiting for him.

"Ever been up there?" Rory asked looking up the stairs.

"Yeah. It's all yucky girlie, but the bed's under a slanty ceiling near a window with colored glass. Me and Auntie Vickie make it into a fort and snuggle and tell secrets."

"Any mirrors up there?"

"Auntie Vickie doesn't like mirrors."

"I don't know why," Rory said. "She's every bit as beautiful on the outside as she is on the inside."

Shane turned to look up the stairs behind him. "Hey, Auntie Vickie, did'ja hear that?"

Rory saw Victoria's rainbow shoes first, her shapely ankles, a raspberry skirt that shared her hips with a lemon shawl, then a lucky babe nuzzling the cleavage of her low-cut lime top. She looked good enough to eat with a spoon.

If not for the children, he'd stop her at the bottom, slip his hands up her legs, and begin the feast.

The babe started wailing halfway down to the kitchen. The shop bell rang at about the same time.

"Get it," Rory said. "I'll take her."

"She's hungry," Shane said.

"Go," Rory told Victoria.

By the time Victoria came back, Rory had finished feeding Jessica her apricot and oatmeal — "barf-bait," according to Shane — and her bottle was nearly empty.

"Have you burped her yet?" Victoria asked.

Rory unplugged the empty bottle, no easy task, and won an earsplitting wail. "Was I supposed to?"

"Uh oh," Shane said, backing up.

"Fast, sit her up," Vickie said. "That girl can hurl."

Up she went . . . and a volcano of high-speed mush shot straight at him . . . cooling as it slid beneath his collar.

Victoria wiped his face with a towel. "Jess holds the long-distance flight record for projectile vomiting."

"Yep, Dad says she could hit the Green Monster from home base at Fenway."

The commentators fell over each other laughing, annoying the hell out of Rory, until the miniperpetrator burped like a sailor on shore leave, and gave him a hundred-watt smile.

Victoria tried to wipe his hair, his shirt, and jeans. He liked her attention, more fool him, especially because she looked apologetic. "You rhymed me into this, didn't you?"

189

"Of course not!"

"Then why do you look so bloody guilty?"

"I . . . have a client in the shop looking at vintage gowns. I forgot I made the appointment, months ago. She's a big-time collector so I can't afford not to —"

"Go, go, go," Rory said, setting the baby in her carrier and taking her to the sink so he could wash his hands. "Lad, you can help me clean up Wee Millie Stinky here."

Victoria returned about a half hour later. "My customer is trying on gowns, so I thought I'd see how you were doing."

Rory handed her the mite, wrapped in a towel. "Here you go, clean and powder-fresh from her bath."

"Do you like my braw gentle bear?" Victoria asked her. "You look so tiny in his big Scot arms."

Her braw gentle bear? This should not please him.

Victoria dressed the babe in what she called a "feety bunny suit," and checked her watch. "MacKenzie, you're starting to sour. You've got three minutes to shower."

"Stop rhyming," he said running up the stairs. "I'll probably slip and break my neck in the shower!" He finished in record time, and when he opened the bathroom door, Victoria gave the mite back. "Mel's running

190

late, and I need to open the shop."

"No problem," Shane said. "Us men can handle one baby girl, can't we, Mr. Mac-Kenzie?"

"Mac, laddie. Call me Mac. I'm not my crusty father."

"Your father's crustier than you?" Victoria asked.

"Keep it up and I'll demonstrate."

By the time his charges napped, Jessica in her carrier and Shane on the sofa, Rory was knackered enough to join them. He should search for the unicorn key, of course, but he closed his eyes and Victoria filled his mind.

He never knew what she'd wear, do, or say, and except for her honeyed spell and exploding rhymes, he didn't care. Her hair was never neat but always an inspiration. She was an inspiration, not unlike the opposite of boring, and, aye, he guessed he'd had enough of that, since he'd never felt so alive.

He genuinely, honestly, liked Victoria, as much as he liked the thought of getting her into his bed . . . for a whole lot more than sleeping.

Vickie and Mel found Rory and the children sleeping in the library, Jess in her carrier by the sofa, blanket to her chin, her cheek resting in the palm of Rory's hand. Rory huffing softly, a besotted Tigerstar in the crook of his arm, Shane under Nana's quilt at the opposite end of the sofa.

"You said he was cold and prickly," Mel whispered.

"Only when he's awake."

Mel tugged Vickie into the hall. "You slept with him, because you like him that way?"

"Sleeping with him was an accident."

"There are no accidents where you're concerned. Be honest. Deep down, didn't you want to sleep in his arms?"

"Okay, maybe when he pets Tigerstar, I wish —"

"Yes!" Mel hugged her. "You and Rory have formed a truce of sorts, haven't you? I mean, I thought you'd come to blows when you met, but from what I saw this morning, you're obviously attracted, or he couldn't have gotten you on that sofa with a gun to your head. It's like magic."

"Rory doesn't like magic."

"That could be a problem."

"*If* I had magic."

"I'm reserving that argument for reinforcements, but answer me this. If Rory tried something, would you let him?"

"She did let me."

Vickie turned with a hand to her heart. "I

did not!"

He stood just inside the library, Jessica's sleepy head on his shoulder. "Tattoo," Rory said.

Mel's radar went up. "Which one?"

Rory did a double-take. "Stars. How many tattoos does she have?"

"Hello, I'm in the room!"

Mel turned on her. "He's seen your stars? He's only been here three days."

"Hey," Vickie said, "there were mitigating circumstances. It's not like he saw the dragon."

"Dragon?"

"You hussy." Mel hugged her. "I'm so proud of you."

"Where's the dragon? Damn. Darn. Never mind." Rory stepped aside to let Shane out.

"Is Dad home yet?"

"Yikes," Mel said. "Let's go, kiddos. We have to pick up your dad at the airport twenty minutes ago."

In the driveway, Vickie and Rory waved Mel off, as if they were a couple, and Vickie unfortunately liked the idea. Thank the stars for Mel and the kiddos after last night.

Her dreams were fantasy, but sleeping in Rory's arms had been real, and wonderful, and alarming, and she wanted to do it again. Never. Someday. Maybe. "Would you like to take a walk?" she asked.

"I'll say it again; you're a mind reader." He took her hand, and as they walked, autumn leaves crisped beneath their feet, a witch swept a sidewalk, a vampire hung a sign, pumpkins sat in windows, haystacks stood on stoops.

"Hungry?" Vickie asked. "You worked hard today."

"Aye, at a labor I enjoyed, though yesterday I'd have said I couldn't abide children."

"You, a stubborn Scot, changed your mind?"

"A braw lad who thinks you're 'a super cool dude' and a wee mite's toothless grin can do that to a man."

Vickie shouldered him. "You're such a pushover."

"Never tell the blatherskites back at the lodge. They think I'm the scourge of Caperglen."

"A scourge? I knew it!"

"Ach, darlin', it takes one to recognize another."

"You can't annoy me," Vickie said. "The shine on your armor's too bright tonight."

Rory checked his watch. "Your blinders are due to fall off any second. I've never seen your approval last."

"You want approval? How do you feel

about running the shop Friday and Saturday? I have a vintage clothing auction in Rhode Island, and if you do it, I won't have to close."

"I'd be honored."

"Add another layer of gloss to your shine. Can I treat you to dinner, Salem style? Not pizza."

Rory pulled her close. "What I fancy," he whispered, warming her ear, "is a snog by the fire."

"Is that as kinky as it sounds?"

"Think of it as . . . lip exercises for two. It's how far we take the snog that counts, and this knight's feeling as if his charger can go the distance."

Victoria's knees went weak. Rory's arm at her waist held her upright as he turned her. "Let's go home," he said, "and I'll pet you like I pet Tigerstar."

Vickie stopped. "You heard that?"

Rory's rusty half chuckle touched her in a physical way, and when they stepped into the kitchen, he swept her into his arms.

"Feeling a surge of testosterone, are you?"

"A rampage."

"Oh goody," Vickie said as he carried her toward the stairs. "Wait, we need a celebratory feast. Fridge," she said, and he lowered her so she could grab a split of champagne.

"It's been chilling since Christmas."

"Then it's as ready as I am."

She snatched a bag of cheese-puffs off the counter.

"You call that a feast?"

"You betcha!"

"Ach, darlin', but a feast is what I'm going to make of you."

Twenty-One

Vickie sighed, lowered her head to Rory's shoulder, and someone knocked on the kitchen door. He carried her over to open it.

The blonde on the stoop pricked Vickie's sexual haze like a pin to a bubble, yet a sense of peace washed over her as well. "Can I help you? Rory, put me down." She handed him the puffs and champagne, and adjusted her clothes. "Do I know you?"

The blonde shrugged. "I'm looking for my grandmother."

The girl's "Will Work for Shoes" tee-shirt, with its funky shoes marching across the front, flattered a pair of vintage jeans and butterscotch leather spikes.

"I'm sorry," Vickie said. "You have the wrong house."

"Nope, this is it."

"I live here," Vickie said, "but the wharf streets are tricky. Come in, and we'll find her in the phone book."

"Did you buy the house from Nana? Can you tell me where she went?"

"I take it you lost touch?"

Shoe-girl looked around, shook her head, and Vickie got a strange sense that everything would be fine, which was weird because nothing was wrong, until a second young woman appeared.

"I can't wait another minute. I have to pee." Goth-girl resembled Shoe-girl, except for her chop-shop hair, dyed blackberry to match her nails and lipstick. She eyed Vickie as if *she* was weird. "You're not Nana." She gave Rory a once over. "You either, hot stuff." She crossed Vickie's kitchen. "Bathroom," she said, waving a hand. "Don't worry, I know the way."

"That was Storm," Shoe girl said. "She's my sister."

"Is that her name?" Rory asked, "or her MO?"

"That's Rory. Don't mind him. He was recently released from his cave. I'm Vickie."

"Harmony," Shoe-girl said.

"Harmony and Storm?" Rory said. "Your mother must have a great sense of humor.

"Yeah, she was a hoot. The day we were born, she taught us hide and seek, and we haven't found her yet."

Twins abandoned at birth invading her kitchen, Vickie thought, feeling as if someone had told a joke and she was the only one who didn't get the punch line.

"Is Nana out playing bingo?" Storm asked, returning.

"Your grandmother doesn't live here," Vickie said, prickling every time one of them said "Nana," which was stupid, because, hell, everybody had a Nana.

"She lives here," Storm said, jeans riding low, cleavage riding high and about to pop from in her "Sleeps Well With Others" tee. A rebel and proud of it, Storm raised her chin and blew a gum-bubble the size of Texas. When it popped, she eyed Rory as her gold-studded tongue pulled it back in, her lipstick stark against the pink gum.

Vickie elbowed Rory. "You're drooling."

He came to. "What?"

"You're such a man." Vickie turned to the twins. "Wrong house." She opened the door.

Harmony touched Storm's arm. "Be nice."

"Sure, Sis." Goth-girl slapped the door to Nana's built-in ironing board. "Ironing board," she said, "puke-ugly coral inside, if nobody's painted it."

Rory opened it, proved Storm right, and

used Shane's favorite gagging symbol.

Goth-girl winked.

Their grandmother had probably been a neighbor, but . . . "How did you know?"

"Were you gonna leave me in the van until morning?" said a clone in a cowboy hat.

Three? There were three of them?

Miss "Save a Horse, Ride a Cowboy," clicked into the kitchen in a thigh-high leather skirt and well-worn alligator boots. "Is Nana here?"

"This is Destiny," Harmony said. "We're triplets, identical, if you haven't guessed. Storm tries to confuse people."

"I can't believe her name is Storm," Vickie said.

"Neither can she. She's been making a karmic joke of it her whole life."

"Stop talking about me as if I wasn't here. Having a dorky name doesn't mean I'm deaf."

"That's true," Vickie said. "But maybe you don't know who you are, so you're experimenting until you find out?"

"Smartass."

"Bitch."

"You should know."

Rory made a noise deep in his throat, which meant he was amused, damn him.

"In case my weird name didn't give me

away," Storm said, "I'm the unexpected 'twin,' the straw that broken the camel's back."

Destiny shook her head. "Get over it. The woman who let us borrow her uterus would have skipped town anyway. And be nice. Vickie isn't her."

"Be nice to goody-two-shoes?"

"She's no goody-two-shoes," Rory said, "believe me."

"You should know." Storm winked.

"I mean, Victoria can be as much of a bitch as you."

Storm huffed. "What am I, the bitch standard?"

Vickie tweaked Rory's beard.

"Ouch!"

"Storm," Harmony said, "everybody calls you a bitch."

Storm shrugged. "Whatever."

"Nana's not here," Harmony told Destiny. "Vickie owns the house, but Storm's been brewing mischief, so we haven't cleared the confusion."

"Spell me!" Storm said, with an "F-you" tone.

"Don't tempt me," Harmony said. "I'll spell you sweet."

Destiny focused on Vickie. "We're looking for Brigit Cartwright; do you have any idea where she went?"

Rory steered Vickie to a chair. "Would you like to sit down?" he asked the girls.

"No thanks," Harmony said. "We need to find our grandmother tonight."

"Well I gotta sit," Vickie said, "because I'm freaked. Our grandmothers have the same name and . . . I'm sorry, but my Brigit Cartwright died four months ago."

Storm slapped her arms against her sides. "We're screwed."

"Way to grieve!" Vickie shot from her chair and wrenched open the door. "I think we're done."

"Storm isn't really a heartless bitch," Destiny said. "We only met Nana once."

"Well, she practically raised me, and I miss her like hell, so pardon me if I throw the bitch out on her self-centered ass."

"Like that hasn't happened yet today," Storm muttered.

"Wait," Destiny said, pulling Storm up short. "This is confusing. It's not like we can have the same grandmother. Dad's an only child."

"So is my father," Vickie said, unease taking root in her mind. "It's not possible, but what the hell, I'm gonna ask anyway. What's your father's name?"

"Patrick Cartwright," Harmony said.

Vickie pushed the door so hard, it slammed. "Why *didn't* I see that coming?"

TWENTY-TWO

"Do I ken some sibling attachment, here?" Rory asked.

"Don't count on it, hopscotch," Storm said.

Vickie sat again, feeling angry, and a lot like crying. "Why didn't Nana tell me about you?"

Harmony took Vickie's hand, and held it. "Nana didn't want to hurt you. It would have hurt you, wouldn't it, to know that Dad had another family?"

"A family he stayed with? Yeah." Vickie wanted to pull her hand free, but Harmony had a calming influence. "He really did a number on my mother, the bastard."

"Not to mention what he did to you," Rory added. "I'd like to beat the bejesus out of him."

"Get in line," Storm said. "Are you her watchdog or her worst mistake?"

"I'm Victoria's roommate."

"Her boy toy you mean?"

"Of course n . . . never mind. Think of me as an impartial observer."

"You looked impartial when you opened the door with her in your arms," Harmony said, letting go of Vickie to take Rory's hand. They stared each other down.

"You're harmless for the most part," Harmony said, letting him go. "But watch that hidden agenda."

"I am not harmless!" Rory opened the fridge and slammed pizza, sandwich meat, and cheese, on the table.

"Harmony can feel your enegy. And Des is psychic," Storm added, "so get used to her know-it-all attitude."

"If she's psychic," Rory said. "Why didn't she know about your grandmother?"

"Nana wasn't open to being read," Destiny said with a shrug. "She was probably stronger than us."

Rory looked confused and appeared to shake it off. "Why did you need her tonight?"

"We got kicked out of school this morning," Destiny said. "Dad stopped paying tuition."

"No surprise there." Vickie opened the box of cold pizza and offered it around. "Aren't you kind of old for college?"

Destiny nodded. "We worked a few years, until Dad came into some money."

"Money?" Vickie looked up. "About four years ago?"

"Yes, as a matter of fact, it was." Destiny took a piece of pizza.

Vickie fell back in her chair. "I knew Nana had a good reason to mortgage the house. Bet Dad drank your tuition."

"Who knows?" Destiny shrugged. "He sold our house and didn't leave a forwarding. Nana was our last hope."

"You don't have a place to go?" Vickie put down her pizza.

Storm hooted. "We're homeless, and you're clueless."

Vickie wiped her hands. "You're homeless, Storm, but your sisters aren't. *They're* staying here."

"Hey," Storm protested. "Don't get all control freaky on us."

"Storm," Harmony chided. "A little gratitude would be nice. Victoria is willing to open her home to us."

Storm tugged on the snack bag until it barfed puffs. "How'd it get to be her home, I'd like to know? We have as much right to this house as she does."

"Wait a minute," Rory said, picking a puff out of Vickie's hair. "If you'd tended your

206

dying grandmother, struggled to pay her hospital and funeral bills and a mortgage to pay *your* tuition, you might have a quarter of a right to the house. Might."

Storm poured a cola. "We don't know for sure that Nana gave Dad the money."

"Don't worry," Rory promised. "I'll find out."

"How do you figure into all of this?" Storm snapped.

"He came to my rescue like a knight on a white charger."

Destiny shook her head. "Don't bet the bank on *that* horse going the distance, Sis."

Rory paled. "I'm paying a thousand a month to live here. How does that sound to each of you?"

Vickie pulled on his sleeve. "Stop it, Rory."

He relaxed his bulldog stance. "Just adding perspective."

"Forget it. They're staying." Nana had said to welcome harmony and destiny, and now Vickie understood that she hadn't been talking psychic awareness. *For you, Nana, I'll even open my home, and heart, to Storm.* "I'll see what I can do about the spare bedrooms."

Worried, Rory followed her. "Victoria," he said, as she stood dazed in a pink-striped room packed with furniture. "Your sisters can sleep on the sofas in the library tonight. We can empty these rooms tomorrow."

"Rory . . . I have a family . . . sisters." Victoria held up three fingers. "Three."

"Aye, and that's a houseful."

"I always wanted to be part of a big family, except . . . I thought it would happen more slowly."

"How are you going to support them?"

"Stop trying to scare me. I'm not abandoning them. Been there, hated it. I'll make the shop pay better . . . knock out the living room wall, buy more stock."

"You're in shock."

"Of course I am." She indicated a room that looked like a furniture warehouse. "Where am I going to put all this?"

"Have a tag sale? It's October. I hear the October tourists are like bats from a cave. They just keep coming."

"It's all broken."

Rory fit a strip of oak trim against a dry sink. "It can be fixed. That's what you hired *me* for."

"Do you think it'll work?"

"Trust me. I'm a master woodworker."

"Not that. My sisters. Do you think they like me?"

"Do you like them?" Rory wiped his dusty hands on her hip shawl to cop a feel.

She stepped closer. "I don't *know* them."

"There you go. You need to get to know each other. The brat is as mad as a box of frogs, but I'm sure she has at least one redeeming quality."

TWENTY-THREE

Vickie hid her face in his shirt. "I don't know *how* to be a sister."

"You're Melody and Kira's in all but name."

Her head came up. "I gotta call them."

"Tomorrow," Rory said, taking Victoria by the shoulders. "Right now, you need blankets and pillows for the library."

She looked toward the stairs. "For my sisters. I mean, they say they are, but they're strangers, aren't they?" Victoria looked as earnest as Rory had ever seen. She bit her lip. "Should I have asked for their birth certificates?"

"I suppose, though they resemble you, and you didn't ask for *my* ID."

"Logan and Mel are friends with a retired judge, who's married to a retired D.A., who had you run through the system. You don't have a criminal record and the references on your website check out."

"Well there's me in my place." He'd not underestimate her again. "Tell you what. *I'll* get their IDs."

Victoria gave him an eye twinkle, an electric one that went straight to his poor upstaged libido, cut off in its prime by intruding siblings. Their presence would hamper his search for the key to the hidden compartment and his ability to get to the unicorn, once he found a key. And he might as well stop trying to charm Victoria into his bed. Her sisters were reading his bloody mind.

When he went downstairs, Destiny handed him their birth certificates before he asked, bang-on spooky. He wondered if he could control his thoughts.

Hell, he didn't *want* to hurt Victoria. He wanted her to be happier and wealthier for his stay, and she would be, if her sisters didn't interfere.

"Fun to have psychics in the family, eh?" Storm said.

"Is that what you do, Storm, read minds?"

"You got it in one, hopscotch, plus Harmony and Destiny have their radar locked on you, too, past and future, so don't you be scamming our sister."

Victoria appeared on the stairs, with blankets, in time to hear Storm's warning, of course. "Storm!" she said, "Thank you for trying to protect me. That's the nicest thing you've done all evening."

Storm slammed the refrigerator door. "Yeah, well I don't like getting caught at it, so next time you *think* I'm being nice, don't bring attention to it. Got that?"

Destiny chuckled. "Remember this 'maelstrom' of warm fuzzies, Sis, because in Stormland, this is a Hallmark moment, and you might want to paste it into your scrapbook. They don't come every year, you know."

"I'll never mention it again."

Storm frowned. "See that you don't."

Rory pushed their birth certificates across the table.

"Yep," Victoria said with a sigh. "Sired by the same loser."

"He's got a lot to answer for," Harmony said. "But we are sorry to intrude on you two."

"Better that you did. It was definitely a case of being saved by the bell."

"Ach, and we agree on that." *Not.*

"Hah," Harmony said to him. "I'm on to your wicked intent."

Storm got in his face. "Not gonna happen, Romeo." She faced Vickie earnestly. "Rent! If we triple up and do chores after work, can we share one room for one grand a month?"

Victoria shook her head. "You'll pay rent when you have jobs, then you'll get a family discount. Tomorrow we'll talk. Right now, I need to get used to having sisters."

Destiny hugged her. "I knew you'd be sweet."

"Duh, you're psychic," Storm said, "but too much sweet makes me barf."

"I like you, Storm," Victoria said, "even though too much crap makes me barf."

"That's my girl." Every minute in Victoria's company pulled him deeper under her spell. Rory almost wished he cared to fight it.

"You can sleep in the library," Victoria said, "until you have bedrooms, then it's Rory's study again."

He looked up. It was their trysting place, and Victoria liked it that way. He may not smile much on the outside, but he was sure smiling inside. He watched her take the blankets to the laundry room.

"Rory," she called. "Can you come in here for a minute?"

He found her staring at the feminine figure he'd created from a wire coat-hanger, hanging on the wall, wearing her cherry teddy. "Ach, I forgot about that."

She took it down. "What was the point of this exercise?"

She raised his temperature just asking. He backed her against the wall, and pinned her there. "I want to finish what we started before your sisters got here."

She sighed and fell against him, so he put his arms around her, and ran his hands down her back to cup her backside and pull her close.

"So you put my teddy on a shapely hanger to cop a feel in the laundry room?"

"Ach no, this is a bonus. That was for . . . inspiration?"

Victoria rolled her eyes, stepped from his arms, and tucked the teddy, hanger and all, into a stack of laundry that she took with her when she left.

After the triplets were settled for the night, Rory led Victoria to the living room. Unwilling to say goodnight, he urged her down to the sofa and thought some soft music would be nice about now.

Victoria got up and put on a CD. "I made this compilation myself."

They snuggled to the relaxing strains of "When a Man Loves a Woman," and "Unforgettable," and pin-pricks ran up his spine.

Victoria pulled an afghan over them. "It's been a long day," she said, "but I wasn't ready to say goodnight."

Did magic enter into her mind-reading, her anticipation of his needs? If so, was this the worst, or the best of it?

Had her ability to read him increased . . . with the arrival of her hauntingly gifted sisters perhaps? Or had their arrival brought *him* a bit of wishing ability. If so, he wanted Victoria in his bed. Now. No, wait. Did using powerful wishes make him a witch? Or would that be a wizard?

The whole spooky thing shivered him to his bones, but having Victoria in his arms calmed him. At home in Scotland, at this hour, he'd be greedy for solitude, but, here, peace no longer appealed. Victoria appealed. He'd been a restless soul, but she seemed to tame the hermit in him.

She rose to ease his sore shoulder before he realized it had gone stiff. He loved her hands on him, and imagined her kneading more sensitive parts. He massaged her nape to give pleasure back, and judging by her sigh, he succeeded.

When the music ended, he sang the first line of "Unforgettable."

"The astrological charts are right," she said sitting back down. "Taureans do have wonderful voices. Sing the rest."

"I only know the one line."

"Try," she coaxed, her whisper arousing.

He pulled her across him, so he could hold her and watch her face as he sang:

"Unforgettable . . . you shine like a . . . star.

Unforgettable . . . my bed's not far.

Thoughts of you in that teddy . . . cling to me.

You do . . . *big* . . . things to me."

She started giggling, and he pulled her against his chest to absorb her happiness.

"I applaud your attempt," she said wiping her eyes.

"My attempt at singing?" he asked. "My attempt at lyrics? Or my attempt at getting you into my bed?"

She rose and reached for his hand. "All three."

"Did I succeed?"

"Not a chance."

"But I want to see your starburst again, and what about that dragon Melody was talking about?"

"Try and I'll beat you."

"Ach yes, beat me."

They said goodnight at his door, her unexpected hug bringing their parts deliciously close, and sadly away again, her whisper-soft kiss leaving him wanting, yet strangely pleased. But when he shut his bedroom door, and saw her cherry teddy on its curvaceous hanger reflected in every mirror, he wanted her more than ever.

"For inspiration," said her note on his pillow.

Twenty-Four

"Ach, darlin', do you mean to inspire our dreams?" Rory settled into bed and closed his eyes, his imagination putting Victoria, square, before him, in nothing but the cherry confection she left to inspire him.

Rory waltzed Victoria among the carousel figures to the rising beat of the music, and didn't slow until they got to the unicorn.

There, he lifted her into the saddle.

As she rode, Rory stood her servant, her slave, her lover. He let his fingers drift through her honey hair, the tendrils at her nape, along her ivory throat and into the curls puddled like silk against her shoulders.

Counter to the unicorn's downward movement, he made rising circles along her spine, and when her horned charger rose once more — nearly as high and hard as he — Rory gave Victoria's breasts his stroking attention.

He opened her bodice buttons and knuckled

her starburst, his fist abrading the ridge of her nipple, almost by accident, and she bit her lip against a sigh.

Foreplay at its slow-stroking, fast-turning finest. A moaning lass. A keen, bull-hung laddie, ready for another waltz, a mating ritual like none he'd known.

Victoria's ride raised the spark between them and built their sex play to a fine pleasure-pain. She begged for his teasing strokes, arched and whimpered as he caressed her low at her center, bringing them both nearer the brink . . . closer to that magic time when he would make her his.

Rory could no longer bear the tease. His body clamored to bury itself in Victoria's willing warmth, so he stole her from her horned beast and brought her to the dragon chariot for a ride with a horned beast of another sort.

Making love to the selkie would be like flying into the teeth of a sea storm. Victoria was like a mer-goddess, waiting to rise from the sea, and his anticipation of the moment when she came into her own turned him to honed steel.

As they rode the dragon, her in his favorite place, straddling him, their clothing turned to wisps of silk whisked from their hands by the breeze that caressed their exposed flesh.

Nothing but a last layer remained to each of

them, thin, silk to the eye, but steel to the hands, like chastity belts for two, a challenge to their sexual hunger, a caution to any good sense that remained.

None did.

Scallops of gold gossamer fell around them, draping them into a lily-scented tent, warm with dancing candle-flames and pulsing flesh. A paradise from which they could view the colorful world around them, a confinement neither cared to escape.

Her limbs were bare to his view, his touch, his lips, with nothing between him and her center but a gossamer wisp of cherry dreams.

She caressed his chest and laved his nipples with kitten-tongue kisses, but his black silk briefs allowed her no access. Ach, but he would have her laving his erect charger, if she could free it.

Victoria released her straps, lowered her confinement, and with her own hands, she presented her pouting breasts, a sensual feast for the taking. An offer he would not refuse.

As the dragon rocked, and the carousel spun, Rory's blood thickened and desire smoldered bright in Victoria's eager eyes.

He suckled her, the lace at the juncture of her thighs abrading his rod, heightening his desire. But how to enter her? Barriers so fine, they barely existed — his and hers — barred their way.

Stroking Victoria, seeking her pleasure point, despite the obstruction, Rory found a slash in the fabric at her center — a surprise, but not. There, liquid fire anointed him, and despite the inferno, he brought her pleasure, amazed that he survived her flame.

"Find me," he said. "Take me home."

When Victoria found the opening in his black silk briefs and closed her hand around his eager sex, 'twas nothing like Rory had expected. Heaven and hell in a grasp, better than a dream, more real than reality, more primitive and agonizing than the most tempestuous of matings.

Victoria cupped his bollocks as she worked him, and though Rory had not yet entered her, he reached a high he could hardly bear.

She watched him losing control, seemed almost to take pride in her power, and though Rory tried to take her with him, he jumped the precipice without her, and fell to a sweet death in a starburst of bliss.

Rory came as he woke, an extended orgasm like none he'd known. "Victoria," he whispered, his fist on his brow. Only Victoria. In her hands, in his dream, he'd taken his pleasure and spilled like a lad. What about her?

Day and night, he focused on burying himself inside her rather than on finding a way to search for the unicorn's hidden compartment.

Was Victoria destined to become his salvation or his downfall?

At breakfast, he scowled at the four Cartwright women watching him. "What?" he asked.

"You were a *lot* happier a little while ago," Victoria said.

Her sisters' gazes moved between them.

Storm put down her cup. "Are you two . . ."

"Snogging? Yes," Victoria said, proudly.

"Shagging, no," Rory corrected.

Storm looked at her clones. "Do you know what they're talking about?"

"No," Harmony said, "but evidently they do."

"We're not playing the blanket bagpipe," Rory said. "If that's what you mean."

"Did I mean that, Des?"

She shrugged. "Beats the hell out of me."

Storm shook her head. "And you call yourself a psychic. Can I have the jelly?"

Clearing the spare rooms of overstock, Rory couldn't get his mind off the feel of Victoria's hands on him, the rush when she cupped him, and her look of power and satisfaction when he was about to lose control.

"Rory!" Storm snapped. "Stop undressing Vickie with your eyes. If you lose your grip on that dry sink, you'll drag her down the stairs with you."

"Storm's right." Harmony said. "You look at her like she's prime rib and you're starving."

Rory met Victoria's gaze over the dry sink and they both knew what he'd been thinking. Her eyes turned dark as amber and Rory growled.

"Get a room," Harmony said. "I never saw two people who needed to get laid more."

"Why thank you, Harmony." Victoria raised a brow. "Don't hold back on my account. You know, I'm beginning to see the resemblance between you and Storm."

Harmony gasped. "Now you're just being mean."

"Hey!" Storm elbowed her. "Whose side are you on?"

"My sister's." Harmony smiled. "I'm trying to guide a dry sink to a safe landing, but my pack mules aren't cooperating, except in their minds."

"Jump each other's bones and get it over with," Storm snapped. "I'm going to the shop to help Destiny."

"Harmony," Rory said. "Maybe you should go work in the shop, too, and send Destiny in to help us."

"Sorry," Harmony said, "I know I make you nervous, Rory, but I couldn't stand to go in there."

"Hey, that's my shop you're talking about, and you've never even seen it."

"It's every antique shop, Vickie, and it's what's inside them that bothers me."

"Like what?" Victoria asked when they set the dry sink down in the kitchen so they could rest.

"Everything," Harmony said. "A three-ring circus forms in my head — generations of sounds, sights, feelings, bounce around inside. Negative and positive energy war for prominence, mostly in antique shops, but in old houses, too, though not in this one. There was sadness and love in this house but nothing scary."

"Glad to hear it," Victoria said, "but let me get this straight. You go near old stuff and you feel . . . what?"

"What their owners felt. I can bring energy into focus by touching something. I can tell a lot from touching things . . . and people."

"That shot was for me," Rory said.

"If the hidden agenda fits . . ." Harmony

turned to Vickie. "Think about getting rid of the negative energy in your stock. Your customers would come back more often."

"Would they? You mean have, like, a negative energy sale?"

"What kind of energy does this have?" Rory asked, signaling for Victoria to pick up her end, so they could get the dry sink to the shop.

Harmony flattened a hand on it as they passed. "Someone kind built it," she said walking with them as far as the shop, "for someone he loved. Wait, there's something in it that we're supposed to find."

"Its empty," Victoria said.

"It's not." Harmony shook her head.

Victoria tilted hers. "Let's put it on the porch, search it, stick a premium price on it, and see what happens."

"Well," Rory asked Harmony. "Will it sell or not?"

"Geez" Harmony said. "What am I a fortune teller? Ask Destiny."

"What are you, if not a fortune teller, because you and the other two broom-riders remind me of Victoria and her rhyming wishes. Does magic run in your family?"

"No," Victoria said.

"Yes, it does," Harmony countered.

TWENTY-FIVE

Harmony walked around the outside of the house from the kitchen, so she was waiting for them when they reached the porch with the dry sink.

"Magic doesn't run in the family in the sense that *everyone* has it," Victoria said, determined to make her point. Perhaps too determined, Rory thought.

"Well, no, the men don't have any magic," Harmony admitted, "But Dad said all the women do."

Victoria laughed. "What does he know?"

"That the witch who built this house came from Scotland and bequeathed one of us a special key and a great deal of magic."

"From Scotland?" Rory asked, setting down his end of the dry sink. "What key?"

"We're heredity Pictish witches," Harmony explained. "Nana told me the last time I visited."

"I thought you only met her once."

"I came a couple of times without Destiny and Storm."

Victoria sighed. "Okay, I give. What does Pictish mean?"

"It's a pre-Celtic Scottish witch tradition. The Picts, who came before the Scots, lived around Loch Ness, where our ancestor's family came from. Loosely translated, Pict means picture or tattoo."

Victoria dropped her end of the dry sink. Good thing he'd already set his down, Rory thought, because he was as shocked as she was. Had her genetic makeup compelled her to get tattooed? And where on her body were the rest?

"Why did she tell you?" Victoria asked.

"She said *somebody* in the family should know."

"I mean why didn't she tell me?"

Storm laughed but not in a good way. "You think a woman from our family wouldn't sense your aversion to what amounts to your own heritage?"

"Nana wasn't . . . I don't believe in hereditary magic. It's nonsense."

"Because your rhyming wishes *don't* come true?" Harmony asked.

Destiny joined them on the porch. "Give Vickie a break. She needs to find her own way like we did."

"Speaking of finding things . . ." Victoria opened the doors to the dry sink and stuck her head inside. "Nothing in here," she said.

"I guess a dry sink will do, if you can't stick your head in the sand," Storm said, and Victoria practically gave herself a concussion as she came out ready to argue. But Harmony held the molding Rory had snapped back on last night, and she was prying a parchment envelope from beneath it."

"Damn," Victoria said. "What made you look there?"

"As I said, things about an object jump out at me. The longer I touched it, the clearer the location became."

"What card is it this time?" Rory asked.

"It's the Star, telling me to open my heart," Vickie said — and her home, she thought, which encompassed her sisters, and maybe Rory as well. She'd need to see her way a great deal clearer, however, before she could even begin to believe the last.

"That's one interpretation," Harmony said. "I see the Star as getting along and letting love flow freely." She gave Rory a look. "Family love." She led the way back around the house and into the kitchen, Rory bringing up the rear, feeling excluded.

Destiny sat at the table and studied the

card. "Hope," she said, "the light at the end the tunnel. But I always look toward the future, and maybe I'm reading for the three of us, not Vickie."

Storm made a snarky sound, opened the curio cabinet, took out an expensive-looking pink-glass bowl, and flicked it. "We could also interpret the Star as a mandate from the universe to share the wealth."

Vickie retrieved the bowl, placed it in its gilded holder, straightened its gilded handle, and shut the glass door. "So much for family love," she said. "That's Nana's prized Victorian wedding bowl. There are some things that should stay in a family, no matter what."

Rory choked on a grape. "Sorry. Went down the wrong way." He went for a glass of water. "We left the dry sink on the porch," he said, after he drank it. "Victoria, you need to price it. Destiny, you can sell it. Storm, you clean it up, and don't cheese anybody off."

"Up yours, peckerhead."

"The first trolley's due," Destiny said, so she and Storm went back to the shop.

An old witch from Scotland, Rory thought. If Harmony had mentioned Lili, he'd have done the Highland fling. Except that Victoria's tattoos now worried him as much as they turned him on.

She fell into the chair across from him, her hair more mussed than usual, looking more dear than usual, which complicated everything. Now that he knew her heritage, he should find the compartment, prove his ownership, and take the unicorn home. She looked too innocent to be a witch, and too much in denial to be anything but. "Bloody hell, you're all witches."

"Being psychic doesn't make somebody a witch," Harmony said. "Destiny, Storm, and I chose to be witches."

Rory grunted. "Storm, we knew about."

"Don't confuse witch with bitch," Harmony said. "It's insulting."

Rory raised a brow, and Harmony chuckled. "Okay, so Storm's both." She touched Victoria's arm. "Sorry to burst your I'm-not-a-witch bubble, but I think using your gift for wishing goes hand in hand with practicing the craft."

Victoria raised her chin. "My bubble's intact."

"Fine," Harmony said. "Do you want to finish cleaning out the spare rooms, or are you going to sit there and let Rory undress you with his eyes all day?"

"He's trying to decide if I'm a witch."

"Hey," Destiny said, coming in from the

shop. "Storm and I cleaned the backroom and found this ring with a gazillion keys on it." She dangled it before them, and Rory figured that finding the key to the case in that mess of keys would take days.

"Want us to hang them in the backroom?"

"Nah, leave them here," Victoria said. "I'll put them in my room."

Damn, Rory thought. There went his shot. Why hadn't *he* found the keys when he . . . "What do you mean you cleaned the backroom? It was neat as a pin. I cleaned it myself."

"Tidy is not the same as clean," Destiny said, grabbing an apple. "I sold the dry sink, by the way, no dickering."

"Is Storm alone with the customers?" Rory asked, and Destiny and Victoria ran. He went back to fixing and moving furniture from the spare rooms.

That afternoon, Victoria eyed her crowded porch. "What do we do at night with all the pieces that don't sell?"

"We can throw a tarp over them tonight, but we should probably clean out the garage." He'd like to turn it into a workshop anyway. He did his best thinking when he was working with wood. And he certainly needed time to think right now.

"Okay, tomorrow the garage," Victoria

said. "If we clear enough space, maybe you can have a small woodshop."

Later, when the girls picked out their rooms, Harmony asked about the other doors on that floor. I presume they're yours and Rory's."

"No, I sleep upstairs," Victoria said. "But, that's Rory's. I don't want to empty this room." Victoria opened the door, and her sisters shrieked. The biggest bedroom in the house was a closet — slanted shelves of shoes on one wall, half a dozen racks of clothes extending from the wall opposite.

"Look," Harmony said. "Shoe heaven!" She threw her arms around Victoria. "I love my big sister."

"Finally!" Storm said. "Saint goody-two-shoes has a weakness, a failing, a *flaw*. No, two. She's a shoe hound *and* a clothes horse."

Victoria laughed as the triplets invaded.

"Where do you keep your underwear?" Rory whispered in her ear. "That's what *I* want to see."

"I can't decide which would get us into more trouble, MacKenzie, your first smile, or your rifling through my underwear."

"Your underwear, up to my elbows, if you please."

"One good smile, you stubborn Scot, and

I'll let you into my underwear . . . drawer."

"Remember last night's dream?" he whispered. "When we got into drawers of another sort?"

Victoria nodded, innocent but seductive, silent but promising, and Rory damned near took her into his arms.

Harmony knelt before the shoes, raised her arms, and prostrated herself. "I worship before the altar of the shoe goddess." She popped up. "Boots, platforms, and Manolos, oh my!" Still on her knees, she walked the length of the shelves, screeched, sat, tried on a strappy pair, and extended an air-tapping foot. "Yes! We wear the same size!"

Victoria joined her on the floor, which was just as well, Rory thought. A bit of distance between them couldn't hurt.

Destiny was as taken with the clothes. "This *can't* be a Versace," she called, holding up a hanger.

"Uhm, yeah," Victoria said. "It can."

Storm raised a minidress by its hanger. "Hey, look at this. Vickie's got a little black slut dress. I like."

"Did anyone feel a shift in the time-space continuum?" Harmony asked.

"Can it," Storm said. "I might wear this someday."

"Good," Victoria said. "Somebody should."

Then they were all four rooting through the clothes, finding outfits that would be "perfect" for, or "hysterical" on, each other.

The sisters were bonding, no magic involved, just the murky mystique of womanhood. And since they were speaking in tongues, Rory left them to it.

Twenty-Six

The warm fuzzies teased Vickie as she climbed the stairs and got ready for bed, but she pushed sentiment away. She'd house her sisters, employ them, and get them to finish school. They were family, but she wouldn't get attached. Family had a way of disappearing. They knew that, too.

Tonight, even Rory had disappeared. And who could blame him for not wanting her, when there were three beautiful women around. Though he did show an interest in *her* underwear.

Oh well, she was too tired to try and understand the male mind and the way it shifted from one brain to the other.

She had come to the carousel to be alone with Rory, but before she found him by the unicorn, she saw that there were people riding the other figures. Girls actually. No, they were women, identical all of them, beautiful, infinitely more so than her, and every one thinner and younger, so why would Rory want her when the goddesses were there?

She came upon him watching them, so she turned to leave, before he could see her, but he caught her hand.

"How can you want me with them around?" she asked.

"Who?" His smiled weakened her knees and her resolve. "I see no one but you," he said, and won her, heart and soul.

Belonging less to herself than to him, she let him lift her onto the carousel, a move that usually meant they were taking another step toward intimacy, except that they weren't alone.

Rory took her by the hand as they passed scores of gorgeous female clones riding different signs of the zodiac, every one on a horse. The Aquarius unicorn rode alone.

Rory had eyes only for her. Imagine that.

The dragon chariot sat empty, as if awaiting their pleasure, but with their audience, it would remain so. As Vickie's heart fell, Rory caught her around the waist, lifted her against him and jumped them from the platform into the grassy center of the kaleidoscopic whirl.

Around they strolled, a short distance, until Rory opened an invisible door cut into the carousel's mirrored octagon center — a private haven at its heart.

Inside, Rory waltzed her in place to the music of the steam organ, her skirt swaying against his MacKenzie kilt, her cheek pressed to his pirate shirt, the thatch of mahogany chest hair it revealed making her want to touch.

Once upon a time, Rory had worn nothing beneath his kilt, and tonight, she'd followed his example, so nothing could bar his way. "My turn," she whispered in his ear, and Rory understood. He had reached the height of pleasure on their last visit, but she had not.

He turned her, and she was surprised to see a brass four poster dressed in scarlet, and tented with white lace. The bed and the gold candelabras on the floor surrounding it were mirrored on every one of the eight walls. In this wonderful place, the mirrors reflected everything but her.

As Rory led her to the four poster, the organ music slowed and softened. "Do ye sleep well with others, lass?" Rory asked, and when she nodded, he placed her in the center of the bed.

He nibbled behind her ear, her temple, her brow, her cheeks, hot with embarrassment for being in bed with him, then finally he devoured her mouth.

Vickie matched his hunger.

When he left her lips, she whimpered, but then he kissed her neck, the hollow between her breasts, then he bared them, so he could kiss her starburst. Then he adored her, giving each breast its aching due, laving and suckling, making her taut with sensation.

Rory returned to her mouth, while she budded and flowered.

By the time he abandoned the meal he'd made of her, Vickie pulsed slick and ready, but her knight continued his slow journey down her bodice. He nuzzled her center through her gown, then he skipped to her ankles.

She gasped with frustration, and he chuckled, and burrowed beneath her gown.

"Rory," she laughed. "Rory?"

He popped from the tent of her gown, and pushed it aside. "I found a dragon!"

"No kidding? Where?"

"Here!" He took cover again, and paid her dragon due homage. So close, she thought, but not close enough. Then he touched her, there, where she wanted him most, and as he unfolded her, like the petals of a flower, she sighed.

Vickie forgot everything but his gentle touch, his whisper-soft strokes that sent shivery pleasure currents to every part of her.

He touched her in new places, deep pulsing

places, and shock of shocks, she felt . . . his beard, abrading, arousing and . . . "Oh!" He breached her with his tongue.

She'd wanted her turn and he was granting her wish, though she'd not expected this, nor had she rhymed a word. What rhymed with tongue and vagina anyway?

But his attention took her thoughts away.

Under his spell, she rode a wave in a storm, wild and wind-tossed, so high, she might fall off, but he kept her from going over the edge. Instead, he raised her higher, until riding the crest became a fulfillment in its own right, the pleasure so keen, she begged for mercy, until Rory lowered her to rest and float on a sunny sea.

The music turned to a buzz, a horrid intrusion that crashed her to earth and reality.

Vickie smacked her alarm across the room and it hit the wall. She hadn't been ready to wake up. She liked dreams better than reality. Rory had turned her into a woman, at last . . . but only in her dreams.

After a sobering shower, Vickie met her sisters in her dressing room, where chatty blood strangers and dysfunctional family ties roared up to nudge at her reluctant heart.

She liked spending time with her sisters,

but after last night, she wanted some alone time with Rory.

When they all sat down to breakfast, she went over the day. "Rory's going to empty the garage and put that furniture out with the rest. Harmony can check the energy on the repaired pieces and I'll price them. Positives on the porch; negatives on the sidewalk, at bargain prices. Destiny can you mind the shop?"

"I love working in the shop, but there's something up with that unicorn. I think it has a spell on it. I sense a strong vibe whenever I'm near it."

"I do, too," Storm said. "But what I sense is passion and lots of it. You should lay hands on it, Harmony."

Rory was beginning to sweat.

"I can't," Harmony said, "unless we move it outside. Otherwise, I won't get a clear reading."

"Forget it," Vickie said. "The thing weighs a ton."

Rory released his breath.

"Storm, will you clean and polish the positive pieces?" Vickie asked.

"Sure, but why don't we neutralize the negative ones, and keep the prices up there?"

Rory looked up. Vickie sat forward. "You

can do that?"

"I'll put sage and rosemary in a lemon cleaner, and afterward, I'll sprinkle sage in the drawers and salt the sidewalk around them."

"Discreetly," Rory said.

"Bummer." Storm smirked. "I was gonna sprinkle the salt while I circled each piece on my broom."

Vickie choked on her Chai.

In the cupboard, Storm found half a bottle of lemon cleaner and less rosemary. "Harmony and I will hit the grocery store," Storm said.

"By 'hit,' I presume you mean 'go to'?"

"Can it, hopscotch."

Rory shook his head. "Here's money and a list."

"We're doing your grocery shopping?" Storm grabbed for the cash.

Rory pulled it back. "Are you eating?"

"Whatever. Hit me." She presented an open palm. "And I don't mean smack me."

They were bonding, Vickie thought. Rory and Storm understood each other. Neither liked people, emotions, or mincing words. Damn.

In the garage, Vickie wasn't ready to talk about the dream, and Rory followed her lead, though his eyes seemed to twinkle more than usual.

Destiny set up sidewalk-sale signs, and by the time the girls got back with neutralizing supplies, Rory was ready to move a sewing chest out there.

As he crossed the garage, Vickie took off her sweatshirt. "There," she said. "That's better."

He turned, saw the "Sleeps Well With Others" tee, and the sewing chest got in his way.

Vickie stood over him, hands on hips. "Hey, a roll and go for the overactive libido set."

"You seduced me."

"Come again?"

"Helluva time to ask." He fixed his gaze on her cleavage. "You might want to ask if anything's broken."

"I can see what's *not* broken."

"I can't help it if I have a huge —"

"Close your eyes," she said.

"Not looking at you won't lessen my reaction to you," but he folded his arms behind his head, and closed his eyes, not in the least self-conscious about his boner.

"Okay," Vickie said. "What did you just see?"

"A neon sign on your great breasts telling me that you're as hot for me as I am for you."

"Storm looks better than I do in this shirt."

"Storm's a kid. You're the woman I want to take to bed, for real."

Vickie knelt beside him. "Are you okay?"

Rory sat up, hooked a finger in the vee at her cleavage and pulled her close, his knuckle against her breast. "Sleeps well with others, eh?"

"That's for you to find out."

"Keep it up and I won't be able to finish the job."

"We're down to the small stuff."

"Not from my perspective." He eyed her breasts.

"They're too big."

He cupped a beefy hand. "Look what they've got to fill, darlin'. Am I gonna have happy hands or what?"

TWENTY-SEVEN

"Hey, you two. Keep it up," Harmony called. "Making out in the driveway is good for business."

Vickie pushed Rory's hovering hand into her lap.

"Even better," he said.

"Go put the sewing chest on the sidewalk," Vickie said, because of the interested customers, and while he did, she sorted smalls. After he'd brogued the socks off the customers, he returned.

"Is anything selling out there?"

"I sold the sewing chest, and Storm set up two bonnie displays, though I made her promise not to give any customers the evil eye."

"And you lived to tell the tale?"

"Let's just hope my charger works when we need it."

Victoria patted the spot beside her on an old throw rug. "Right here."

"So you can check my charger?"

"So we can finish sorting."

"Ach, right. So, after we sort, then you'll have your way with me?"

"Sort."

Rory took the carousel painting from the box he'd left it in and showed it to her.

"I was sixteen when I painted that, around the time the dream became seductive," Vickie said, "so I directed my confusing new energy into the painting."

"This canna be us, then."

"Look at the color of the man's hair. I had to go to Boston to find it because I couldn't find the perfect color around here. The name on the paint tube was *mahogany.*"

"Us fifteen years ago, when I only started dreaming about you four months ago, and we didn't meet until five days ago?"

Vickie liked the heat in his gaze, a seductive here-I-am mixed with a cocky your-loss-if-you-don't-hop-on.

"When I close my eyes, I can feel your lips on mine," she said. "I could fifteen years ago, and I can today."

"Let's make it real starting now." He leaned forward but gave her a chance to say no.

Afraid to break the spell, Vickie nodded.

Rory took her in his arms and touched his

lips to hers in real time, not dream time. He smelled of spice as he opened his lips over hers, ravenous and seeking sustenance.

More to the point, they fed off each other, his hand sliding down her spine, pulling her against his heat, sinking them into the familiar: into a powerful, physical manifestation of the dream, comforting, arousing, and . . . alarming.

Vickie felt as if she stood on a nonexistent carousel spinning counter to the norm, turning so fast they couldn't go back the way they'd come. The floor beneath her feet picked up speed, made her dizzy, and unwound her world.

She came up for air, while Rory continued to nibble the sides of her mouth, her neck, her cleavage at the vee of her shirt.

"I have a confession to make about some of our dreams," she said breathlessly.

Rory looked at her through a smoky haze of desire.

"Our foreplay has started to make me come as I wake up."

Rory dug his fingers into her waist. "You, too? I'm glad."

"How could I not when you were —"

"As greedy and out of control as a lad?"

With a rush at the memory of him coming, Vickie opened her mouth over his, and

Rory cooperated.

"Last night was amazing," she said.

"Aye, but I want to do all of it for real, ye ken?"

"Your brogue thickens with your rod, did you know that?"

He kissed her again, and she climbed into his lap, or he put her there, and he crushed her breasts against him, abraded them, and made her want more . . . until she heard a subtle cough.

Rory cursed and Vickie looked up.

Her sisters stood just inside the garage.

"The shop's closed," Destiny said.

Harmony curtseyed like a maid. "Bedrooms are clean and ready. And that was yesterday. Today we —"

"Yeah," Storm cut in. "Breakfast is ready."

"Can it, brats. We get the picture." Vickie untangled herself, rose, and straightened her clothes.

"My shock-shirt!" Storm accused, but she couldn't hold back a grin. "Way to get your sexy Scot in the sack, Sis!"

"I thought I was her worst mistake."

"Mistakes can be sexy."

Supper, not breakfast, was ready.

The triplets said it was good, but Vickie didn't taste it, and Rory pushed it around on his plate.

Her sisters mocked them until they finally went to bed.

In the library, she and Rory kissed in every position but the one they really wanted. The girls were too close. Sounds would carry. They needed to get away. Vickie sat up and fluffed her hair. "Rory, you know that auction I have to run this weekend?"

"Aye, the one that'll have me running the shop."

"Come and be my escort. The girls can run the shop."

Rory held her face between his hands. "I'll come all right. You only had to ask. You're not afraid anymore?"

"Of you coming? What made you think I was?"

"Ach, darlin', your fears are about *you*, not me, and I mean that in the most literal and sexual of ways."

"That's a weird take on —"

"My take, as you call it, is that you feel safe exploring your sexuality in dreams, but when you're awake, and we get close, you're as frightened as a fawn in a glen. A man senses these things."

"Then your psychic powers are bonkers. Get with the program, MacKenzie. I want . . . what you want. And when . . . it . . . didn't happen just now, I thought my wishes stopped working. I was thinking of a rhyme, like . . . 'put your penis in my wee-ness.' "

"Enough with the rhymes," Rory said, kissing her knuckles to soften his disapproval. "Bloody hell. What does it say about me that I want it to come true? Wee-ness?"

Vickie worried that their time hadn't quite yet come. Was that what Rory sensed?

She also worried about what she'd set in motion by asking him to the auction, but she wanted their dreams to come true, most of the time.

At breakfast the next morning, she broke the news to her sisters. "Rory and I are going to Rhode Island for the weekend. For work," she added when they grinned. "Do you think the three of you can run the shop without us?"

"I can," Storm said. "I've been waiting for a shot at polka dot walls."

"Imagine the money we'd make if we sold our shoes," Harmony said, but she fell forward laughing. "Like I'd give them up."

Vickie looked at her crowded kitchen table, and realized she had all-out embraced change with Rory and her sisters, though sometimes she wondered where her peace had gone. It didn't matter. She had a family, and she liked every crazy minute.

"What kind of work thing is this?" Harmony asked.

"A vintage clothing auction to benefit the Pickering Foundation. "My friend Kira is the special events coordinator. I volunteered months ago."

"Did you bring formal evening wear?" Vickie asked Rory.

"Aye, I did, since I thought I'd take one or two of my clients up on their age-old invitations while I was here in the States."

"Great. Pack it for Newport."

"More important," Storm said. "If you brought jammies, *don't* pack them."

Rory's expression remained stern but his ears got red.

"Oh, get a room and get it over with!" Storm snapped.

"They are," Destiny said, "in Rhode Island."

TWENTY-EIGHT

Friday morning, before she and Rory left for Newport, Vickie held her first shop meeting, despite Rory's disapproval.

"Before I make you my official employees," she told her sisters, "you should know that I want you to finish school. Salem State is down the road, so you can live and work here when you're not taking classes or studying."

"You are *not* paying for school," Storm said.

"She already did," Rory said.

"Who asked you?"

"Right then. I'll just keep out of this, shall I?"

"See that you do. This is between me and my sister." Storm crossed her arms. "I refuse to go back to school."

"Of course you do," Rory said, eliciting a look before his chair cracked, and shifted. But he jumped up in time to keep from hitting the floor with it.

"Sorry," Vickie said. "I should have warned you about that chair."

"I'm not sure it was the chair."

"No school," Storm repeated.

"Victoria," Rory said. "After the girls graduate, you can set up a tuition repayment schedule so nobody is overburdened, meaning you, or feels as if they're taking advantage, meaning Storm."

Storm harrumphed, nodded once, uncrossed her legs, crossed them the other way, and looked out the window.

That girl did *not* like being understood, Vickie thought.

"Let's settle the rent," Harmony suggested.

Victoria folded her hands. "I'm suspending rent for anybody who goes back to school."

Storm wilted. "Son of a switch."

"Now that's settled," Vickie said. "Destiny, you're shop manager, for the weekend, and Storm, I'm giving you artistic license to showcase our stock in any way you'd like while I'm gone."

"Harmony, how do you feel about being my buyer? That way you can work for me without stepping foot in the shop."

"I like the idea."

Vickie took an envelope from her stack of notes. "Here you go; act like a buyer."

Harmony whistled at the cash inside.

"Here's a list of the clothes I bought last year, where I bought them, what I paid, and what I sold them for. Use it as a guide, and have fun."

"Can I check yard sales?"

"Yes!" Vickie gave Rory an I-told-you-so look. "I've found great deals at the older houses. And this is the best time of year. There's a list in the paper."

"But shouldn't I come with you to Rhode Island, if I'm your buyer? It's a clothing auction, right?"

"I bought what I wanted from their stock when I set up the auction, so, not this trip."

Harmony laughed. "True or not, you get an A-plus for quick thinking, Sis."

"Rory," Vickie said. "You're next on the agenda."

"Thanks, boss." Rory yanked open a folder. "Here are your paychecks." He handed one to each of her sisters.

"You only worked half a week, and that's what Victoria is paying you for, because she didn't want to leave you without funds, or offend you by giving you a handout." He turned to Storm. "*No* smutty tee-shirts on the job." He stood. "Now let's get the hell

253

out of Salem, while I'm still in a good mood."

"Looks like you're in for a blast, Sis," Destiny said.

"Your sister's thinking with her heart, where you're concerned, not her business sense," Rory said.

"Yeah?" Destiny countered, "and what are you thinking with, where she's concerned?"

Fifteen minutes later, as Vickie maneuvered her aging Civic through Salem's bustling streets, she peeked at Rory from the corner of her eye. "You think they're gonna skip with the cash and whatever else their van will hold, don't you?"

"I don't know them well enough to judge, and neither do you, but they've got the skipping gene from both sides of the pool. Even if they stay, they could turn your shop tail over teakettle."

Vickie chuckled. "They'll do me proud."

"I hope you're right."

"Storm might bite a few people."

Rory's expression relaxed as he knuckled her cheek. "I might bite you."

"I'll drive faster."

He touched her leg. "Let's take it slow. Make it last. How much time do we need to get to Newport?"

"No more than an hour and a quarter, if

the traffic goddess smiles on us. Why?"

"I'm greedy for time alone with you, ye ken?"

"Now who's psychic? What do you have in mind?"

"Call Kira and tell her we might be late."

"No need."

"Ach, sounds like we read each other's minds." Rory took her hand, squeezed it and held it against his knee.

Vickie slid it higher up his thigh, and while he raised a brow, she wallowed in the feel of her hand covered by the cool silk flesh of his.

"Kira and Jason are expecting us around four," she said.

"Good, let me borrow your cell phone, and remember where we were." He took a tiny address book from his breast pocket, dialed, had a business-friendly conversation with somebody named Charlie, and netted them a peek at a "vintage Looff," whatever the hell that was.

"I have directions from Route 95 South," he said.

Before long, they pulled up to a private gatehouse. The attendant heard Rory's name and went back inside for an envelope with his name on it.

"Drive," Rory told her.

The lakeside estate was closed for the season. It had a carousel, also closed. "This is the place," Rory said.

Vickie stopped the car, and Rory came around to open her door. He took a key from the envelope. "Several of the most beautiful carousel figures I've restored are here," he said, leading her to the back door of the pavilion.

She went into the dungeon first. "Wait here," Rory said.

"Sure, until somebody throws a bag over my head and carts me away."

Rory chuckled and the lights came on.

"You're right," she called. "This is one gorgeous carousel." It came to life with colored lights and upbeat echoing music from a fabulous central showpiece organ.

"It's a Looff, circa 1895," Rory said, setting her on the rotating platform. After he joined her, he led her to a whimsical jumping giraffe, and lifted her into its high-backed saddle. "I restored this beauty," he said. "She almost looks like she's smiling, doesn't she?"

Vickie felt like a princess with her prince beside her. Rory's hand rode her thigh. Never had she enjoyed a split skirt more. With her Victorian blouse and kitten-heeled shoes, she felt feminine, and desired, and

. . . petite. She laughed.

Rory's stroking thumb raised her pulse and eased her fears. She wanted whatever they could have this weekend, and she'd never felt this way before.

He showed her a playful winking sea-horse that she adored. But beside a coral iridescent mermaid, he took Vickie's hand and ran it along a wave in the mermaid's flowing hair, and Vickie knew that she was seeing and touching a work of art with a sculptor's eye.

"Feel the life in her hair, the waves made by the sea. Your hair is wild and elemental like this," Rory whispered, his lips grazing her lobe. "But it's alive and pulsing with energy."

He touched one of her curls to his lips. "Someday I'm going to carve a mermaid with hair exactly like this." He ran a hand through her hair, and she shivered. He was a sculptor adoring a fine piece of art, and she felt humbled and, strangely . . . beautiful. "Your hair will inspire me forever," he said. "*You* will inspire me forever."

With his hand over hers, they stroked the mermaid's figure, along her fin and up to her hips, dipping into her waist and out again to cup a breast and finger a barely there nip. "This is what I'm going to do to you tonight, and more," he promised.

Vickie responded by turning her head to feel Rory's breath on her lips like a caress.

Their kiss was hungry, ravenous, nature at its most basic, the giving and taking of breath with mating tongues and willing bodies.

They rose together, and he took her to a one-seater dragon chariot, beautiful, but not nearly as grand and enticing as the dragon of their dreams. She touched his chest and felt the beat of his heart. He put an arm around her, covered her hand, and leaned his head against hers.

"Cherry teddy," he said.

"Black silk briefs," she replied, watching him react, wishing she had the "bollocks" to reach for him. "It's getting late," she said, because it was, not because she wanted to go. She never wanted to leave this spot.

He jumped off the carousel first, clasped her around the waist and lifted her down as if she weighed no more than a feather.

They heard someone calling from outside.

Rory stole one last kiss beside the carousel, the music too modern, and the lights too bright . . . very much, yet not enough like their dream.

"Is this it?" Vickie asked as she heard a key at the door. "Have we fulfilled some prophecy, with a kiss beside a carousel?"

"Not as far as I'm concerned," Rory said. "Charlie," he added as he turned. "Meet Victoria Cartwright."

"Miss Cartwright. Well, now I can see what finally brought our Scot to America after all these years." Charlie gave Rory's arm a mock punch. "And you said you'd never leave Scotland."

Back in the car, she and Rory held hands.

"Scotland has older carousels," Rory said. "I'd like to show them to you."

"I'd like to see them." But they made no plans.

On the back roads to Newport, they saw children flying kites on leaf-strewn village greens surrounded by gingerbread houses, steepled white churches, and brick town halls.

Vickie rolled down her window. The sights, sounds, and apple-orchard scent, would always remind her of Rory after this.

All too soon, they entered Newport proper, a seaport where three-masted schooners floated beside catamarans, power boats, yachts, and fishing boats. Pricey condos rose over the harbor with a view toward Goat Island and the bridge beyond.

Driving the hill from Thames toward

Bellevue, Vickie bit her lip. "There's something you should know about Kira."

"Kira who suggested you cook my picture in honey?"

"Oh yeah. That makes the news easier to break. She's a witch."

"And you?" Rory asked.

"Until recently, I was certain I wasn't."

"Recently?"

"Between my sisters, my Pictish heritage, and my rhyming wishes, never mind our dreams, I've had good cause to wonder."

Rory scratched his beard, a sure sign of concern. "Surely if you turned your back on your power, and tried not to harness your wishes, there'd be no reason for you to claim your magic . . . if you have any."

Vickie shrugged. "I'm not certain it's all that simple. This is Bellevue Avenue," she said, hooking a right and changing the subject. "You can see the mansions between the trees. Not all of them belong to the Pickering Foundation. The really famous ones belong to the Historical Society, and some are privately owned. That's Kira and Jason's Cloud Kiss over there."

"Impressive," Rory said.

A minute later, she turned into a driveway. "This is Kingston by the Sea." The manicured front lawn made a great first impression, she thought, with its tiered gardens and ageless trees dressed in autumn hues.

"Kingston lives up to its name." Rory whistled. "A view of the sea to the horizon."

Vickie nodded, driving around to the side. "This is where Mel shot her cooking show with the bees."

"Aye," Rory said, "I recognize the patio where I saw you in costume after the program."

"That dress is up for auction tonight. I can't believe you remember me from the program."

"Never forget the dreams, darlin'." Rory stroked her from her cheek to the pulse point at her neck, and she shivered as Kira and Jason stepped outside to meet them.

Rory reclaimed his hand and got out of the car.

"Vickie! We wondered what happened to you," Kira said hugging her as they met on the patio. "This must be your hunky Scot." She kissed Rory's cheek. "Welcome to Newport."

Vickie introduced Rory to Kira's husband, Jason. "Funny thing happened on the way to the auction," Vickie said. "My sisters turned out to be great shopkeepers."

"I still can't believe you have sisters," Kira said.

"Versatile and identical sisters."

"Ach, and a wee bit scary," Rory added, his throat chuckle pronounced.

"Oh, talk some more," Kira said.

Jason took his wife's arm. "Never mind the brogue. Mind the sleeping arrangements."

"Oh, right. I saved a room for you at Cloud Kiss, Vic. One room. I didn't know Rory was coming, and the house is full, but I'll see if I can find a sofa or a —"

"We'll share," Rory said.

"Excuse me?" Vickie tripped over her own feet as she pulled him aside.

"We're going to share," Rory repeated.

"A room?"

"Aye, and a bed, and shower, if I have my way."

"One bed?"

Rory shrugged. "I canna decide whether you're hopeful or fretful over the possibility."

"Neither can I."

"Fair enough."

"Why don't I just go and ask Kira if it's one bed or two?"

"Now, darlin', don't go spoiling our fun. You're missing the point of a runaway weekend."

"I am?"

"Aye. Let a bit of excitement and spontaneity into your life. Personally, I'm hoping for a dwarf bed where we'll have to sleep one atop the other, and you can be the princess I kiss to sleep."

"You're fracturing the fairy tale."

"I'm making a better one. We frogs have ways of making princesses sleep, you know."

"Oh?"

"Lass, it's not like we haven't cohabitated already." Rory combed his fingers through her hair and tucked a strand behind her ear, while Vickie tried to find her place in the conversation.

"But it's not like we've shared a room."

"Dreams are more intimate," he said. "I've touched you in silken places with my hands and my lips, and even with the tip of my tongue. You do think it's talented, my tongue? Ach, what a striking shade of pink you've turned. Admit it, or my manly pride will be cut to the quick."

"It's getting warm out here, don't you think?"

"I certainly do, and I think deep down that you'd like for us to do everything that we do in dreams."

Vickie sighed. She couldn't hide from the truth, not with Rory so close. "Heaven help us," she said. "One room it is."

"We'll share," Vickie repeated as they returned to their interested hosts.

Kira beamed, Jason scowled, and Vickie kissed his cheek. "I can take care of myself, Jay. It's not like he's a big bad Ice Wolf or The Best Kisser in America, or anything scary like that. He's just a tame old Scot."

Rory and Jason had a scowling face off, but fortunately, nobody got pinned to the boards.

TWENTY-NINE

"We hired an auctioneer," Kira said, leading them down an elegant hall to their dressing rooms, "but, Vic, I'd like you to describe the outfits so that when we open the floor to questions before the bidding, you can answer. Nobody knows vintage clothes as well as you."

Vickie changed into her gown, and reviewed the program on the stage podium as she waited for a glimpse of Rory in his tux. She lost that hope when she saw him, but who cared?

In a regimental dress kilt, sword, tartan drape, and all, Rory caused a stir.

Cameras flashed.

Men stopped talking.

Women turned, gaped, drooled.

In his MacKenzie tartan, a black dress jacket with epaulettes, pins, sword and medals, his mahogany mane tame, more or less, Rory jumpstarted Vickie's heart and a whole lot more.

When he met her at the base of the stage steps, she wondered what he was wearing beneath, but he took her hand, turned it, and kissed the inside of her wrist with a heart-pulsing old-world intimacy.

Then he stood back to admire her. "I didn't know you were modeling your gown from Melody's show," he said. "You look more beautiful tonight than you did then, and even better than in my dreams."

"When I said formal dress, I didn't know you'd be wearing Scottish formal."

"Am I embarrassing you? Would you rather I left?"

"No. No. You're yummy. I mean, they think so."

Women came from every direction, svelte beauties all, but Rory shook his head, focused on her, and presented her with a folded tartan scarf. "I'd be proud if you wore my colors."

Ignoring the malnourished models, Rory awaited Vickie's response as if her answer mattered.

"I'd be honored," she said softly.

Before a hundred rich, chic, sexy guests, Rory draped a band of MacKenzie tartan over Vickie's right shoulder then crossed and pinned it at her left hip.

"The pin is beautiful, Rory. A thistle-topped silver sword."

"Aye, with the MacKenzie crest. It's the family kilt pin, but I always carry a spare."

His navy and emerald plaid accented her pale blue gown and gave her a sense of belonging . . . to him and to this august gathering, if only for the night.

Like magic, Rory had sought her out when he could have any woman he wanted. Why?

On stage, during the auction, as she described each gown and fielded questions, her fear melted as Rory stroked her with his gaze, like warm fingers along her skin, first here, then there, and — ooh! — there, too.

"Last up is my gown," Vickie said, removing Rory's colors for the bidding, "a redingote dress by Felix of France, circa 1898, in pale blue with wide-spaced, navy pinstripes. Just to be clear, the tartan doesn't come with the gown, and neither does the Scot."

Only the men laughed as Vickie turned to the auctioneer who would handle the bidding.

Rory tried to outbid a diamond-studded surgically perfected playgirl used to getting her way, but nobody was more stubborn than her Scot.

The price rose so high, Vickie wanted to

tell Rory to stop, except that he must have a special someone in Scotland to give it to. Plus there was the marvelous money they were raising for the boys at St. Anthony's, the orphanage the Pickering Foundation supported.

At a quarter past fifteen-freaking-grand, implant-girl slapped the table and gave up the fight. Rory had won the gown, or lost his mind. Vickie wasn't sure which.

Between ticket prices, program ads, donations, and auction profits, the event exceeded expectations and topped half a million dollars, for dresses that had been locked in a preservation vault for years. Most would never have met their potential, no matter how many special events the foundation held, and they'd kept a great assortment.

Stage lights dimmed, the orchestra began playing dinner music, and Rory caught her in his arms at the bottom of the stage steps, and twirled her until she was dizzy. "Ach, you did it, darlin'. What a night. Dinner, shall we?"

"As soon as I change my gown," she said.

"Ach, darlin', but you're already wearing it." He offered his arm.

"Oh no! Rory, please tell me that you didn't buy this expensive gown for me."

"Who else would I buy it for, I'd like to know?" Rory leaned close. "I've peeled you out of it, ye ken? How could I let anyone else wear it?"

"You did that in dreams, not in real life."

"Ach, now, and that's what I'm working on, isn't it?"

Going in to dinner, Vickie felt like Cinda-freaking-rella. Who would have thought she would get the hunkiest Scot at the Crystal Ball?

They dined tête-à-tête on coquille St. Jacques and crème caramel at small round tables dressed in black and white, sipping champagne and recounting wicked dreams beneath a mist of gold stars.

But they were awake, Vickie reminded herself, and they planned to share a room later. The stakes were rising like the tides she thought, but she was so happy floating, she didn't care if she drowned.

When dress-up prep-school Barbie batted her lashes and asked Rory to dance, Vickie's bubble popped, but Rory turned the girl down gently.

"Crivvens," he said as she left. "Poor bony-arsed lass. I hope she grows a figure soon."

Vickie chuckled. "Jail bait."

Rory took her hand beneath the table and

rubbed her palm against his thigh. "Making you jealous fills me with —"

"Testosterone?"

Later, as she stepped into his arms for the first waltz — he in his kilt, possessive and strong, and she in her vintage gown — she knew that they had done this before.

Déjà vu? Or destiny?

"I feel as if we've done this before," Rory said, "and not in our dreams."

"Not you, too?"

"It's like destiny," Rory said, and Vickie shivered.

He blew in her ear and she warmed. "Mmm."

"I'd rather kiss you warm. You only have to ask."

"Now?"

"Aye, sure. Why not? I might as well be a pariah in your country as well as my own."

"You're a pariah?"

"Most hermits like it that way."

"Oh," Vickie said, still struck by his offer. Good thing he held her as they danced, because the offer made her think of him beneath her skirt in the dream, and her knees were about to fail her. "I'd rather wait on the kissing . . . and such . . . if you don't mind."

"Until?" he asked.

"I don't know," she said. "Later? Maybe."

"Later, definitely." Rory twirled her dizzy, and she clung, their hearts beating one against the other.

But the Crystal Ball ended too soon for a cowardly princess who did not want her prince to see exactly how well-fed she looked beneath her carefully chosen camouflage.

THIRTY

"It's too small," Vickie said. Though the exquisite Gothic four-poster, draped in teal and turquoise like the sea outside their wall of windows, looked rich and decadent, it might as well be flashing the word "sex" in neon.

"Crivvens, no. There's room for all seven dwarfs, the three bears, and us, too."

Vickie shook her head. "Noooo, that's baby bear's bed, and you're the big bad wolf."

Rory hugged her, used her head as a chin rest, and sighed. "Ach, and I'm not going to eat you, darlin', but if I do, you'll thank me."

Wary of the thrill that ran through her, Vickie sighed and assessed her wolf in shining armor. "Okay, so let's say the bed's just right."

"It's too big. This wolf dreamed about using you as his mattress, ye ken?"

"That's *not* what you've been dreaming

about." Now why had she gone and mentioned their X-rated dreams?"

Rory stepped back and grinned, a real grin. His first. A wet-your-panties, take-me-I'm-yours grin. The kind that makes a woman forget her name, trip over her feet, and pant, and want, and offer herself for the living fantasy.

"I . . . need to use the . . . dressing room." Vickie scooted inside — an actual dressing room, as it turned out, so elegant it had a fainting couch.

A minute later, and before she could gather her wits, Rory knocked and joined her. "What do you think you're —"

"Shh." He crossed her lips with a finger, uncrossed her arms, and unbuttoned her gown at her left shoulder, then at her right hip. "I wanted to be sure I could get it off you without breaking the mood."

"What mood?" Centipedes were freaking clog-dancing in her stomach.

He turned her to face the full-length mirror. "Look at how beautiful you are."

"Stop your bletherin'," she said, quoting him and making reflected eye contact.

"I thought you hated mirrors," he said.

"I'm not looking at myself. I'm looking at you."

"Aren't you taking a leaf from your mother's book by not seeing yourself . . . the way she didn't see you?"

"Just the opposite. By not looking at myself, I'm trying *not* to be like her. She looked at herself too often and hated what she saw. I accept myself as I am."

"But you canna see how beautiful you are."

Vickie laughed. "I see myself in this dress every night in our dreams." She turned to face him. "I know what I look like."

"I don't think you do," Rory said, "but we'll save that discussion for another day, shall we?"

"No. Kiss me." To turn Rory's thoughts, Vickie leaned in and raised her arms to toy with the hair at his nape, obliging him to open his mouth over hers . . . but stealing her breath, and another piece of her heart, must have been his idea.

He cupped her bottom to bring her closer, and teased a breast through the fabric of her dress. He branded her with the heat of his hands and the promise of more, while fire licked at her center, and dreams came to life.

When Rory pulled away, Vickie lost her balance, but he steadied her, chuckling in his throat the way she liked. And his eyes held a hint of mischief that she wished she could sew into a small satin sachet to keep beneath her pillow.

Rory wanted to initiate Victoria, gently, into the beauty of her own body, and into the joy of mutual pleasure. But she had started by breaking his heart. She'd stood near the bedroom door like one of her antique paper-dolls stuck to its stand. Then she made straight for the dressing room like a mechanical windup toy. Well, he was having none of it.

"Lass," he said, turning her so she could see the bed through the open dressing room door. "You can have your own space on your own side. Or you can sleep in my arms in the middle, and I'll hold you while you do."

Victoria didn't say a word, so he led her by the hand back into the bedroom. "You can also run and hide in the attic, ye ken? I'm sure there's one here at Cloud Kiss."

Victoria shoved his arms away. "You're lower than a wolf — you're a rat!" She stalked away.

"The worst," he said, but he'd made her fighting mad. Perhaps enough to stop running from mirrors and family and her own sexuality, and who knew what else? Her heritage came to mind as a need that she might be running from, but Rory dismissed the notion as foolish.

Victoria raised her chin and looked him straight in the eye, her fear receding . . . or her determination taking charge. "Can we take this a step at a time?"

"Ach, darlin', nothing would make me happier."

She laughed and he didn't know why. "What?"

"Your smile. It's like —"

"My what?" Rory touched his mouth and traced its shape. "Aye, I think it is a smile." He went to the mirror to be sure. When his reflection grinned back at him, Rory shook his head, stretched his lips, and worked his jaw. "Must take care," he said. "Don't want to strain anything." But he grinned again, picked Victoria up, carried her to the bed, and dropped her in the middle. Then he tried using her as a mattress.

"Bathroom?" she asked.

"Not right now, thank you," he said.

"Sword," she said, "bruising my leg."

"It's not *that* long." But he grinned again.

"The real sword, Sherlock. Your dress sword. Take it off."

Rory rose from the bed and unbuckled his sword belt. "Right. I'll get rid of the kilt, too, shall I?"

"And lose the sporran. It's been trying to

have sex with me."

"The horny beast." Rory started to unhook his sporran from its chain but Victoria sat up. "No, wait," she said. "I've decided that I want to take it off you myself."

Bloody happy day! "Either I've died and gone to heaven, or we're dreaming," he said.

"I think we're really doing this." She confirmed as much as she slipped off the bed and came his way.

"We are?" Rory cleared his throat in an effort to tone down his excitement. "We are. But, one step at a time, mind, and at your pace."

"My pace. Okay, so when you undress me, stop at my underwear."

"You prefer to sleep in your underwear?"

"No, but I want you to remove it beneath the covers."

Ach, and that wasn't *all* bad, Rory told himself. It meant they were definitely getting under the covers . . . together. "Aye, I can do that, but may I counter your suggestion?"

"Counter away."

"I remove your dress first, so you're wearing only your underwear when you undress me."

She was seriously considering it. Hot damn.

"Only if I can get you naked and have my wicked way with you, however I want, for however long I want, after I undress you."

Rory nearly came. "You strike a hard bargain, Cartwright." He was going to have to be one bloody strong Scot this night. "Aye, lass. Do as you will, but be kind."

Victoria pushed him down on the bed, straddled him, and went for his doublet. But Rory pushed her button-hungry fingers aside and finished unfastening her dress first. "You look too fine in it, darlin', to let the likes of me go tearing it off you. Besides, remember our deal. You in your undies first."

As he slipped Victoria's dress off her shoulders, he nearly lost his breath. She was wearing some of the best vintage underwear he'd seen in her research book. Whatever it was called, it barely covered her lush bodice, while it pushed her breasts up as if presenting them for his delectation.

He untied her petticoats, one after the other, in a provocative rustle of silk and satin, and tried to push them over her curvaceous hips. But it was no easy task undressing her, with him on his back, and her on top of him, so he tried reversing their positions, but they ended up rolling on the bed entangled in her petticoats.

Rory stopped laughing when Victoria suddenly hovered over him — no more petticoats — looking like a wet dream come true. He slid his palms up each side of her corset. "What do you call this rod-stiffener I get to remove by brail later?"

"A swan-bill corset from 1876," she said.

"And the ruffle above it?"

"Don't laugh. It's a breast enhancer. I'm playing mix and match era-wise. I know, who needs a breast enhancer less than I do? But it works for the costume. Vintage underwear is hard to come by."

"You look good enough to eat, but even I suspect that the pink satin ruffled knickers under my hands are from another century."

"Late 1930s, early 1940s, from France," she said, trying, but failing, to appear immune to his touch.

She shook her head and pulled his arm away, as she tried to get him free of his constraints. "And what do you call this jacket?" she asked.

"A regulation doublet, Prince Charlie style."

"Hmm. Nice. Very black-tie dressy."

"As you see." He flicked his black silk bow tie.

"And a dress shirt, too, not a pirate shirt."

"Those are Jacobean shirts. Have I worn

one since I arrived?"

"Only in our dreams."

"It's hard, isn't it?" he asked.

"Is it? Wait, let me check beneath your sporran."

"I don't mean that *I'm* hard, well, I am, but —"

"I'll say." She pushed the sporran aside and knuckled his length through his kilt, and he closed his eyes and rode a wave of pleasure. Between that and the hand she splayed on his pecs, Rory felt captivated, enraptured, enslaved — which should send him running for the Highlands.

He closed his eyes. "I *mean,* it's difficult not to confuse our dreams and our real lives."

"Sometimes, I prefer one to the other." Victoria sat back, teasing his erection with her buttocks. She tilted her head. "I believe I need a sexy Scot fashion show."

"By all means. After you," Rory said. Victoria had to hop off him, so he could get up.

She'd stolen his doublet, vest, and shirt, so he rose wearing only his tie, kilt, and sporran, garter-flashed hose and shoes. He postured and posed and Victoria applauded. Then he slid his sporran to his hip and did a six-step Highland fling, humming the tune for the Ghillie Callum as he did.

"Stop," Victoria said. "Let me have your briefs. That'll make your fling way more entertaining."

Rory grinned in earnest, at Victoria's inner vixen shining through. She got off the bed, knelt before him and slipped his briefs down his hips without touching that which most wanted touching. Then she climbed back on the bed and sat cross-legged to watch. Well aware of his man parts flinging, Rory danced with an extra bounce to add to Victoria's viewing pleasure.

She fell back on the bed holding her stomach, laughing so hard, she could hardly breathe — and what a sight, in pale blue heels, gartered stockings, and a corset that would make a Victorian hooker proud.

Rory laughed as well, as he dragged her from her giggling fit to fling with him. When she kicked off her shoes, her inhibitions seemed to go with them, and her vixen came out to play in truth.

A corseted tart and a kilted Scot, they danced and made merry like never in his wildest dreams, except that this, too, suddenly seemed like a memory.

Fun, Rory thought it was called. All-out laughter. Not sex, or foreplay . . . well, maybe a bit of foreplay. His charger was up for anything. But fun, too, the old-fashioned type that required two people who genuinely liked each other, and a lot more caring than he should be willing to admit.

Rory stopped and wrapped his arms around Victoria in a way he'd never done, in a way that was meant to show her that he cherished her. And though he had no right, he gave her a forever kiss, one filled with hope.

She understood, and when they came up for air, eager yet guarded, they consumed each other with their gazes for a long time, there with the moonlight spilling through their wall of windows, until he began to waltz her in place. Barely moving, lost in each other, serenaded by a wailing of wind and a lapping of surf on the shore, Rory knew he was falling in love.

"I like you, Victoria," he said, the understatement bringing tears to her eyes, though, under the circumstances, the truth would have been more brutal.

"I like you, too. Damn you."

"Damn me?"

"We don't even live in the same country."

No, but they were tuned in to the same channel. "Aye, but we're in the same country now."

"I know," she said. "I know." She knelt

and slipped off his shoes, one by one. Then she slid her hands up his legs, beneath his kilt . . . and she fondled his sex.

"Mighty me!" he shouted at the unexpectedness of it.

"Mighty you is right," she said, peeking beneath his kilt.

"I didn't think you'd do it," Rory said when he caught his breath. "Didn't think you had the guts. This isn't a dream after all."

"I'm not gutless, MacKenzie."

"Aye, I know that now, and there are plenty more ways for you to prove it," he said, biting off another shout.

"Patience, laddie. I'm biding my time and trying to make it last," she said.

"You're killing me is what you're doing."

"At my pace, you said."

So Rory groaned, made the supreme sacrifice, and let Victoria Cartwright have her very wicked way with him.

Thirty-One

Still on her knees before him, Victoria got him hard as a claymore while he tried not to embarrass himself.

"I hoped you'd go commando," she said.

He covered her hands with his kilt between them to cool his blood. "I didn't want to cause a scandal at the auction," he said, "and you have had a wee bit of fun with the briefs."

"Now and in the dream."

"Aye. We know a lot about each other, don't we?"

"Except for why we've been dreaming the same dream."

"Aye, and that's a corker."

"Did you come to Salem to see the unicorn or did you come looking for the source of your dreams?"

Rory thought about how to extract himself from the quicksand of her question without telling her a pack of lies. It'd serve him right if he sank to his eyeballs. "I came for both," he said, and that was the unvarnished, though unembellished, truth.

She pushed his staying hand aside and went back to her torture, testing his length, his thickness and depth, spreading the droplet at the sensitive tip of his shaft like dew, challenging his control.

She cupped his bollocks in both hands and thumbed the base of his rod until he groaned and stopped her again. "You're killing me, darlin'. I'll be good for naught if you keep that up."

She unclipped his sporran chain and placed the sporran on a chair, then she unbuttoned his kilt, and it fell, but got caught on his rod, and hung there like a flag.

Because he loved the sound of Victoria's laughter, Rory stood there like a fool, his kilt at half mast, just to entertain her.

After she finished laughing, she unflagged him, folded his kilt, and set it aside. Then she stood and walked round him, as if he were up for auction.

"What do you bid?" he asked.

"A night in your arms," said she, tugging the quilt from the bed.

He followed her to the wall of windows with the sea beyond. Victoria sat cross-legged, and tugged him down, so Rory sat behind her and draped the quilt around them both, her back against his chest, and he kissed her nape, behind her ear, the hollow at each shoulder blade.

"Tell me about your home," she said, and as he described Scotland's fields of heather and wildflower glens, he began to stroke her inner thighs, from her knees toward her center, coming closer with every pass, until the hitch in her breath told him she was ready.

When he separated her, she laid her head on his shoulder, and when he found the center of her pleasure and stroked her there, as softly as a sigh of wind, she arched and invited more.

Rory had never made such slow gentle love, neither had he craved a woman's pleasure more than his own.

She turned, so her soft panting gasps warmed his neck and he bent to kiss her brow.

He watched the exquisite passion in her expression and felt a responding surge at the power of her climax. Then she came for his mouth, kissing him, milking him, with a primordial instinct that mimicked the sex act, and while she devoured him, he made her come again.

She whispered his name and begged for more. She cried out his name, and went limp in his arms. "Enough," said the conqueror of the multiple orgasm, but jings, she'd had a jolly go.

After coming back to herself, she must have noticed his rod prodding at the base of her spine, because she stroked her way along his thighs, until she found him behind her, and with her hands, she made him sigh, and wish, and ponder the future in a new and frightening way.

"Take me to bed," she said. "Take off my naughty undies so there's nothing between us, and hold me while we sleep."

Naked and highly aroused, Rory took Victoria's hand as they stood.

"Doesn't that distract you?" She pointed to his ready sex.

"It'll only distract me if you don't finish what you started. Then there's the matter of the price you mentally tagged on it the day I walked into your shop. You never told me my estimated value."

Victoria gasped. "How did you know?"

"I read it in your look."

"It was embarrassingly high, so you can stop probing and leave me some dignity."

Rory liked that he could read her, that he'd been able to since the first. Scary that.

He put her dress on a hanger in a Scottish minute and knelt before the selkie in her sexy vintage undergarments. "A feast," he said, "to nibble my way into."

She stopped him midreach. "Under the covers, if you please."

Rory sat on his heels and watched her try to hide her panic. "What's spooked you, lass? Am I going too fast? You're trembling like you've got the toothache and the drill's on the way. You're not afraid of me?"

"Can we get under the covers now?"

He pulled the blankets back, and she scooted into the center of the bed, her pink ruffled backside a mighty fine distraction.

When he slipped in beside her, she put a subtle distance between them.

"Don't be frightened, darlin'. I'd never hurt you."

Victoria sighed and rose up on her elbow. "Listen, Rory, you might as well know now. I may be a woman of today, but well . . . I'm not."

He rose up to face her, elbow to elbow. "Care to translate?"

"I have no real experience. Something always got in the way, if you get my drift."

Rory tried, but Victoria wasn't making it easy. "Like guilt or fear, you mean?"

"No, like a false alarm in my college dorm

that made the guy in my bed run down the fire escape and sprain his ankle."

"You let that stop you from letting him into your bed again?"

"He never came back again, and well, there were other accident-prone partners. One guy got a concussion when my bed broke. Another got leg cramps. Another had a sneezing fit every time he reached for me."

"Do you feel as if they abandoned you?"

"Like my family, you mean? No, but it's obvious; don't you see?" Victoria fell back against her pillows.

Victoria . . . beside him in bed, teasing his poor neglected cock with her erotic under-pinnings, but keeping her hands to herself, and warning his away with her look.

"I don't see," Rory said, trying to ignore the poor neglected fellow beneath the covers weeping for a warm place to go.

Victoria sat up. "You *gotta* make me say it!"

"I feel like a cad, but I'm sorry. I don't understand."

"Okay, I'll spell it out. Every screw-up, thankfully, kept me from baring my 'well-fed' self to their disappointed eyes. There. Are you happy now?"

"I have you in bed and I'm about to get you naked, so yes, I am happy. As for what you just told me, answer a question for me. Did you . . . *wish* . . . they'd not see you naked?"

"Of course n . . . no. I don't think so. I wished I had a better body . . ."

"So you did wish."

She lay facing him. "I didn't rhyme, if that's what you're suggesting. Do you think I subconsciously saved myself by using my magic?"

"The magic you say you don't have?"

"The magic I'm beginning to think I *do* have."

That was a blow. Magic had destroyed his family and now he was falling for a . . . No, he wasn't. He was in lust. That was it. Lust. "Tell me you're just trying to scare me out of this bed," he said.

"I'm being more truthful with you than I've ever been with any man who made it past my bedroom door."

"For the record, I never made it past your bedroom door," Rory said, "but, warning well taken."

He brought her close, pulled the blankets up to her chin, and began to undress her beneath the covers. "Let's get you out of these things so you can sleep comfortably."

She started to protest and he kissed her to shut her up. "I'll have no protests. It's you who doesn't think your body's perfect, not me, and I'm not going to see it, even now, not in real life, though I'll get hard and heavy touching every inch of it, and you can bet your swan-bill corset on that. I wouldn't run if the roof fell in, so you can drop the scare tactics. I'll survive and enjoy the night, because *you,* Victoria Cartwright, will be sleeping in my arms."

"Oh, Rory," she said, covering her eyes. He made free with his hands as he un-hooked her corset garters and slipped off her stockings beneath the covers. But she kept her eyes covered until he undid the last of her corset laces. No touch of his warmed her, no stroke made her sigh. It was as if the passionate goddess reflected in the window-glass minutes before had turned to ice.

However, when he pulled her bust im-prover out to examine it in moonlight, she uncovered her eyes, and snatched it away.

"You're beautiful," he breathed against her ear, trying to prove as much while paying homage to every inch of her unresponsive skin with his adoring hands. "You'll like sleeping in my arms so much that I won't be able to keep you from my bed when we get home, no matter how I try to fight you off."

A stronger sense of *déjà vu* hit him at the sight of her in moonlight, watching him, her expression soft, her blond hair fanned out on the pillow beside his.

"Wouldn't your sisters tease if we slept in the same bed every night, or every afternoon," he said to inject a non-threatening note of reality.

"In broad daylight?"

Rory chuckled and settled them with her head on his shoulder. "Oh, aye, afternoons are the best for a snog, and a whole lot more, with sunshine on your lovely curls everywhere." He knuckled her at the apex of her thighs, and she shivered, but she kept her legs tight together.

"Don't worry," he said. "I won't do that again, not even if you beg." Her chuckle against his chest warmed and relieved him of concern. "On the other hand," he said at her ear, "if you try and have your wicked way with me during the night, I might be forced to cooperate."

Vickie woke in the middle of the night as if floating in one of their dreams. Rory had stripped her naked, and though he never saw her, he knew by what he touched that she was hardly slender. He didn't turn away, and neither did the bed break or the roof fall in, which she took as a good sign.

He kept his brawny arms of silk and sinew tight around her, tangled his legs with hers, until her knee rode his rod, and he stroked her hip while he whispered the outrageous things that her "perfect" body did to him.

Vickie thought he believed what he said, because the evidence lay large and thick between them.

He ran his foot along her calf. "I watch the curve of these legs whenever I can," he said, "the turn of your ankle, too, and every other part of you that's not hidden by scarves, shawls, or capes."

"You're being an idiot," she said.

"Ach, woman, I'm not an eejit, I'm a man bewitched by your perfection," he'd replied, however false his words.

Smiling at his version of "idiot," Vickie's heart was warmed by his foolish re-assurance. His earnest look somehow managed to calm her even in moonlight, so she kissed him.

Rory accepted the kiss, and took it to a higher level, to a safe place filled with arousal and silent reassurance, talented lips, roaming hands, and shivery strokes in warm secret places. Vickie had never spent a better time in bed.

Brock would be useless to her after this.

Poor Brock.

This time when Rory breached her with his touch, Vickie welcomed him. She buried her face in his shoulder, while he brought her release, more times than she wanted to count. And while he did, Vickie discovered with the flat of her hand that the planes and angles of his chest were hard-muscled, his abs washboard-firm, his chest hair satin, not steel wool.

She traced the hairline from his navel, and he took to holding his breath, and when the source of his gasping pleasure nudged her palm and begged like a kitten for a petting, she closed her hand around it.

Power, Vickie felt beneath her fingers, a surging power looking to be unleashed, harder than muscle on the inside, and softer than silk on the outside.

She liked his deep guttural moan against her neck and felt suddenly in charge, because his "ach, darlin'," and "aye, lass," and "mighty me," spoke not of control but the loss of it. Then before she knew why, he'd removed her hand from his sex, pressed kisses to her knuckles and his erection to her hip.

"Don't you want more?" she asked.

"I do, and from any other woman, I'd take that as an offer and never look back. But this is you, Victoria, and I ken that you're not ready, which is fine, darlin'. In good time," he said. "Sleep now. Sleep for knowing you're safe in my arms."

If Rory hadn't come to see the unicorn, Vickie would think she'd "rhymed" herself the perfect lover, because he was the man she wished would worship her bod, were it good enough, and his was the rod she wanted most to adore . . . with more than her hands, if only she dared.

She'd especially like to cup and caress him, milk him and make him come, as she held him in her warm deep-aching center, if only she were not so afraid of where that would lead, or more to the point, where it could never lead.

Yes, she could take this man inside herself and feel complete. She could reach the stars in his arms and sleep beside him for the rest of her days —

Except, she couldn't.

Nobody stayed that long.

THIRTY-TWO

Rory's smile grew as he woke. Victoria had fallen asleep cupping his bollocks. His erection had come back to life as he tongued the nipple she'd placed before him in her restlessness, as if his mouth was what she sought.

He wished for a day he could explore to his heart's content, a day he could bring her the ultimate pleasure, with a deeper understanding of her needs, and perhaps his own, where she was concerned.

In the dawning light, surprised he'd slept at all, Rory watched Victoria for nearly an hour, wondering how he could have found the major portion of his soul on the other side of the world.

He thought of Caperglen and the trust he'd recovered by locating the unicorn, the respect of the cheering villagers, the back slaps, everything the MacKenzies who'd come after Drummond had sought for centuries.

Not only could he not let his village down
— he couldn't let the MacKenzies down,
past and future. His sons should be able to
hold up their heads in Caperglen, though
his heart would remain in Salem.

What did it matter if he never had sons,
which he wouldn't, because . . . Well,
because their never-to-be mother slept
beside him, and they lived two worlds
apart, and he had to return the way he'd
come.

Unlike Drummond, Rory couldn't bear
the thought of taking another to his bed,
though perhaps his father had been right,
and women were ten a penny, and shagging
one was as good as another.

But this was Victoria, damn it to bloody
hell, and one or both of them would be
disappointed whatever choice he made . . .
as if he had a choice at all.

She woke with a feline yawn, her hip
against his boner, not the least aware of his
discomfort, but seeming delighted to have
caused it, judging by her hip-wiggle and
eye-twinkle.

She pulled the quilt around herself and
knelt over him, then she began to lower the
sheet as if to expose him, but he held it in
place.

"Can't I just see it?" she asked, looking her fill at him tenting the bed.

Rory scrubbed his face with a hand. "You lower yours; I'll lower mine. Ach, and here comes himself with some silent begging of his own."

"Wow, it's waving."

"That's usually the way it works. Wooden chargers are frisky of a morning, especially when they have a naked audience of the female persuasion of whom they're very fond."

Victoria got closer. "His charger got bigger."

He tugged on her quilt. "You're getting way more of a visual than I am. At least give me a fair peek."

She huffed, let him lower the quilt to expose her gorgeous breasts, and he traced her rose areoles, until her nipples pebbled, and he remembered how he'd suckled her in the night.

He tried to tug the quilt lower but she held her hand firm. "That's enough for one day."

"Ach, darlin'. Are we doling it out now? How many times do I have to tell you that I could make a feast of you everyday?"

"I appreciate the sentiment."

"But you don't believe it."

"You're a man. I rest my case. Look, it's getting small."

"Way to shrink a man's pride, selkie."

"Is *that* your pride? And it's insulted?"

"Yes and yes. It's a fine knight's charger, and it has a code of honor, you know."

"What can I do to make up for my insult?"

"Give him a stroke."

Victoria laughed and Rory grinned, a newfound ability he rather liked, because it lit Victoria from the inside.

She reached. He held his breath.

His charger rose to greet her, and she slid a finger down its length. A sheet between them, and still Rory was ready to spill.

He grasped her quilt. "Now if you'll just —"

The sound of a gong damned near knocked him out of bed. "What the bloody devil was that?"

"Get up," she said. "Breakfast in thirty minutes. Then we can tour some of the mansions before we go home."

Home . . . to Salem in Massachusetts of the USA. Amazing thought.

Victoria stood and arranged the quilt around her like a toga.

"I'd rather tour the bed," Rory said.

"Oops," Victoria said when he stepped on her quilt from behind. She turned to peer down at him, randier than a cock in a hen-house at dawn.

"You should be honored, darlin'. That's all for you."

"Oh."

"Because of you, I should say. Because he slept against your perfect bottom." Rory found the opening in the quilt, and ran his hand up the outside of her leg until he stroked that very bottom. "You got him all primed in the night, and he woke ready for action, ye ken?"

"Oh."

He slid his hand around to her front to see if she was as ready as him. She sighed, gave him room, and he found her wet with morning dew.

"Ohh," she said, watching his face as he watched hers, which resulted in a distinct change in his size, and her lubrication.

"I could do this all day, ye ken?"

Victoria's voice became a sigh, and her eyes glazed over. She was going to come any self-serving minute with no thought to *his* pleasure. Funny, he'd always thought that was the man's job.

Rory pulled her back so she fell atop him on the bed.

"Oh!"

"Have I ever told you how much I like

you when you lose your vocabulary?"

"That sounds like an insult."

"Quite the contrary; it proves you're a woman of passion. My favorite kind."

With him nestled against her, her movements brought his charger into play, without her taking him in, of course, and she stole her pleasure to the max, with him still hot and primed.

"Ach, darlin'," Rory begged. "Bide a while and come again to give me some relief, will you? Just close your legs and hold me there, until . . . ah yes . . . that's my darlin' girl," and Rory grasped her bottom in his hands and worked his poor homeless charger, so primed it was willing to settle for a thigh-tup.

Like a rocket, he settled, and fast, while Victoria rose over him and came again, the hussy, collapsing atop him like a wet blanket afterward the two of them breathless, sticky, and sated . . . more or less.

"Wow," Victoria said raising her head.

Rory stroked the damp hair from her brow, kissed it, and nuzzled her ear. "You do know that I'm bound and determined to show you how to do this right, if it kills me."

"I'm willing to take the chance," she said.

THIRTY-THREE

Late that afternoon, coming around the half-circle of Pickering Wharf, Vickie saw a crowd at the shop.

"People are standing in line," Rory said.

She parked in the driveway and ran up the porch steps while customers told her to get in line, but Rory stopped to charm them.

Her shop looked bright, organized, interesting. Storm had done an exceptional job. Small changes, big effects. A splash of blues here. Reds there. Colors that led the eye to treasures whose prices had risen. *Hmm.*

"What's happening?" she asked Storm, bagging purchases.

"You know Des. She can't keep her mouth shut when a customer's future jumps out at her. I swear, she's reading half the people who come in."

"You mean Destiny is telling fortunes? For profit?"

"No, geez, get a life."

"I didn't mean to sound critical, but so many customers."

"They're buying, too. I'm sure Harmony's positive energy is part of the draw. When she sits on the porch, customers gravitate to her. Maybe they sense her connection to the past; I don't know. Others are here for Destiny's spontaneous readings."

"Well, between the three of you, you've turned my shop into a happy place."

"Duh, we are witches."

"You're proud of that." It was often difficult to tell with Storm.

"It's a gift. We're lucky."

"You never tried to fight your powers, any of you?"

"As far back as I can remember, we played with them."

"That could have been a triplet thing, right, if you read each other when you were small?"

"No," Storm said. "That's different. We communicate with each other without words, but we can't *read* each other."

"So how did you know you had a gift?"

"We were always fascinated by the craft, so we read books about it."

Storm went back to help Destiny. "We felt a calling to be witches, even before we knew about our Pictish heritage."

"That's true," Des said, ringing up a sale.

Rory came to the counter. "The power of three, is it?"

Destiny looked at Vickie. "It might be the power of four soon."

"It might be the power of a law suit," Rory said, "if you promised Victoria's customers anything tangible with your fortune telling."

"Nah, Des gave a couple of off-the-cuff readings, and the word spread. We're open to talking 'shop,' and people like that." Storm eyed Rory. "Some people are fascinated by us."

"Looks like the attitudes have taken over," Rory said.

Storm frowned. "The attitudes?"

"You've got it and you're proud of it," Vickie said. "Why pretend?"

"So, did'ja get laid or what?"

Rory coughed. "None of your business," he said, but he regarded Vickie with so much heat, she thought she might melt.

Storm cracked up. "You did! I knew it!"

Rory ignored her. "You don't mind that they're admitting they're witches in public, Victoria?"

"I'm as surprised by their comfort with the subject as you are," Vickie said, "but this is Salem, and they make mc think I should take stock of my own wish craft?"

"Because it's frightening?" Rory asked with hope.

"No, because maybe it *is* a gift." Vickie got behind the counter to help her sisters.

Rory shrugged. "I'm off to check the computer. I want to see if I received the translation of your mantel carving."

After supper, Rory went upstairs and Vickie tried to convince her sisters to go to a movie, but the know-it-all triumvirate pretended not to understand.

"Damn it," Vickie swore. "I don't even know how to get you out of here. How am I going to tell Rory what I want?"

"Walk us to the van," Destiny said. "We're going to a movie."

"About damn time," Vickie grumbled.

"Hey, Sis," Storm said as they climbed into their van, "just tell him you wanna get laid. Guys don't need finessing, *ye ken?*" She wiggled her brows.

Harmony pulled Storm in. "Throw some bath salts in the Jacuzzi, light some candles, get in, forget your towel, and call Rory."

"Yeah," Des said. "He'll take it from there."

So much for their sensual interlude, Rory thought as he paced the library. The minute they got home, reality had beckoned times three, with spiked hair, witchy attitudes, and fortune-telling shop girls. Damn.

They had enjoyed touring the mansions and acting like . . . a couple. He'd loved Victoria in her black jeans and red cape, not to mention her red polka dot blouse and headband. He'd thought all day about peeling the layers away, and here he was spending the evening alone.

When his pacing took him to the fireplace, he ran his hand over the carving. "Welcome home, Rory," it said. Imagine that.

He took one of Victoria's woodcuts off the shelf, and realized there was a tiny design in the corner that he'd seen on the Paxton Wharf painting, either a "V" or a Lily.

Victoria's ancestor had carved the woodcuts and painted Paxton Wharf. Looking at the woodcuts again, Rory remembered something, a woodcut to match these, "Lovers," on a shelf in *his* workshop as far back as he could remember. Lili. Lili *was* Victoria's ancestor. The damned unicorn was probably Drummond's. Rory almost wished it wasn't, but he wouldn't worry about that until he could prove it.

Right now, he was thinking about the sound the painting made when he moved it, as if something was loose inside. He went to his room for the painting, brought it to the library, and with a sharp old letter opener, he pried up a back corner.

"What are you doing?" Victoria asked.

"I thought I'd lost you to the Attitudes."

"They've gone to a movie."

"That's fortunate."

"That's bribery."

"I just made the connection between the tarot card woodcuts and your ancestor, and I want to see what's sliding around in here."

"I'm not sure I do."

When he peeled enough of the back away, they saw the old envelope.

"It's yours," Vickie said. "I gave *you* the painting."

But he handed the envelope to her. "Read it for me, then."

"It's the Empress." She laughed.

"You want to share that joke?"

"Sure," she said. "It means I want to get laid."

"Glory alleluia," he said, not caring about Lili or the unicorn. He led Victoria to the stairs. "Wish I'd found that card the first day."

"It wasn't time."

"Which translated means?"

"I have no idea."

"You scare me."

"You should be scared. You're the first

man to step foot in my attic retreat. If the roof's ever going to fall, this is the night. Ready for another concussion?"

"I'm up for danger," Rory said halfway up the stairs. "Hell." He took her hand and placed it over his zipper. "I'm just plain up. Want to see what we can do about that?"

Victoria wiggled her brows. "Yeah."

Just inside her room, she turned to him. "Remember what happened at Cloud Kiss this morning?"

"Every minute."

"I know we didn't do it right, precisely." She toyed with the buttons on his shirt, "but do you think you could show me how it all works first, before we take that final step?"

Final step? Rory sat on the bed beside her. "You're not a virgin, Victoria?"

"I'm not?"

"Are you?"

"I already said that no man has ever —"

"You said the men who climbed into your bed got injured. You said no man had seen you naked. But some man could have breached you beneath your skirt."

"Are you making fun of me?"

"I'm making fun of every man who's ever come near you and lost his shot. I'm also trying to understand the facts. Have you ever had intercourse with a man, Victoria?"

"No, never. It's sad to admit at my age, I know, but —"

Rory stood to digest her startling information, and when he looked back at her, she'd pulled up the corner of the quilt, though she sat there fully dressed, which he definitely needed to do something about. Hell, she looked scared.

He swore, knelt by the bed, and took her wee cold hands in his. "The final step, you said. Final is final, darlin', ye ken? A frightening thought for a virgin, never mind a man who's never deflowered one."

"Well, I may not technically be a virgin."

Rory sat back. "You just *said* . . ."

She opened her nightstand and showed him a white vibrator shaped like a cock with a butterfly on it. "Brock here might have devirginized me," she said.

"Jings, you named it?"

"Well, yeah. Don't you think 'Brock the Cock' has a certain ring to it? Besides, who else's name am I gonna call out?"

"He's that good, is he? Of course he would be, wouldn't he, with his rhyming name and all?"

"Oh for pity's sake, there's no spell on it; it's just your everyday, average BOB."

"I thought it was Brock."

"B-O-B: Battery Operated Boyfriend."

"Mighty me. You Yanks have names for everything."

"I don't think Brock is as mighty as you. Besides, this is Brock the third, and it was actually Brock the first who —"

Rory stood and went to the window. He wasn't happy about competing with a state-of-the-art cock named Brock.

"Do you blame me?" Victoria said. "Look, you've got a boner bigger than Mount Everest, and *you* don't want me."

Rory chuckled when he turned to her. "Ach, darlin', that's how much you know. Men don't get hard looking at lasses they *don't* want."

She dropped the quilt.

"That's right," he said, returning to the bed. "You're getting it. We get hard over a lass we want to shag. Ach, and here's me bigger for telling you so. What's taller than Everest?" He slid the headband from her hair. "I'm humbled to be your first *man*. I only hope I can outperform my predecessor."

"Hey, your charger doesn't need batteries. I'll save a fortune!"

"No, I'm *not* super-charged, and I'm no fairy-tale knight, either. I'm naught but flesh and blood, but I'm honored that you want me anyway."

"You won't give my secret away?"

"What? That I'm your first man, or that you wear out Brock cocks like socks?"

A bonnie sight: Victoria giggling. "You rhymed," she said.

"Jings. Is my cock going to fall off?"

"No, but your socks are."

"Mighty glad to hear it." Rory crossed his heart. "Your secret is safe. My honor as a Knight of the Sacred Star, and that's a royal promise."

"Well could you just give me the royal shaft instead? I need to get laid, MacKenzie. Slip it to me, will you . . . after you show me how it works that is."

"Ach," he sighed. "You're asking a lot of my old-fashioned charger. He hasn't the coming power you have, lass, which is quite the capacity, I might add, if last night and this morning are any indication. And you want a demonstration *before* the main event?"

"Brock could do it."

"Throwing down the gauntlet, are we?" Falling deeper under Victoria's spell, Rory unbuttoned his jeans. He didn't care if she was using magic or not.

Ready to outperform, and survive, anything she cast his way, he was, by damn, getting under her, over her, around, and inside her, as many times as he could before he inevitably expired from a lethal case of bliss-induced exhaustion.

THIRTY-FOUR

"Oh," Victoria said as his jeans puddled around his ankles. "He sure looks like he has enough spunk to do the job."

"That much and more. He's been standing at attention, waiting for your command to charge, for more than a week."

"He doesn't seem to mind my well-fed self, I'll give him that."

"Ach, you need more than lessons on how my charger works. You need lessons on your female power. Here's one of them. You might have figured out by now that my mouth is often short-circuited by my charger, which also sometimes overrides my brain, especially when you're around. That's what happened the day I met you."

Victoria leaned back on her elbows and crossed her ankles. "Do tell."

Rory stepped out of his jeans and sat beside her. "The wind toyed with your honey hair, ye ken?" He toyed with it now, just because he could. "It tossed your slithery skirt up and about so it bared your legs while it caressed and revealed your delicious figure to my goggly eyes. You stole my breath, Victoria. I was so bloody enchanted, I couldn't think, and I felt like an eejit for staring, so I said something nonsensical just to break the silence. Please forgive this daft Scot for his first bletherin' words, will you?"

"I'll think about it while you show me what you've got."

Rory grinned and opened her blouse. "Ach, and I'm fond of a scarlet bra on a woman." All systems go.

She stopped him from getting at the front hook. "Nice try, MacKenzie, but bring that big boy up here."

"Not so soon, darlin'. He's up last, and I want to take this slow." Rory got on the floor and started nibbling at her toes, until she fell back on the bed laughing. That accomplished, he climbed back on the bed and straddled her.

When he saw her surprise, he went for the zipper on her jeans. But he got distracted by her pout and had to make a meal of her with his kiss. All his parts went on alert as he tended to her breasts.

"I wanna get laid," he said, repeating her request, "the four nicest words in any language. Help me pull down your jeans, will you, darlin'?"

"Are you saying my hips are fat?"

Whoosh. All systems down.

He sat up. "Victoria," he said, hand on heart. "I love your hips, I love your lips. I love your thighs, I love your eyes. I love your toes, I love your nose. I love —"

Victoria scrambled out from under him and stopped when she reached the wall. "Shuddup!"

"Right." Rory understood. He'd felt the quiver up his spine too late. "Love," a terrifying word. Now he had to make up to her for scaring her half to death.

He grabbed her by the ankles and pulled her back down to revel in, and reveal, each of her lush curves by explaining the glory of them . . . from his *cock's* point of view.

"Wait," she said. "We have to give him a name. He deserves better than a pronoun."

"What name?" The pronoun in question was shrinking.

"How about Lance?"

"How about I kill myself now?"

"That would put this on a par with my standard sexual encounters."

"Lance, it is." Problem was, "Lance" wasn't seeing any action beyond the palm of Victoria's hand. And she insisted on keeping her bra and knickers on, no matter how often Rory moved them aside. Every time "Lance" got close, she shied away, which Rory took as a sign to go slow.

After Victoria came another thirteen times, she sat up and laid him back, the object of her interest pointing heavenward. "Okay, now, before you turn me into a woman," she said, "show me exactly how this mega-charger of yours works."

"Have you ever seen a grown man cry?" Rory asked, "because I'm tearing up here."

"You rat! I knew you couldn't bear to do me!" She shoved him off the bed.

"Huh?" He elbowed his way up and off the floor, and got shoved on his arse again.

"Screw you, MacKenzie, if you can't bring yourself to —"

"Oh for —" Rory pulled her to the floor and pinned her beneath him. "Hell, you made me sprain 'Lance' when he hit the floor, and I can *still* show you how much I want you."

"Well put your Lance where your mouth is."

He reared back. "I think that's illegal."

"Bite me."

"I'd love to."

"Don't."

"That's it. Enough with the fight, sass,

and general lack of cooperation." He switched their positions so she was on top. "Just put your hand here." He closed her hand around him, and taught her the move. "Keep it up, and in about ten seconds, you'll see how it works."

Rory tried to grab some control, despite Victoria's endless teasing, and he had a handle on it until Tigerstar landed on his chest, and he short-circuited.

"Ohhh," Victoria said. "So that's how it works. That makes me hot."

"Wonderful," Rory said on a weak-limbed sigh, while her cat climbed over his face. "The good news: it'll last longer next time. The bad news: next time will take a few minutes."

Rory put Tigerstar in the wardrobe, with an apology, and a blanket, and he left the door open a crack, with a chair to keep it from opening any wider. Then he made Victoria come again, then she made him come again, then he needed a short recess to pass out. "Do you know the story of the unicorn and the maiden?" he asked.

She shook her sleepy head. They were so entwined, he couldn't tell where he began and she ended.

"First of all," he said, "the unicorn is a rare beast for he's fierce, yet good, selfless, solitary, and he can only be captured by *unfair* means. It's the perfect job for you."

Rory checked to see if Victoria got it.

She was smiling like a Cheshire cat. "You're not the unicorn. You're the dragon."

"Why? I have a great horn."

"But you breathe fire. The unicorn is the matchmaker. It's the dragon I'm supposed to vanquish, or tame."

"The unicorn *canna* be tamed, except by the most perfect of maidens. That's you. And when he finds her, the unicorn is at his weakest, because he stops whatever he's doing, even if he's running from hunters, and he lays his head in her lap."

Rory laid his head in Victoria's lap, kissed her wherever he could reach, and he sighed in contentment. Then he remembered that the maiden could become the unicorn's downfall, so he let Victoria doze.

Rory couldn't sleep. The harder he tried, the more wide awake he became. Panic began to ride him for what he felt . . . for Victoria, and for what he hadn't accomplished.

Falling for Lili's descendant was not the reason he had come to America. He had a mission. A MacKenzie had taken Caperglen's prosperity, a MacKenzie must restore the possibility of it. He'd told himself so often over the years, 'twas a wonder he could forget so easily.

He blamed Victoria.

Rolling toward her, he took in her scent: lilies, lavender, and the musk of sex, and he felt the breath sigh out of her. When exactly had he fallen all the way? The first dream? The first day on her porch? At Cloud Kiss? Tonight when she introduced him to Brock?

It didn't matter. Loving Victoria was, in fact, insane. He needed to choose sanity and purpose. He needed . . . to find . . . the key-ring she kept up here.

Rory moved her hand from his chest, kissed her knuckles, and eased from her bed.

Tigerstar pounced, claws out, and Rory yelped as much in surprise as pain. Then the cat wailed, a sound loud enough to wake the house. How she'd gotten out of the wardrobe, he'd never know, but this was payback.

Victoria sighed his name in her sleep, and Rory's heart stopped, but then he heard her soft snuffling snore. Breathing again, he put Tigerstar on the stairs and shut Victoria's door.

She was some sound sleeper. She lay on her belly, moonlight caressing the base of her spine where a yellow quarter moon made love to a red-orange sun just above the band of her scarlet knickers.

A third tattoo, now of all times. Rory wanted to climb back into bed and kiss her just there. He also wanted to go looking for any tattoos he might have missed.

He chose sanity, instead. He felt along the top of her desk, opened drawers, her bureau, her desk, her nightstand, and found the keyring beside Brock. Giving in to his evil side, Rory placed Brock gently in the wastebasket by her desk and covered it with half a box of tissues. Then he grabbed his jeans to muffle the sound of the purloined keys, and made his getaway.

The attic stairs creaked like a canny Scot's rusty purse, so loud that Rory stopped and waited for Victoria to call his name. He would gladly have turned back, but no call came, so he continued on. At the bottom of the stairs, he pulled on his jeans. Crossing the second floor was tricky. Every other floorboard creaked. Why had he never noticed that before?

A door squealed, and Rory hooked a left, walked into a two-ton ceramic frog . . . and broke a toe.

Flat beside an ornate umbrella stand, Rory waited, blinking tears of pain from his eyes, thinking, *bad karma bad karma,* until Storm returned from the bathroom. After that, he continued on. Hard to go down stairs with nine good toes and half a hop, but he managed . . . without passing out.

He stopped in the kitchen for an ice pack and tied it to the top of his foot with Victoria's "bitch, bitch, bitch" dishtowel. "Dumbarse wanker," he said, "besotted by the witch you're screwing, and not in a *good* way."

A minute later, he hopped toward the moonlit Plexiglas unicorn case. Despite his aching foot, he began trying keys from a ring that must hold a hundred.

He'd rather be upstairs making love to . . . no, not love. Though, bloody hell, what was it then? His feelings for Victoria were more than friendship, and more than lust, though friendship was definitely involved. What the bloody hell did you call that?

"Insanity," Rory said.

Once upon a time, he would have considered the unicorn a lucky find, but no more. He didn't deserve it, and he didn't want it. He wanted to climb back into Victoria's good graces, slip into bed beside her, slip into her, and forget Caperglen existed.

Why couldn't he?

He'd send a letter, care of the Sacred Star. Say he was staying. He didn't have to say he found something — no, he found someone — better than the unicorn. A small matter, after generations of pariahs searching for the thing . . . and a father driven to drink because of it. The key he'd been trying turned before he knew it . . . an anticlimax of dishrag proportions.

"Fate," he said, putting his hands to work, not in the preferred way, with Victoria's tattoos to find, but searching for Drummond's secret compartment.

Finding the wanking latch annoyed him. He kicked off the blasted ice pack. It hurt more than it helped.

Life would have been easier if this was the wrong unicorn. "But when was life ever easy?" He needed another bloody key to open the bloody compartment. "Bloody MacKenzie curse!" he snapped.

"Bloody MacKenzie thief, more like!" Victoria's voice cut through the darkness, the emptiness in his soul, rushed joy in . . . and raised the hair at his nape.

Rory dropped the hundred-key ring on his broken toe.

THIRTY-FIVE

When the light went on, Victoria raised her chin, her glorious eyes bright with fire and fit to slay a dragon. "Man, I hate to make you come then kick your ass in the same day," she said.

More sorry to disillusion her, Rory couldn't work up a dram of elation at finding Drummond's unicorn. Instead, he was, foolish him, happy to see Victoria, even though she now knew what an arse he was not to have told her the entire truth.

"A sin of omission?" she asked.

A perceptive witch . . . with whom he was deeply in lust, aye, and a dangerous case he had, for he'd rather have her trust than the unicorn he'd searched for his whole life.

He wished he knew if there might be some forgiveness in her, but she gave nothing away. He condemned the foolish thought, turned and continued his search. "I need a smaller key to open the hidden compartment."

"Do you plan on making cheap copies?" she asked, "or are you trying to steal the original? It's worth a cool quarter million, you know."

"Double that," he said. "It's a Drummond."

"In that case," she said, "triple it."

"No, because this *isn't* the last of his zodiac figures. "I have the other eleven."

"You what?"

"I own the carousel. It's missing only this unicorn to make it whole."

"But the experts said . . . Who *are* you?"

"Your worst nightmare, is, I believe, the correct Yank cliché." He didn't bother to say that her family had stolen it from his. "Drummond was a grandfather on my father's side."

"That's another lie. His name would have been MacKenzie."

"It was. Drummond Rory MacKenzie. The family called him Rory, and everybody else called him Mac, so he chose Drummond for his art. By the way, your mantel carving says 'Welcome home, Rory.' Bit of a kicker, isn't it? Considering."

Vickie wondered how she could be so bloodthirsty that she wanted to hurt those same parts of him that she had adored just a short while ago?

No sooner did she think it than Rory yelped and cupped himself. She'd somehow zapped him in the balls.

"Retro," she said. "I don't need to rhyme. My magic must give me what I want, whether I know it or not."

Rory took a few deep breaths, and Vickie was afraid she'd really hurt him, though she shouldn't care.

"Proud of yourself, are you?" he asked.

"You have no idea." She flashed a fake grin while fighting the tears threatening to melt her hard-candy shell.

"For your information," he said straightening with a wince. "That was a wee zap, nothing more. Surprised me is all. And I'm not stealing the unicorn's design. I own the signed original. I brought it with me to show you. The proof that this is a Drummond rests in the existence of a hidden compartment beneath the saddle, and I just found it."

"Your ancestor might have carved it, buster, but my ancestor left it to *me!*"

"Lili, you mean?"

Vickie felt the weight of Lili's sadness, probably because this man had just turned his back on *her,* as some man — possibly even Drummond, himself — had turned his back on Lili. "Guess you're one in a long line of MacKenzie rats."

Rory's usually direct gaze slipped away. "You don't understand."

"Oh, give me credit for some sense. Speaking of which, I'm calling the police." Vickie picked up the receiver on her wall phone.

"You might not want to do that, because I can prove the unicorn is mine," Rory said, though his troubled expression contradicted his words.

"Lili left that unicorn to me. I have the will, and this is not Scotland. Possession is nine-tenths of the law here, and if a compartment exists in that unicorn, whatever's inside it is mine as well. Step away," she said, pointing with the receiver, proud of her cop-show con.

As if she wielded a gun, rather than a phone, Rory did as he was told. He musn't watch his lodge "telly" very often.

She stretched the phone cord to its limit as she felt beneath the unicorn's saddle for the latch that Rory said was there. "You're right," she said. "It needs a key."

"Aye." Rory bent to retrieve the hundred-key ring and he held it out to her.

"It's not *here*," Vickie said. "I didn't know the compartment existed. Why would I have a key to it? Besides, that latch requires a much smaller key." She snatched the ring from his hands. "I *know* what each of these opens."

Rory gave her a nod of respect; a bit late, she thought.

"I suppose the key might still be in the wardrobe where I found the unicorn." Vickie slammed down the receiver and led the way back through the house. "Your ass is grass, MacKenzie."

"Understood."

"I hate you."

"Aye. I hate me, too."

He dropped the towel and ice pack in the sink.

"What are you doing with those?"

"I injured my —"

"Never mind. It's your karma. I also plan to beat you later. Better still," she said. "I'll sic a witch with attitude on you."

"Crivvens, I didn't kill anybody."

She indicated that he should precede her up the stairs, as if she were wearing a gun or something, but at least he'd get the idea that *she* was in charge.

"I think a witch with attitude already brought me to my knees tonight."

"For the last time, I am *not* a witch!"

"So *you* say . . . on and off. But you

zapped me in the bollocks without raising a brow. That's the scariest witch magic of all, ye ken, the frontal attack?"

She might have laughed if it had not been for the musk of sex that greeted them when they stepped into her room. "Back to the scene of the crime," she said, ignoring the bedding on the floor. But she remembered the power of his sex in her hand, the stream of his come, and the same excitement shot through her now as it had then. And she was still technically a virgin, damn him!

Vickie pulled the wardrobe door open so hard, it hit him and bounced shut again. Rory caught the door the second time, and propped it open with a chair. The scent of lilies wafted into the room as if on a spring breeze.

After a minute of looking into the darkness, they stepped in, bumped shoulders, and pulled away.

"Ladies first," Rory said, tipping a nonexistent hat, like a fool. A yummy fool, damn him. Vickie searched the wardrobe floor so the fool wouldn't see the embarrassment heating her face.

Beside her — too close beside her — Rory searched the wardrobe's upper reaches. The need for sex with the traitor became strong. Desire purled through her and settled deep in her pulsing womb.

Finding nothing, she rose, and hit her head on his jaw.

"Argh," he said. "I don't have enough hands to hold everything that hurts."

Vickie saw stars, too, and Rory's hot hands caught at her waist, as he fought a battle with his greedy grasp.

"I hate you," she said, cupping his jaw to soothe it.

He stopped fighting his instincts, grasped her tight, and pulled her against him. "You should hate me."

They stared into each other's eyes. Enemies or lovers?

"I have other parts that hurt, too," he said.

She cupped his balls through his jeans.

He winced but he didn't pull away.

They'd neither of them dressed for their midnight trek to the shop. He wore unzipped jeans. She wore his gray oxford shirt, because it smelled of him, but she'd removed her bra and panties, thinking she'd join him in the shower when she didn't find him in bed.

He bunched it in his hand, his fists now riding the undercrest of her breasts.

"Bollocks," he said, lost in a fury of his own making.

In tight, dark quarters, bodies touching,

the musk of anger and desire rising, Vickie wanted Rory's lying lips against hers. "MacKenzie, I'm going to hurt you, if you don't kiss me soon."

He came for her in a blink.

Greedy. Ravenous.

Mutual starvation.

Satisfaction guaranteed.

Sighs and moans filled their confinement — his moans, her sighs — as they rediscovered each other's bodies, their vocalizations blending and adding to the frenzy.

She slipped a hand into the fly of his jeans . . . and found him. "Remember, I'm using you," she said, "like you used me."

He tore his shirt off her back, and bared her to his mouth. "I deserve nothing less."

She liked the power of his rod in her hand, and she went for his balls, too. "You deserve another zap."

"They've had a hard night."

"It's gonna get worse."

"Is that a promise?"

"It's a threat." She zapped him again, just to prove she could.

He yelped. "Your aim is off. You got me in the rod. I rather liked it."

"Figures."

"You must be working on your emotions," he said, "and the rod is what you want."

Damn it. He was right. And she was gonna have that big boy. She brought it toward her center.

"No," Rory said through gritted teeth as she stroked herself with the head of it. "Not this way," but he surged, nonetheless, so she arched and took him in with a great deal of satisfaction at getting her own way.

Despite the surprising size of him, Vickie sighed in relief, because Brock had done the deed, and the discomfort was minimal. She felt herself stretching, finally becoming a woman, but . . .

"This doesn't feel quite as good as I expected. Are you doing it right?"

"According to the manual," he muttered, and damned if she didn't soften toward him, the rat.

"I'll take it slow," he promised, "and make it good."

He moved so slow, he soothed the ache and increased it at the same time.

"You can go faster than that. What'd you do, take lessons from a turtle?"

He firmed his lips. "I didn't want to hurt you."

"Too late for that, MacKenzie, but I want you anyway. Heaven knows why, because I want to hurt you, too, but I'll save the torture for another time."

"Don't stop now. I think you're doing fine."

"Just don't forget that I'm using you."

"I know, but jings, I'm feeling cocky, anyway . . . though I know I don't deserve it."

"You sure as hell don't," she said. "But I wanna get laid, and you're the designated boy toy. You already screwed me over once tonight, so you may as well do it again. Just try and get it right this time."

"You really know how to turn a man on, you know that?"

THIRTY-SIX

"Victoria," Rory said, wanting to make slow delicious love to her more than he wanted air in his lungs — except that he'd be her first, then he'd have to leave her, like everyone else in her life.

"Finish what you started, damn it. Forget about Drummond and his unicorn for a minute. Right now it's you and me, and the big 'O.' "

"As long as you put it that way," he said.

He did want to be the man to give Victoria her first non-plastic induced climax. He wanted her to feel the life-force raging between them. "Wait," he said. "Protection."

"Pill, and safe as a virgin."

"Celibate as a damned cloistered monk."

"No wonder you're so quick on the trigger."

"I resent that. That was you teasing me for a week."

"Shut up and screw me, damn it, and try to go the distance this time."

He'd go it by damn, until she bloody begged. Rory buried himself to the hilt, again and again.

"This is exactly what I want," she said, moving with him, and bringing him deeper.

"Aye, and don't I know it. Of course, I'm just taking my punishment."

"Something inside me tells me different," she said, laughing and dislodging him, but she rocked him back in, using her female instincts to good advantage, he thought.

"My hyperactive charger? Wait," he said. "The girls are looking for us." Rory was wild to move. Didn't dare.

As rigid as they held themselves, their bodies moved of their own volition — him throbbing to go deeper, her pulsing to pull him in.

She arched the slightest bit; he surged in quiet triumph, both of them moving in a slow silent mating, the danger of being caught adding a frisson of fear and adventure.

Another arch, another surge, and Rory had to kiss her, or shout his triumph.

He heard footsteps on the stairs. "Come down here!" Storm called.

"Shut the door," Victoria said.

Rory slipped from inside her and caught the wardrobe door, but he kept it open a crack and stepped close to listen.

"I'm going up," Destiny said.

Victoria reached over and pulled the door shut.

"My cock!"

Vickie knelt to soothe it. "You poor bent thing."

"I'm telling you, we have to open the shop ourselves," they heard Storm say.

"What about Vickie?" Destiny asked.

"I sense the present," Storm said, "Remember?"

"Oh, you mean Rory and Vickie? Cool." The footsteps receded.

"Storm sees snapshots of the present in her mind," Victoria said.

"Then she must be laughing her arse off. You broke my cock!"

"Oh, I did not. Look, it's as hard as ever."

"Well, sure, with you kissing it and rubbing it against your cheek, what do you expect?"

Victoria took the poor maimed thing in hand, and put it where they both wanted it, then with her hips, she began a slow-rising torment, literally, sort of.

Before long, Rory took the lead, never more determined to last, and never more in tune with bringing his mate to climax.

He was her first; he couldn't take her in a frenzied rush. He'd done enough damage. Then again, so had she. "Come with me, Victoria."

"Lift me against you. I need to get closer, bring you deeper."

Ach, and how could he argue with that logic? He lifted her and she wrapped her legs around his waist, turning him into Brock on speed.

"Jings, I love your arse in my hands." Rory got a rush just saying it.

She frenched him as he worked inside her and took him half-way to heaven.

"You feel so good." Victoria sighed. "Soo good."

He made it last, and last, until Victoria cried out, and set him off, and they touched the stars together.

More a cataclysm than a climax, Rory thought, breathless, his heart pounding, with Victoria limp and sex-drunk in his arms.

Still bearing her weight, he fell against the wardrobe at his back, rattling it, and something fell, bounced off his shoulder, and hit the floor with a clink.

Victoria stood away from him, the separation rushing cold air between them.

Rory pushed the door open to shed light on reality, in the form of a small, filigreed key.

It was like having a helping of hot passion followed by a serving of cold remorse. Rory picked up the key, Victoria watching as if in a trance.

"Thank you," she said, leaving the wardrobe. "That was nice."

Nice? "Bloody hell, nice. It was bloody freaking glorious!"

With a look to rival the attitudes, Victoria tossed her wild blond mane into further disarray, turned her back on him, and slipped into her robe. "I wouldn't know," she said. "I have no baseline comparison."

"Well, now that you do, let's give it another go." Rory tackled her from behind, and took her to the bed.

Having been dropped in the center of it, Victoria narrowed her eyes. "Why didn't you just throw me over your shoulder and carry me up your tree?"

Rory straddled her, caged her in, his hands on either side of her head. "Do you want another go, or not?"

"Not," she said, taking him in hand, bringing him to life, and putting him where he wanted to be. "Better than nothing," she said.

Hours later, he'd given her plenty to compare it to, and he'd proved his staying power as well. Hell, he was the king of staying power.

Around noon, someone knocked on her door, and when Rory opened it around two, he found a tray on the landing with Chinese take-out containers and plastic utensils. "This is going to cost us," Rory said, setting the picnic between them amid a clutter of disheveled bedding.

"Don't," Victoria said. "I'm not ready to let the world in. Besides, the witch-made happy faces on these containers are enough to keep me here for another two hours."

They stayed, in fact, for three.

"A couple more hours, MacKenzie," Victoria said as they started to search for their clothes, "and I'll have caught up with my friends who lost it in high school."

He hooked a finger in her scarlet bra and pulled her against him. "I'm game to try," he boasted, though he was pretty sure she'd worked his charger into a coma.

"Give me the key," she said.

He searched his naked body for pockets "I think you have it."

"You picked it up off the wardrobe floor, remember?"

"And you snatched it from my hand."

"Then you tackled me."

They strip-searched the cyclonic bed, and came up with a naked mattress.

After remaking it with clean linens, they crawled around on the floor, with no luck, so they moved the bed from its alcove.

"I still haven't forgiven you," Victoria said, picking the key up off the floor on the far side. "I can't believe I let you —"

"*Begged* me. *Used* me."

A protest forming on her lips, she changed her stripes. "You're already on my hit list, MacKenzie, so let's just call this a draw."

"Fine, don't admit it. Fury begets passion, ye ken, and desire has been simmering between us for days, intensified by the dreams in which we play it out. No wonder our primal urges won out. You canna fight destiny, darlin'."

"Don't talk to me about destiny. You're a skunk."

"I am. I admit it."

"So stop stinking already."

"You know, my inner animal has a bad case of multiple personality disorder. It doesn't know what kind it is. A rat, a wolf, a skunk, a unicorn, or a dragon."

"Give up your claim to the unicorn and you'll be my knight in shining armor again."

"Victoria, there are extenuating circumstances."

"Aren't there always?" She left him to eat her dust.

And well she should. He deserved to choke on it. His responsibilities were about to separate them, and he'd remain sorry forever. Like Drummond, he thought, going downstairs.

Why did this situation remind him of Lili and Drummond all of a sudden?

Vickie left Rory to make dinner while she went to work for the first time that day. Her sisters' grins as she passed through the shop annoyed her.

She sat on a rocker beside Harmony who was tending the sidewalk sale. "Between trolleys?" Vickie asked.

"Between orgasms?" Harmony replied.

"Jealous?"

"Exhausted?"

"Nah," Des said, coming outside. "They slept all day."

"Not," Storm said, behind her.

Vickie winced. "How vivid are your 'in the moment' snapshots?"

Storm rolled her eyes. "Not to worry. The better I know you, the less I can read you. You're my sister, after all, but your satisfied expression has 'I got laid' written all over it."

Actually, Vickie thought, they'd made love, but Rory probably didn't think so. Besides, she should hate him, not love him. "I was using him."

"I sense something more, something magical," Harmony said. "Did you use some kind of spell on him?"

"If you must know, I zapped him in the nuts."

"Yes!" Storm high-fived her.

"My wishes got away from me."

"Oh, oh," Destiny said, "Witches are supposed to harm none. Negative as well as positive energy will come back to you times three."

"But I'm not a witch."

Vickie didn't appreciate her sisters' amusement, but the camaraderie was painless to embrace, as long as she remembered that they'd leave at some point.

They positively tortured her and Rory through supper, and after they went upstairs, she and Rory went back to the shop to open the hidden compartment.

"I'll do it," Vickie said, elbowing him out of the way. "It's *my* unicorn."

Rory combed his beard. "The latch isn't easy to find."

"Yeah, but I'm searching with the lights *on.*" Vickie's heart beat as if something momentous was about to happen, while the word destiny, and an image of them making love in a rowboat, of all things, filled her mind's eye.

As she slipped the tiny key into the tiny lock, her hand trembled.

When it came to raising the heavy, hinged lid — the massive piece of wood that formed the saddle and cantle — Rory leaned over and helped her, until it rested on the unicorn's rump. "Thank you," she said, idiotically glad he stood beside her.

She stopped shutting him out, and together they explored the narrow entry to what appeared to be a wider cavity.

She removed a book. "A diary," she said opening it. "Lili's diary!"

"And these are Drummond's letters," Rory said, unfolding the top one. "Here he's breaking his engagement to Lili."

"His engagement? Your Drummond was *engaged* to my Lili? We're connected through the past? Did you know that when you tricked your way into my home?" *And my heart,* she thought sadly.

Rory fingered his beard. "I wasn't sure until last night in the library when I realized that the signature marks on your wood-blocks, and on my painting, are lilies."

"But you always suspected that this was Drummond's unicorn. You lied to me."

"No, I said I came to see the unicorn, which was true. Without the compartment, that would have been the end of it."

"Would that have been the end of us as well? Don't answer. That was sophomoric of me. I don't want an 'us.' "

"Right," Rory said. "Plus the unicorn has a compartment, but more important, Drummond's signature is on this letter breaking his engagement to Lili, which proves the unicorn is mine."

"What convoluted route did you take to get to that conclusion?" So much for being glad he was here.

"Drummond didn't love Lili, which is why she left Scotland. Therefore, he wouldn't have sent her the unicorn of his own free will, which proves she bewitched him."

"What a crock," Vickie said. "One letter can't possibly tell the whole story. To learn the real truth about the past, we should sit down and read all the letters from the beginning."

"I can tell you the real truth."

Vickie scoffed. "That would make a nice change."

THIRTY-SEVEN

"I mean, the truth about the past, but I deserved that."

"Ass-on-right, you did. So, tell me already."

"The villagers thought Lili was a witch, so my family pressured Drummond into breaking his engagement to Lili." Rory shrugged. "They said she'd ruin the family, and she did."

"My stars! Will you stick with the freaking facts!" Vickie went to sit at Nana's old table.

"Facts. Right. I have a handwritten family history at home in Scotland that'll tell you everything in detail."

"Who wrote it?"

"Drummond."

"Did he by any chance color his story with the same self-serving crap you just handed me?"

"He was less prejudiced against Lili than later generations, I'll admit. I'll also admit that I've always thought Lili's curse on the family, and on Caperglen, was foolishness."

"I don't care what anybody says, you have potential, MacKenzie."

"Unfortunately, I've changed my mind. Lili's granddaughters have turned me into a believer. Mostly the Attitudes, at first, but your frontal attack hit me hard, in more than the expected way."

"Oh, your poor zapped bollocks. Like I didn't soothe the hell out of them afterward."

Rory grinned and Vickie tried not to let her reaction to the phenomena temper her anger. "What happened between our greats anyway? More truth, if you please."

"They were engaged and I think they were lovers."

"And in love," Vickie added.

"I don't know. I do know that after Drummond broke their engagement, Lili became a pariah in the village."

"Takes one to know one," Vickie said. "Poetic justice at its finest."

Rory conceded the point with a nod. "Before Lili sailed for America, she sent Drummond a note asking him to meet her by his carousel." Rory frowned. "What's always bothered me is that he went."

"Because he loved her."

"She wanted him to come here to America with her, but he didn't," Rory said. "However, in his history, Drummond wrote that he 'refused the risk and ended as Lili predicted.' They never saw each other again, as far as I know. Before he died, Drummond broke up the set of zodiac figures and sent Lili the unicorn. The carousel hasn't worked since."

"That's it?" Vickie said in exasperation. "That's your proof that Lili bewitched Drummond?"

"He'd dumped her years before, then he sends her the unicorn? Even your sisters said there was a spell on it. What else could it be?"

"Love," Vickie said. "You don't sit on a wharf and watch for a ship that never comes, if you're not in love with the man you're waiting for."

Rory shook his head. "But they married other people."

"Which doesn't mean they stopped loving each other. Drummond probably had to carry on the line. Was he any happier than Lili?"

Rory smoothed his beard. "No." He sighed. "As a matter of fact, he wasn't."

"I rest my case," Vickie said. "And since you shared your knowledge —" She hesitated. "You did tell me everything?"

Rory scrubbed his face with a hand. "Aye, I did."

"Good. Now this is what I know: Lili left the key to the wardrobe, with the unicorn inside, to the daughter who would inherit her magic and complete her spell."

Rory's spine went broomstick straight. "What spell?"

Vickie held up Lili's diary. "I'm hoping the answer is here. But suppose our dreams are the spell?"

"To what purpose?" Rory asked.

"Okay, this is some heavy speculation, but hear me out. Suppose we've become like a conduit between them, because together we're blood to both of them, and they're the ones meeting in our dreams."

Rory stood up so fast, his chair fell over. "That's not bloody funny," he said. "Besides, your sisters could have opened the wardrobe, and I wouldn't have been attracted to them."

Vickie was sadly glad to hear that. "None of Lili's descendents in a hundred years succeeded in opening the wardrobe, until I tried. If I had failed, the key would have been left to my daughter, not to my sisters."

"So *you* inherited Lili's magic?"

"I wish I knew."

"Just don't rhyme anything, right now. I'm edgy enough already."

"Then you might not want to hear this. The note on the key said that when I opened the wardrobe, I'd meet my destiny. That's why I called the unicorn a match-maker." Vickie went to the shop window remembering the first time she saw Rory out there. "So," she said, hugging Lili's diary. "Did Lili bring us together? Is our attraction the result of a spell?"

"It feels real," Rory said, coming up behind her and placing his hands on her arms.

She stepped from his reach. "No, it feels *unreal.* What do you know from real? You've been faking it since you walked in."

"In the wardrobe, in bed," Rory said. "There was no faking it for either of us."

"Don't count on it."

He mocked her self-preserving lie with a chuckle. "I know what's real from fake, make no mistake."

"That's rich, because I don't, and I'm supposed to be the witch, while you've been acting since you got here."

"Withholding information, yes. Everything else was real. Victoria, heed my warning, if you suspect you're a witch, stop using your magic."

"Warning? Do you think I have control over my wishes? It's as if my emotions are in charge. When Nana was dying, I wanted her to live with such an intense longing, she had to beg me to let her go. She said she couldn't stop suffering until I did, so I accepted the inevitable, and she passed."

Rory looked so shocked that as Vickie went into the house, she was glad he followed, damn him. "The unicorn is mine. These are mine." She held up the diary and letters. "We're caught in some old history is all." A past that she wished wouldn't destroy a future she couldn't imagine without him. "I have to get some sleep so I can open the shop tomorrow. I can't let my sisters run the place into a profit, now, can I?"

Rory tried for a grin, but he couldn't pull it off.

"Maybe you should find another place to rent," she said, wanting him to argue.

"I'm staying until I talk you into selling me the unicorn. Then I need to take it home to Caperglen."

"Good luck with that." She was being vague, to keep him when she knew she should let him go. What a kick in the ass to fall in love at this late date with a lying son of a Scot.

Rory walked up to the second floor beside

her. "You know your mantel message says 'welcome home,' but you should know that a hundred years later, you made me feel at home and welcome."

Vickie swallowed her sorrow. She couldn't speak. As she made her way up the attic stairs alone, she didn't look to see if Rory watched; she felt his longing warming her back.

In bed, lonely without him, though he'd only spent the afternoon here, she sorted Drummond's *and* Lili's love letters by date, and read them first to last. Then she read Lili's diary.

At three in the morning, Vickie had more answers than either she or Rory could have imagined. She spent another half hour trying to decide whether to take the information to Rory, then another few minutes with her hand on his knob — enticing thought — before she got up the nerve to go in. When the creaky door didn't wake him, she thought of a few moves that would.

When she climbed into his bed, he turned her way, took her in his arms and hugged her. "Victoria," he said, "Sweet Victoria," then he continued snoring softly.

He'd automatically turned to her in sleep.

How could she fall deeper in love with a rat?

As she expected, his charger responded first, and after some fondling play and raspy promises, she woke him up.

"Between you and your cat, I don't know which is worse," he complained, but at her insistence he sat against the headboard, and let her read him their ancestors' letters in the order they were written.

"Drummond returned Lili's letters to her in the unicorn so their letters would always be together?" He repeated with disbelief after she finished.

"According to one of his letters. Sounds like love to me." Vickie leafed through the diary. "Lili says, right here, see? That Drummond said there was no joy left in him without her."

"That wasn't in any of his letters."

"I know. It's the one note I can't find."

"Hell, maybe they were in love. What else did you find in the diary?" Rory began to turn her into a midnight snack.

She liked it, but rallied. "Pay attention. Lili's last entry says she planned to put the diary in the compartment with the love letters and — brace yourself — cast a spell on the unicorn to bring her and Drummond together again."

"Ach, but they're dead."

Vickie twirled the chest hair around Rory's nipple. "Yeah, I thought of that, and I'm kinda worried that's the spell I'm supposed to complete."

"Crivvens." He stopped her roving hand. "As in raising the dead?"

"I hope not," Vickie said. "I don't know how. Do you think we're pawns in some ancient game of magic?"

"That's bloody frightening." Rory pulled away. "But I'll go you one better. Are we star-crossed lovers reunited by a vengeful curse?"

"Have you ever read anything about reincarnation?" Vickie asked. "Because I believe in it."

"I think I'm me," Rory said, "I canna be Drummond because, unfortunately, I canna carve as well as he did."

"Then why does their loss feel like ours?" Vickie rubbed her arms. "I'd rather be reincarnated than cursed."

Rory touched her cheek. "I wish I could say that I *didn't* feel their loss."

"For now, let's not let their loss be ours." Vickie unbuttoned her nightgown. "Let's celebrate life and stop worrying about dead ancestors."

"I'm for celebrating," Rory said, pulling

her gown over her head.

Though they began in a sexual frenzy, Rory wanted to slow the pace, so he caught Victoria's fast-working hands and held them between his own. "Let's make this last." *A lifetime,* he thought with regret.

Afraid they were doomed to repeat their ancestors' mistakes — that this was all they would ever have — Rory worshipped Victoria, every scintillating inch of her. He gave her his slow adoring attention in a last attempt at showing her the beauty in her own body.

He kissed the starburst at her cleavage. "Your breasts are magnificent even without the tattoo."

"Ugh. They're shaped like waterballoons."

Rory hid his amusement. "They're pert, perky, and perfect. Surely, you canna deny that your waist is just right? Look it fits the span of my hands."

"*You* have gorilla hands, huge, like your cock."

"Okay, the cock comment is a turn-on, but your self-deriding comments are anything but."

"Good, so stop pretending I'm something I'm not. You're pissing me off."

Rory gave up the crusade, and worked at

helping her endure the ultimate foreplay . . . as many extended sexual orgasms as she could bear.

When she threatened to pass out, he slipped inside her, and realized he was probably making love for the first and last time. An ill-fated love, aye, but a forever love, nonetheless.

They fell into a physical and emotional afterglow with such a potent mystical aura, Rory experienced the kind of panic that Drummond must have felt when Lili sailed away. The thought of losing Victoria made him ache. "Victoria, if you'll just stop using your magic —"

She sat up, using the sheet like a shield — never a good sign — her eyes turning a vulnerable molten gold.

Rory felt the breach growing between them but he was helpless against it.

She blinked away tears, though not a drop spilled over. She moved away and sat straighter. "You know what I think. I think it's time for me to admit that I can't separate myself from my magic, not even for you. The fact is, whether I want it or not, witchcraft is part of who I am, and if you can't accept that, then you can't accept me."

"Victoria, I —"

"No, let me finish. I saw right away that

my sisters had magic, and I accepted them. Why couldn't I see or accept myself and my own magic?"

"Your sisters are loose cannons."

"That's where you've got it wrong. I'm the loose cannon, sitting still and letting my magic blow up in my face."

"And in my bollocks." His piss-poor go at levity failed miserably.

"My sisters," Victoria said, ignoring him, "are smarter than I am. They accepted their destinies, embraced them, and enjoyed their powers from the start. It's not too late for me to take control of my gift, my magic, and my life, and that's what I intend to do."

"What about us?" Rory asked, knowing there could never be an "us" between them.

"I'm a witch, Rory."

"I understand that you think you are, but —"

She rose like a goddess in an armored toga. "We had a fine affair," she said, "but we're not reincarnated lovers. I would, as a matter of fact, prefer a real love to one conjured from the past."

THIRTY-EIGHT

Rory circled the bed to try and make her understand. "Victoria, I canna stay." He hated the truth of it. "I have obligations you don't understand."

"Go back to Scotland, then. But what's with the obligations? Tell me what's so important back there. You owe me that much."

"Aye, I do." Rory tried to keep from taking Victoria in his arms. "I owe you more. You brought me back to life, you see?"

"Your obligations?" she repeated, ignoring his unspoken plea, and retreating inside herself, by the look of her.

He sat and tugged on her sheet, until she had no choice but to sit beside him, or lose her armor.

"You'll listen because our time is running out and I want you to understand the whole of it. Will you?"

"I'll listen, but I won't like it."

"Hell," Rory said. "I don't even like it. I was born into a family with one goal, an ancient quest to find the zodiac unicorn carved by their ancestor."

"Rather narrow-minded, don't you think?"

"You know that without the unicorn, the carousel stopped running. But what you don't know is that the carousel once brought great prosperity to Caperglen. Without it, the village went into a decline and never recovered."

"So the villagers are poor?"

"And so angry, they won't take a dime from me. To this day they blame the Mac-Kenzies. That's why I'm a pariah. They're a superstitious lot, who think Lili cursed Caperglen by bewitching Drummond into sending her the unicorn."

Rory took Victoria's hand, grateful she let him. "They have the daft notion that if the unicorn is returned, and the carousel is opened to visitors again, Caperglen's prosperity will return as well."

With a finger to Victoria's chin, Rory turned her to face him. "I don't believe it, ye ken, but settling Drummond's debt to Caperglen is the only way to repair the MacKenzie name. You should have seen them cheering me off. I got a taste of MacKenzie respect, the kind I'd like for my descendents, if I ever have any."

Rory fell into the depths of Victoria's gaze. He didn't want descendents without her for their mother. He hoped she felt the same, but whether she did or not, he had to go. "The Caperglen villagers have it right," he said. "Because of Drummond, we've all been cursed, you and I most of all."

Victoria rallied. "Because of Drummond, you said. Not Lili."

"Aye, perhaps so."

"You really are an eejit, to use your word. Lili watched the wharf for Drummond to come for her, for years. She *loved* him. The carved welcome on the mantel proves it. Their letters prove it. There was no curse, Rory. Admit there was no curse, only love, and a lot of destructive village gossip."

Rory smoothed his beard. "We dreamed about each other before I saw you on the antiques show, Victoria, before we met. Doesn't that smack of magic?"

"I'll admit that maybe our meeting was part of the spell Lili cast on the unicorn. But if she cursed Drummond or Caperglen, she would have admitted as much in her diary. She had no reason not to tell the truth. She wrote everything down, spells and all, before she locked her diary away. She loved him and she said so. She cast a spell to preserve the unicorn, and she said so. She cast a spell to reunite them after they were dead, and she said so."

"That's true," Rory said.

"Kira said that magic or not, we choose our own destinies."

"You think I want to leave you?" Rory shouted.

"You think putting Lili's unicorn back on your ancient carousel will make it run?"

Rory released his breath. "No, but I'll have paid the family debt to Caperglen. The villagers will have nothing more to complain about. If the carousel doesn't run, the locals won't admit they were foolish, but they won't have cause to look down on the MacKenzies any longer."

"Your name means more to you than you mean to yourself."

"I stand by my responsibilities. This is Drummond's debt, so it's my debt."

"Drummond's, not Lili's."

"Aye, you win."

"Like hell I do."

Rory ignored her pain, he had to. "I owe my father," he said. "Being a pariah broke him."

"But it won't break you?"

"It put me into hibernation, until I saw you." Rory toyed with a rosebud on Victoria's discarded nightgown, and brought it to his face for a memory. "It took Lili's descendent to wake me."

"Lucky freaking me." Victoria opened his door. "You need to take your unicorn and go home."

"I'll top your best offer," he said following her.

Destiny whistled. "Congratulations, Sis!"

Rory looked down at himself, dragged Victoria back into his room and shut the door. "Name your price for the unicorn. Make it high."

"To salve your conscience? Spell you! The unicorn belongs to you, not me. Go home. I'll ship it within the week, but you go today. Now. This minute."

Rory didn't take the blow well, but he pretended differently. He caught Victoria's hand to stop her from opening the door. "One bit of advice. Don't tell your sisters that you think they're fat."

Victoria gasped. "That's a rotten thing to say. They have perfect figures. They're not the least bit fat."

"Aye, their figures *are* perfect."

Victoria looked as if he'd slapped her.

He grabbed her hands to keep her from bolting. "You're missing the point, lass. You wear each other's clothes, you and your sisters. Your figures are interchangeable. We just saw Destiny wearing the dress you were wearing the first time I saw you on the porch. Think about it."

Victoria's brow furrowed, but he didn't expect a lifetime of distorted self-perceptions to change at the first sign of logic. She retrieved her hands and stared at the floor.

"I know you need time to digest the unarguable," he said. "Your figure is as good, better, in my estimation, than your sisters'. Your cheeks are rosier, your eyes brighter, your heart softer, your smile unmatched."

He tipped up her stubborn chin one last time. "Victoria, if you plan to accept yourself as you are, magic and all, accept the truth about your physical self. You're beautiful, and not only in my eyes."

She opened his door without a word.

"I'll need two hours to teach your sisters the bookkeeping system," he said. "I'll be out by noon."

Victoria nodded. "Teach Storm. I'll be at Melody's. I want you gone before I come home."

The woman who owned his heart didn't look back as she left him.

No good-bye. No thanks for the extraordinary shagging, for being her knight and making her a woman . . . and of course for deserting her after all of it.

Half an hour later, Rory stepped into Victoria's shop for the last time.

"We know," Destiny said.

"Then you know what I'm going to do before I go."

Destiny handed him the bills, all the bills, including the mortgage. Rory got on the computer and transferred money from his bank to each of Vickie's creditors. "You're not to tell your sister. She'll figure it out, eventually."

Storm sighed. "Don't worry. We don't want to get rhymed black and blue."

"She's not abusive," Rory protested.

"No," Harmony said with a wink, "but she's got a hell of a frontal attack."

Rory winced just remembering.

"Vickie hurts as much as you do," Storm said, which about broke him.

At three, Rory's plane climbed above the clouds to take him to a place that no longer felt like home. He saw a rainbow that made him think of Victoria, and he focused on it, as if losing sight of it would prove he'd lost her for good, but he had, because he had no choice. The thought of living without Victoria seemed like a heavier burden than the debt he owed Caperglen.

Who would have guessed that ridding his village and family name of a century-old curse would destroy his life?

Thirty-Nine

Vickie entered a house that no longer felt like home. As her tears began to fall, the clouds opened up, while the sun made rainbows everywhere but in her heart.

Her sisters cried with her. It was nice having family who cared about her. But without Rory, she was as lost as when Nana died. More lost than when her mother died. "You don't have to tell me that I've drawn the Death card," Vickie said. "I need to accept the inevitable. It's over."

"No," Storm said. "You need to lose that attitude."

"Look who's talking!" Vickie laughed as she cried.

"Every end means a new beginning," Harmony said, "plus the Fool card opposes Death and reaffirms a new beginning, as the Empress means rebirth.

"You're on a path of sweeping change," Destiny said, "which isn't a bad thing."

"Thanks, Des, but I already figured that out." Vickie stepped into her arms. "Why did that rat have to come here?"

"You had his unicorn."

"Storm." Harmony glared at her.

"Right. *Why* is he a rat?"

"He left. He has no loyalty."

"Hopscotch? He may be a rat, but he's a loyal rat. He's being loyal to an entire village."

"Well," Vickie said, "if you put it that way. Okay, so let's call him 'Saint Rat.' He still freaking left."

Vickie stripped Rory's bed of its lavender sheets with a healthy fury. But when she went to stuff them in the washer, she took one of his pillowcases, inhaled his scent, and put it aside. She found her own sex-scented sheets in the hamper and couldn't get those in the washer fast enough.

With Nana's old max-capacity front loader, Vickie planned to wash Rory MacKenzie out of her life. She added detergent and slammed the door, but the extra pillowcase sat there mocking her.

"Spell me!" she said, throwing it in with the rest. She turned the dial so hard, she snapped it off, which really made her cry, because she couldn't afford a repairman.

The tumbler cranked as it picked up

speed, as if the washer was going into orbit. Great, her personal dirty laundry circling the earth forever.

Too full, too full, too full, it said on a cranky tumbling scold.

Crying was ridiculous, Vickie knew, but she couldn't stop. Neither could she stop the deluge of water suddenly pouring from around the washer door, because she had no control button to turn off.

Her sisters stopped at the door when they saw her standing in two inches of water.

Storm left and Harmony quirked a brow. "So, Miss I'm-not-a-witch, now you've got the weather and the washer crying with you."

Storm returned with a tool box, hammered down the enamel around the control stub, and turned the washer off with a pair of needle-nose pliers.

"Thanks, Sis. Now I won't have to pay a repairman."

Storm opened the washer door and it barfed sheets, also weeping.

Harmony took Vickie's arm. "Come on. I'm going to draw you a bath of cedarwood, lavender, and patchouli oils to help you calm down."

A few minutes later, Vickie sat on the edge of the tub. Her bath smelled wonderful, but she wanted to share it with Rory. Tigerstar catapulted into her arms, knocking her back so she hit the jets switch, but the tub wasn't full enough, so streams of water shot to all parts of the bathroom.

Scared, Tigerstar howled and jumped to a shelf that snapped, and slid her into the tub. With another howl, her cat flew straight from the water and into the hall.

Vickie followed the sound of crying and found Tiger under Rory's, no, Nana's bed.

"What's wrong?" Harmony asked, getting on her knees beside Vickie.

"Tigerstar's scared or hurt." Vickie wiped her eyes, and Harmony rescued her shivering cat, wet, but undamaged.

Vickie couldn't say the same for her bathroom. She'd left the water and jets going. It was a disgrace, and below it, water dripped down her living room walls.

As Vickie surveyed the living room, a drop fell from the ceiling and hit her where her heart used to be.

"Geez," Storm said. "The universe is crying with you. We have to do something about this."

"No, *I* have to do something about it," Vickie said. "I have to accept my magic and learn to control it . . . thereby destroying any chance of ever having a relationship with Rory."

"It seems to me that you made the decision to accept your magic when you used the key to the wardrobe," Harmony said, "which gave you the unicorn, which brought Rory."

"In other words," Vickie said, "I am who I am."

The minute she woke the next morning, Vickie speed-dialed Kira, then she winced when she saw that it was only six.

"Are you up?" Vickie asked when Kira answered.

"Sure, we're having a morning tickle fest, four in a bed," Kira said. "Did you vanquish your dragon?"

"No, but I did send him packing."

"Ah, Vic. I'm sorry."

"I need your help."

"Sure, what can I do for you. Wait. Travis! Zane! Don't tie your father to the bedpost. He's a *good* cowboy." Kira giggled. "Best rider in the east."

Vickie rolled her eyes. "Ki-ra."

"Oh, yeah. Sorry. You were saying."

"I'm a witch and I need to learn to control my magic before I have to build an ark."

"Drew the Magician card, did you?"

"Figuratively speaking."

"I'll come on the weekend and bring my copy of *Magic for Thickheaded Witches in Denial.*"

"Cute."

"Maybe we can do a sleepover, like the old days, and spell you into shape. Call Mel, and invite your sisters, if you don't think talking about witchcraft will freak them."

"They'll survive."

It was a regular witch fest.

With four teachers, Vickie went on magic overload, but she learned a lot.

"The magic is going to happen anyway," Kira said on Sunday afternoon as they said their good-byes, "so you have to learn to control it, especially since it's strongest when your emotions are."

"And after she has sex," Storm added.

"You had sex!" Kira said.

Storm hooted. "Don't tell me Rory was your first?"

"Don't worry, Storm. You'll never know."

Three days later, Vickie brought in the mail. "It's the fifteenth. I know, because the movers are coming to crate the unicorn today, so why don't I have a stack of bills in my hand?"

"Beats me." Destiny shrugged.

"The trolley's here," Storm said.

Vickie got on the computer to check.

"Paid!" she snapped. "That cranky, narrow-minded obsessive rat paid for Nana's funeral!" She hit a few more keys. "The mortgage, the hospital bills; they're all paid!"

"And your problem with that would be?" Des asked.

"I'll repay him, by God. Or I'll kill him. Either way, he'll get what he deserves. He had no right!"

"Uh, yeah, he did. You made him the bookkeeper."

"I didn't make him my savior."

Destiny tilted her head. "In some ways, you did."

"Sometimes having psychic sisters sucks."

"Sometimes being psychic sucks," Storm said, joining them. "That was Rory's way of paying for the unicorn. So get over it."

"The unicorn belonged to him, damn it."

"You may as well get into a super-snit and be done with it," Storm said. "Our tuition is paid, too. Now we have to get our degrees. Sheesh. How rotten can a man get?"

"The bastard," Vickie snapped.

"At least you don't have to go to school. Rory promised to come back and kick butt if I didn't, and frankly I've had enough of the scum-sucking Scot."

"You have?"

"Hah, I knew it. She loves him."

"I do not."

"Don't lie to your baby sisters." Storm wagged a finger. "It sets a bad example." Storm put her hands on her hips. "You know every time we talk about Rory, I get a mental picture of Lili's diary."

"That reminds me," Harmony said, "I've been thinking that I'd like to hold the diary to see if I can sense Lili."

Vickie got the diary and handed it to Harmony.

"My goddess," Harmony said. "Lili was some powerful witch. Oh, and this is her Book of Shadows. Her spells are all here."

"I wondered," Vickie said. "But do you know what's not there? The spell that I'm supposed to complete."

"I still can't believe that the one who wanted magic the least is the one who inherited Lili's powers." Storm rolled her eyes. "And you do need that spell. It's the most important one."

Harmony looked at her watch. "The unicorn. Vickie, go stand beside it before the freight company comes. Close your eyes, relax, and concentrate on the events that have surrounded it."

"Can't hurt," Vickie said. She opened the case, smelled lilies, and thought of Rory.

She stroked the dragon around the saddle, and thought of Rory. She closed her eyes, and thought she should open the compartment. When she opened it, she thought of Rory.

The compartment was empty, of course, which suddenly seemed wrong.

Vickie slid her hand inside, bottom to top, side to side, and found a surface that felt different from the rest, smooth, and a bit puffy, like old wallpaper. It clung to a top wall deep into the cavity just beneath the dragon. She had to stand like a contortionist to chip away at a corner with a fingernail while trying to keep the paper intact. At the bubble, the sheet came free, and a card fell into her hand.

The Lovers. One more piece of the puzzle. Love, bonds, a union . . . figuring out what you want and staying true to yourself.

On the parchment, brittle and ragged around the edges, Vickie found a poem in Lili's hand. Drummond had scrawled a note at the bottom. "There was no joy left in me without you." The words she and Rory had been looking for.

The poem sounded like a prophecy in rhyme. A rhyme. "Oh my stars. It's the spell. Harmony, Destiny, Storm! I need you."

FORTY

Before the unicorn was due to arrive in Caperglen, Rory hired as many of the villagers to repair the Immortal Classic as were willing. Many didn't come because they didn't believe Victoria would send the unicorn. Rory knew better.

Craftsmen repaired the steam engine that turned the carousel, others, the steam organ. Carpenters checked every pole and beam, hinge, and gear. Rory made needed repairs to the zodiac figures.

In many ways, he believed that in retrieving the unicorn, his life-quest had been realized, but when your greatest goal is realized at the ripe old age of thirty-six, there was less a sense of satisfaction and more of a gaping hole in your future.

Carving horses twenty-four/seven would no longer be enough.

Rory blamed Victoria . . . the way he'd blamed Lili before her, his conscience suggested, but he ignored it.

He should be relieved to be free of Victoria, free of all the Cartwright witches of Salem, Massachusetts. Rory scratched his wilding whiskers. *Ach, and there's too much work to be done to wallow in useless emotions.* This sense of loss was a figment of his imagination.

He went to talk to the carpenters rebuilding the pavilion so the sides could come off. The roof now duplicated the top of the carousel.

When he installed the unicorn, an open carousel would sit in the center of a grassy field, like it did a hundred years before — a field that would be overgrown with lilies come spring.

Lilies of all things.

Why had he never made the connection before?

He'd recognized the scent when he stood beside the unicorn in Victoria's shop.

Victoria, who'd taught him about home and family, iron skillets of ripe pumpkins, children flying kites on a green, witchy sisters, soft music, cherry teddies, and satisfying snogs by the fire. Damn, but he missed her.

The unicorn arrived late on the 30th. He

would set it in place in the morning. Halloween, of all days. Salem would be hopping. He wished . . .

Rory tossed his trousers at the wall and sat on the edge of his bed. Since he'd come back, he'd buried himself in carousel work by day, but by night, he had no control over his dreams.

Trying not to fall into the sleepy arms of despair, he picked up a book, a roaring good mystery that would keep him awake all night.

The carousel looked lonely dressed in colored lights and turning to a tune that now seemed oddly sad.

Victoria never came here anymore.

Rory circled the carousel, feeling foolish in the kilt she loved, aching to see her tiger eyes bright, her gown a touch of the magic past.

Her caress, he missed. Her kiss. Her. He missed her.

He called her name.

Shouted it.

Cried it out.

She didn't come.

He sat on the dragon chariot alone, and the dragon wept.

On Halloween, Rory woke with a groan, got

up, looked in the bathroom mirror, and grunted at the salty tear tracks on his cheeks. Then he climbed into the shower, where grief didn't matter.

He went out before dawn and set the unicorn into its rightful place for the first time in a century.

After the workers arrived, Rory got the word that all systems were go. He told everyone to stand back, reminded himself that his quest had been worth everything, and he pulled the lever.

No lights, no music. The carousel failed to turn.

Tradesmen checked their work. Every bolt and gear looked perfect, but no amount of repairs could bring the Immortal Classic back to life.

What would it matter if they did?

One by one, and then in droves, the villagers deserted their pariah, turned savior, turned failure.

He'd grown up lonely, but it hadn't mattered, because he had a goal. Now the realization of true loneliness slapped him in the face.

Rory checked the works one more time, and pushed the lever again, with no luck. Then he sat in the dragon chariot, for hours it seemed. He'd fulfilled his goal, but his dream had died without Victoria.

In its place lay an ocean of loneliness.

He might as well be Drummond in his old age.

Rory sat straighter as he saw the correlation between Drummond's "madness" and his own. They'd both denied their hearts, because of outside pressure.

Rory got a visual of Victoria reaching into the unicorn's compartment, a strong memory, often happened in their dreams.

He rose and threaded his way around the zodiac figures, faster and faster, until he reached the unicorn, unlatched the compartment, and opened it, but the single sheet of parchment was too old to be a note from Victoria.

Disappointment threatened to swamp him, until he read the tattered old poem.

Life is like a carousel, a dizzying affair,
First color and music and nary a care,
Then ponies aplenty and unicorns rare.
Later heights to meet and lows to bear,
Dreams to fulfill with wind in your hair.
Make the journey with joy, bright
    and aware.
Reap peace and love if you meet the dare.
Refuse the risk and end alone in despair.

Despair — Rory knew it well; it had become his companion, day and night since he left Salem. And no amount of attention to the carousel had helped.

Beneath the poem, written in Drummond's familiar hand, Rory read the note Lili had referred to in her diary. "There was no joy left in me without you."

Carved into his library mantel was a message Rory had known his whole life: "Make the journey with joy."

A wave of understanding hit him, and he swallowed a rush of sorrow for his ancestor, and for himself.

Centuries of agony over a once-in-a-lifetime love denied, and did he learn from Drummond's mistake?

Yes! Finally! For the first time in his life, Rory cared more about the present and the future than the past, more about a person than a chunk of wood.

Life with Victoria would be all short-circuiting appliances, falling objects, and rhyming wishes with repercussions. "Crivvens, I canna wait," Rory said, travel plans forming in his mind.

He'd get the carpenters to seal up the carousel tomorrow, before he left for Salem. He only hoped Victoria could forgive him.

His beautiful, wonderful loose-cannon

witch held his fate in her magical hands.

Then again, they'd made love without harm coming to him, which must mean that she wanted him, else something would surely have killed him, given the fun they'd had. "Let's hope she still wants me as much as I want her. Ach, and stop talking to yourself, you dotty, lovesick fool."

He'd start a foundation to support the carousel as a museum piece, and let a board of villagers do what they pleased to advertise it and improve village prosperity.

But first he was going home to Victoria.

With the poem still in his hand, Rory turned to set his plan in motion, and he saw a chimera . . . Victoria, carrying a broom, wearing a witch's hat and cape, crossing the field, coming his way, her cape flowing behind her in the wind.

And him, so blessedly grateful that she had anticipated his needs once again, he could barely breathe.

She saw him, hesitated, dropped her broom, and ran.

Rory caught her up and twirled her in a circle as he kissed her all over her face, the way she was kissing him. Desperate, hungry, grateful.

They stopped to drink from each other's lips, tears salting their reunion.

They laughed and kissed again. He touched her cheek, her hair. "Is this a Halloween trick? Are we dreaming again, or are you the best treat I ever got?" He held her face between his hands. "You're *really* here."

"Where I belong, beneath a starry, pale blue sky at dusk, kissing you beside the Immortal Classic Carousel, just like we dreamed."

"You never looked like a witch in our dreams."

"Besides the fact that it's Halloween, the costume is a symbol. I want to be sure you understand who I really am."

"I ken, and I want you the way you are. I want us the way we are, except together, forever. I wouldn't change a thing . . . well, except maybe one."

"Which is?"

"I really hate the name 'Lance.' "

Victoria laughed, tossed her hat in the air, and untied her cape so it drifted on the breeze and pooled in the grass. "Our dreams were in the past. Our life is in the present."

"And the future," Rory said, skimming his hands up her sides. "Your little black slut dress," he said. "I'm glad. You look so beautiful in it. And beneath it?"

"That's for you to find out."

"Kiss me, then," he said, "and make all

our dreams come true."

In the midst of that magic kiss, the music began, the colored lights flashed, and the Immortal Classic Carousel came to life, all twelve zodiac figures together for the first time in a century, a MacKenzie kissing his witch beside it.

Their laughter broke the kiss. Rory turned Victoria, so he could hold her against him while they watched the bright-flying whirligig. "I see you brought your magic."

"You needed it."

"Aye, and badly." He nodded toward the carousel. "Look at the rounding boards, the shields and paneled mirrors, the central starred cornice," he said. "They were all painted by Lili. The unicorn's tartan is the Lockhart tartan, or the Loch Ness tartan, I should say, which is where Lili's Pictish family came from. It's the only figure on the carousel without a MacKenzie tartan, and it's not been painted over; I checked."

She turned in his arms. "So Drummond always meant the unicorn to be Lili's?"

"Aye, darlin'. The carousel and its magic belong to both of us."

"Both? Are you admitting to having some magic of your own?"

"With you as my destiny, how can you doubt it? You're mine, but not because of any spell, ye ken? Because you own the missing half of my heart. I love you."

"Lili was right," Victoria said toying with his sporran and turning him to steel. "By opening the wardrobe, I met my destiny. Yes, our love is real, but it did take a bit of magic to bring your fire-breathing self to my door."

"Aye, but you tamed me."

"Oh, I hope not. No more fire?" She pouted so beautifully, he was forced to kiss her again, and they both caught fire. Then he unzipped the front of her little black dress, unhooked her fine strawberry bra, and found her bright Pictish starburst. "Oh, aye, and here's our blaze. There'll always be fire in our bed, darlin'."

"And in our chariot, our wardrobe, or wherever our dreams take us," Victoria said. "Speaking of which, where should we live? In my world or yours?"

"How about in both? I could carve magical carousel figures in Salem. And your sisters could run the Immortal Classic when we're in Scotland."

"That's what Des said when she kicked me out the door." Vickie looked around. "Where's your house?"

Rory pointed. "There, the top o' the hill."

"Rory, that's a castle."

"It's a moldering old heap is what it is, but wait till you see the library. Why did Des kick you out? She didn't use magic did she? You came of your own accord, Victoria?"

She cupped his cheeks, her touch a blessing. "Hell yes, I came on my own. The plane wouldn't go fast enough; I nearly flew in on my broom."

Rory chuckled. "My world was bleak before I met you. You bring a joy that I canna live without. You, I canna live without. Will you marry me?"

"First, I have a confession to make."

"Aye? I'm braced."

"My magic is strongest when my emotions are. I accept that, and so must you, though now I can control it, for the most part. But be warned; marrying you will make my magic stronger, and having our babies will amplify it."

He had to kiss her again.

She came away with bright cat's eyes. "You do realize there are triplets in my family?"

Rory laughed outright. "Ach, but I'm in for a wild ride, aren't I? Say yes."

"A dizzying affair," Victoria promised.

Rory put her on the carousel, and climbed up with her. "Care for a ride on your dragon?"

"Yes please," she said with so much modesty, he laughed.

"The tarot Chariot," she said, "can also mean coming out on top."

"Who?" Rory asked. "Me or you?"

"We could take turns."

"Ah, that's my sassy selkie bride."

He took her on his lap and handed her Lili's poem. Vickie read it aloud, as she knew she must to complete Lili's spell, hoping that wherever they were, the poem and Lili's magic would reunite them.

Then she and Rory settled in for a snog, and a whole lot more . . . until the scent of lilies called to them.

As they looked up, two figures appeared, as if from nowhere.

A braw man in his kilt walked around the outside of the carousel from the left, and a bewitching young woman in an old-fashioned gown circled it from the right, their sum and substance, color and depth, growing strong when they saw each other.

Vickie and Rory clasped hands as the couple ran into each other's arms.

"It's All Hallows Eve," Victoria whispered. "Souls walk the earth tonight."

"Aye, I ken," Rory said. "It's Drummond and Lili."

"Oh, I hope so."

"I know so. I have their portraits."

The reunited lovers kissed as if they hadn't seen each other in a century. Heart-wrenching, and damned near embarrassing to witness.

Victoria laid her head on Rory's chest, tears coursing down her cheeks, and Rory held her close, as their ancestors clasped hands and walked toward the sunset, and eternity, together again at last.

To their surprise, Lili stopped, turned, and blew them a kiss.

"Journey with joy," came her blessing on the wind.

ABOUT THE AUTHOR

For **Annette Blair,** writing comedy started with a root canal and a reluctant trip to Salem, Massachusetts. Though she had once said she'd never write a contemporary, she stumbled into the serendipitous role of "Accidental Witch Writer" on that trip. Funny how she managed to eat her words, even with an aching jaw. After she turned to writing bewitching romantic comedies, a magic new world opened up to her. She loves her new home at Berkley Sensation.

Contact her through her website at www.annetteblair.com.